One day this precious child sleeping in my arms will be an old man complaining of creaking knees and fingers that no longer do his bidding. I will urge him to do as his father and I have done: to do his best each day with what little or much God has given him and to hold all things lightly in his open palms so that he might best have them available to offer to those with greater needs.

Prudence Willard
Marietta, Ohio
June 15, 1859

Secrets of Wayfarers Inn

Family Secrets
River of Life

SECRETS OF
WAYFARERS INN

River of Life

KATHLEEN Y'BARBO

New York

CHAPTER ONE

July 1
Marietta, Ohio

Q uilts!" Tessa Wallace made an abrupt right turn into the newly renovated quilt shop. Though breakfast at the tearoom next door had been the first item on their agenda for today, she just couldn't help being distracted by a look inside the new quilt shop. "Look how beautiful! This was definitely worth the wait."

It had just been a few weeks since the Sassy Seamstress had reopened one street over from the inn. Tess and her two best friends had been dying to go beyond just peering through front windows filled with stacks of fabric, quilts hung on antique ladders, and the most adorable handmade accessories.

However, they'd made a pact not to go see what the new owner had done with the place until they could all go. With the repairs in progress at the inn as well as all the other demands on their lives, they hadn't found a day to go together until today, the first day of July.

Today was meant to be a respite from all of those repairs and demands. Before they left this morning, they'd agreed there would be no discussion of the inn today, and then with pinkies interlocked they sealed the promise.

So instead of thinking about how the lovely items she saw here and there would fit into the decorating scheme of Wayfarers Inn, Tess distracted herself by concentrating on the many changes that had been made to this building. The previous owners had not spent much time improving the condition of the interior or adding to the inventory in the past few decades.

The result was a hodgepodge of fabric, mismatched how-to magazines and craft supplies, and the lingering smell of live bait they sold to tourists who rented boats at the docks nearby.

Tess couldn't recall the last time she'd visited the place, but then she had never been much of a crafter. Or a fisherman.

She inhaled. Somehow the aroma of bait had been replaced by the loveliest fragrance. Unless she missed her guess, that was Yankee Candle's Market Blossoms, her favorite. Because the candles filled any space with the fragrant scent of blossoms and berries, Tess had already packed away two of them to use in her new rooms at the inn once she moved in.

She glanced around the inviting space, allowing her attention to rest on the goods so artfully arranged on shelves and tables around the room. A lovely soundtrack of dulcimer music played softly, and a television behind the counter was silently showing an episode of the Arts & Antiques Network's *Quilt Mysteries* series. A stack of the series's episodes on DVD rested nearby.

The restful atmosphere was exactly what they hoped to accomplish at the inn. Perhaps she should ask the name of the dulcimer music. It would be lovely to have that playing downstairs as guests came in.

Oh. No. Not today.

Tess returned her attention to the colorful fabrics standing at attention on the shelf to her right. Truly, she hadn't expected to find anything on their visit to the Sassy Seamstress, although she had thought perhaps to see if the new owner did alterations or made curtains and slipcovers.

Between the calorie-laden, hurry-up-and-eat meals and sweet treats they had been consuming on the run and the fact that half of the vintage furniture they had found to go into the inn would need recovering, a good seamstress who could let out skirts as well as cover windows and parlor furniture would be invaluable.

Tess had pulled out a bolt of fabric in a lovely shade of gold with burgundy and green dots when LuAnn Sherrill caught up to her and shook her head. "Don't you think this would make fabulous pillows for my new sitting room?"

"Oh no you don't," LuAnn told her as she looked at the price per yard on the end of the bolt. "We have a plan and a budget, and we absolutely cannot deviate from either. I don't care how beautiful...oh! Look how pretty."

Her nearly reformed list-making friend tucked her three-ring organizer back into her purse, now distracted by a beautiful quilt in red, white, and blue that Tess's grandmother would have called a hen and chickens pattern.

Tess thought briefly of her own list, a bucket list she and her late husband had created together on their last anniversary. Theirs had been a long and loving marriage but not nearly long enough. After four years, she still missed Jeffrey dearly.

Tess still hadn't had the courage to unfold the list she kept in her wallet and begin checking off the items they had agreed to do together. Someday she would. She smiled as she returned the bolt of fabric to its place on the shelf. Indeed, someday when she was ready and when reading that masculine scrawl didn't bring back fresh pain.

For now the Lord had certainly provided a remedy for that pain in the form of two best friends who likely had no idea how very much they helped to heal her heartbreak when it rose up. Three best friends for life, they were, and their motto said it all: "We will never be boring or bored, and we will never act our age."

So far that had meant being there for each other during happiness and heartbreak, pregnancies and adoption, full houses and empty nests. She tucked those memories back into her heart and smiled. Yes indeed, despite the loss she would never get over, she was a blessed woman.

Still, from a business standpoint, Tess knew all too well the odds of turning the Wayfarers Inn project into a profitable venture. With the Lord's help—and with plenty of elbow grease—they would beat those odds.

In the meantime, even if they never had a paying guest—perish the thought, of course!—the fact Tess would be living in a lovely old inn made her happier than anything had in recent memory. She had a purpose again, even if that purpose on most days was to rein in LuAnn's endless additions to plans and lists and to convince the third member of their trio that there was nothing to fear but fear itself.

As if on cue, the third member of the Inn Crowd, Janice Eastman, joined her, her smile broad. "Oh Lu, that is just gorgeous. Wouldn't it look beautiful in the parlor at the inn? It's the perfect thing for the Fourth of July."

"I think so too." LuAnn turned back one corner of the quilt to inspect the lining. "I can't decide whether to hang it from the railing, hang it from the wall, or just drape it over the back of one of the sofas. If we were up and running and could actually put a float in the town parade, I'd say this quilt should have center stage." She turned toward Tess. "What do you think?"

"I think both of you need to remember that there are neither railings nor sofas to drape anything over this Fourth of July, and anything hung on those walls will either get painted over or covered in whatever dust the contractors are kicking up. However, if you want to climb into the back of my son-in-law's red pickup truck and ride down the street behind the Marietta High School band wearing that quilt, I can certainly make that happen. The rest of it, not so much."

"Party pooper," Janice said with a laugh.

"May I remind you that we all agreed this afternoon would be a break from discussing the inn?"

"Well, of course," LuAnn said with a shrug. "But this is just so fun and pretty."

A blue-eyed young woman in her midtwenties, her dark hair tied up in one of those messy buns Lizzie favored, stepped from behind a quilted curtain at the back of the store. She wore stylish jeans, sneakers, and a red T-shirt that said *A clean house is a sign of a broken sewing machine.* A name badge in the shape of a spool of thread proclaimed her to be Wendy.

Something about Wendy seemed vaguely familiar.

Marietta, Ohio
July 1, 1859

"There will always be a need, Wife," Jason Willard said. "Let someone else take over now. Our son deserves a mama who's living and not one who gave her life to save someone else."

"Please lower thy voice, Husband," Prudence said gently as she focused on the swaddled babe sleeping in her arms instead of looking up at the husband she knew had only her best interests at heart. "I've only just got him settled and neither of us wants to hear him fuss again so soon, do we?"

As if he knew they were speaking about him, Moses opened his eyes to look up at Prudence. Her heart lurched. What a beautiful boy he was. Fat and happy most of the time with only the slightest complaint when he thought he might be missing a meal.

Born the day of the great Marietta fire back in May, little Moses was already a full month and a few days old. The child was his father made over in every way but one: he had his mama's eyes.

She had seen those eyes on the day he cried his way into the world and had known this one was strong. This one would live.

So while Jason had gone off to town to stand alongside the other men and do what he could to stop the flames that were taking building after building on that cold day, Prudence stayed home and held her son, wrapped in the quilt dyed blue for loyalty and red for freedom, while she prayed. Prayers of gratitude mingled with pleas for those in the path of the blaze.

Jason had come home in the early hours of the morning, his clothes smelling of smoke and ash dusting his face and hair. More than two dozen buildings were lost to a blaze started by two young fellows bending lead in a barn. She added a prayer for those two as she tucked her husband into bed then fitted herself against his side to attempt whatever sleep Moses would allow.

Prudence smiled at her baby boy and traced the dimple in his chin. Someday he would be a man who did great things, this much she knew in her heart. Like Mary in the Bible, this mama held tightly to the promise the Lord gave her regarding her son and said nothing to anyone, not even Jason.

"Prudence," Jason said, his voice softer this time but still full of the concern she knew came from a place of deep love, "thou hast not answered me."

She looked up now, shifting Moses to her shoulder to rub his tiny back as she regarded her husband with what she hoped would convey the respect he deserved as head of this household. "To my recollection, thou hast not asked a question."

He would, though, and Prudence knew it. Though Jason's injuries made him unable to fully participate in the moving of the parcels, as those they aided along on their journey on the Underground Railroad were called, he would have been doing the same work alongside her if he could.

Oh, but he did worry. About her, and now about their son.

Prudence faced him now, her heart soft toward this man God had given her and yet knowing that with one word Jason could put an end to the work that meant so much. It was his right to do so, but she prayed now that he would not exercise that right.

"Do not thee worry," she told him with a smile. "Thou knows it has been months since I've done anything but help with the quilting. What harm can come of that?"

Jason traced the line of her jaw with his knuckle, his smile matching hers, and then rested his palm atop hers on their son's back. "My love," he whispered, "if thee were any other woman, I would agree."

Her smile faltered. Did he know?

She returned a happy expression to her face. "Thee wouldn't have it any other way, would thee? Perhaps thee wishes to have married a more docile creature."

Her dear husband paused, his gaze seeming to search her face as he appeared to be considering the question. "The truth?"

"Always," she said even though she was not certain she wanted to hear it.

"Then no," he said gently, "I would not have it any other way but not because it is easy for me that thee are not a docile creature." His fingers tenderly traced the length of her jaw. "But because this is the way God created thee, and it is thee I love just as thee are."

"And I love thee, my husband, with all that I am," she said. "But there are times when things would be much easier had He made me different than I am."

"That I do agree," Jason said. "But much as it would be simpler, what about all of those on the other side of the river who need thee?" He shook his head. "Need us," he corrected. "What do they know of easy?"

"Indeed thee speaks the truth," she said.

"And thee has a plan," he told her as he stepped away. "Should I ask what that plan might be or accept that thee and the other ladies from church are merely gathering on this July evening to make a quilt for a good cause?"

Prudence stepped back into his embrace. "Oh, Husband," she said as she rested her head against his strong, broad chest, "that is exactly the plan, and the cause is one thee and I would stake our lives for. So what is a little quilting with friends, some of whom are new friends and some old?"

"It is a worthy cause indeed," he told her. "So be sure thee take that goose with thee."

She looked up at him and laughed. "Whatever for?"

He shook his head. "With all the noise she makes at the slightest whisper, who better to alert thee to additions to thy quilting circle, wanted or unwanted?"

So he did know.

Prudence reached up on tiptoe to kiss her husband lightly on the cheek. "The Lord will protect us all, goose or not," she said, "but I wager Patience will do her part for the cause."

Chapter Two

W elcome to the completely new and reinvented Sassy Seamstress. I'm Wendy Wilson." She offered a broad smile. "May I help you ladies?"

"Well hello there," Tess said with a smile. "Thank you, but we're just browsing. I do love what you've done with the place. It's absolutely gorgeous, and the sales floor looks to have been completely restocked."

And re-scented, she thought.

"Thank you. I never thought I'd get the smell of fish out of here." She shook her head.

Tess laughed. "According to my friend Winnie, the bait was the store's biggest seller."

Wendy nodded. "I believe that. The inventory was included when I bought the place, and I couldn't believe what was still being offered for sale here. It was like a museum of the seventies and eighties. Can you imagine it? That was so long ago."

"I can," Tess said as she thought of how recent the seventies and eighties seemed to her.

"It cost a lot more than I expected to get things up and running again, and I had no idea the previous owners had run up so much debt when I agreed to take over the..."

Wendy's voice trailed off. An uncomfortable silence fell between them.

"So there's plenty of history here," Tess offered for lack of anything else to say. "You know this building was one of the ones that burned in the fire in May of 1859."

"That explains all the soot I found when I uncovered the old brick walls in the back of the store."

"Apparently more than two dozen buildings were damaged or lost." Tess shrugged. "And all of it started by a couple of kids melting lead in a barn. I mean, hot lead and a wooden barn. I cannot imagine telling my kids that's an okay thing to do. Here, take the matches and lead and go on out to the barn. What can happen?"

The joke seemed to fall flat. Or perhaps Wendy was one of those serious sorts who considered everything before responding.

"Yes, well, anyway," Wendy finally said, "I've always wanted to own a shop like this—not just quilts but all sorts of sewing crafts—so this is really a dream come true."

"I know a little about chasing dreams, so congratulations on making yours happen," Tess said, even as she thought about how far they still had to go to make the dream of a bed-and-breakfast out of the Wayfarers Inn happen.

"Oh." Wendy gave Tess a sideways look. "You're the lady I saw coming out of the old inn one day last week. I recognize your red hair. It's lovely, by the way. Your hair, I mean, although I've always thought Wayfarers Inn was lovely too."

Tess laughed. "If you've seen me coming out of the inn, then I apologize. I've been tackling the project of removing the paint from the kitchen cabinets so we can get the kitchen up and running. I'm sure I will never get all of the paint chips out of my hair. I have to agree about the inn, though. It is lovely. Or it will be again once we're done with the renovations."

"That's a big job," Wendy said. "Just the work I did on this place was enough to make me never want to tackle another home improvement project. I'll stick to sewing, thank you very much."

They shared a smile. "I'm beginning to understand how you feel, although I haven't sewn anything since home ec class in seventh grade. My mom was a great sport about the apron I made her, but then what mother doesn't love anything her child makes?"

"That's true. My mom was so proud of the pot holders I made her when I was in the Girl Scouts. They were just awful, but she refused to throw them away." Wendy's smile faded into a nervous laugh. "So, would it be weird if I told you that I know why you're here?"

"Maybe," Tess said as she studied the girl's expression. "But probably not. Try me."

"Well, you probably think you're just shopping, but I might have prayed that you would stop by someday."

"Might have or did?" Tess asked.

"I did," Wendy admitted. "A few times, actually. Is that weird?"

"Praying is never weird, Wendy. However, I'm curious why you would pray that specific prayer."

Wendy leaned in. Her expression told Tess she seemed to be considering what she would say next. "I heard lots of things about the ladies who bought the inn. I stand here most days looking out the window when there are no customers, and I see you going in and out a lot."

"I guess I do that," Tess said. "All three of us are buying the inn, but my part of the deal is to oversee the renovations. That's probably why you see me more than the others."

"Well, anyway, with your red hair you remind me of someone who was dear to me. I've felt a little lost since moving here. Every time I see you out at the inn, I think of my mom. And that makes me happy."

"Oh, Wendy, I understand that lost feeling, and I'm very glad seeing me makes you happy." She embraced the young woman. "Why don't you come over and say hello next time? I'll give you a tour of the inn."

"Thank you," Wendy said. "I would like that very much."

"Excuse me, how much is this quilt? Oh, and this one too?" LuAnn said from the other side of the aisle. In her arms were two quilts, one that matched the wallpaper sample she'd picked for her room at the inn and the other obviously an antique pattern in colors of red, white, and blue.

"You better go on and help LuAnn. I guarantee she's going to be one of your best customers." Tess paused. "And the next time I'm outside the inn, I'll try to remember to wave at my new friend."

Wendy gave Tess a grateful look and then nimbly stepped around a stack of shipping boxes that blocked the aisle. "I'll have to check and see," she told LuAnn. "Do you mind waiting just a minute?"

"No, that's fine, but I also have a few questions about the type of quilt it is, what sort of batting is inside. Things like that."

"Ask away," Wendy said. "I'll see what I can tell you and look up anything I don't know. Oh, and in honor of the Fourth of July, everything in the store is discounted through Saturday."

While she and LuAnn discussed the quilt and then the history of quilts in the area, including something about General Lafayette and a famous River of Life quilt, Tess feigned an interest in a stack of fat quarters artfully arranged on a display table near the front window. What lovely colors.

Though she'd never had the patience to take up the skill required to piece, she'd sat at her mother's and grandmother's knees and watched them work their magic turning these oddly cut swatches of fabric into the most beautiful pieced quilts. Just when she thought a design would not come together, it always did.

When she was a little older, Tess had been trusted to cut some of the simpler designs. She'd even sewn a few seams for her grandmother once Nana's eyes got bad. And she'd certainly been called upon to thread a few needles for her.

If only she'd paid more attention when she had finally been old enough to learn. By then, Tess had long lost interest in quilting and turned her enthusiasm toward boys and then later, as a young bride, to making a home and eventually raising her children. Perhaps she and Lizzie could take a class together someday. Of course with her happily married daughter busy chasing three-year-old triplets, someday could be a very long time from now.

Then there was the well-known fact that Tess had absolutely no crafting skills. None. Not even a little.

While she could run a business like nobody's business and balance a ledger—without resorting to a computer or fancy calculator, thank you very much—her skills with anything resembling a craft were sadly lacking. Poor Jeffrey. How many ruined holiday projects had he either endured or, more often, successfully completed for her?

Her lack of craft skills had become a joke between them. Every time she threatened to start another project, he would remind her about the Christmas wreath she once set on fire or the Easter centerpiece that exploded all over his grandmother.

What would he have said about the inn project? She exhaled and then smiled. Likely Jeffrey would have rolled up his sleeves and jumped in to help wherever he was needed. However, he would absolutely forbid her to go anywhere near a glue gun.

"I'm so glad I found the perfect quilt for my bedroom. Truly though," LuAnn said once Wendy had skittered away to do her research, "this other quilt would look glorious as the centerpiece of our Fourth of July decorations next year."

"LuAnn," Tess said, grateful for the change of topic to one that had nothing to do with how much she missed Jeffrey. "We had a deal, and I plan to stick to it."

"We won't say anything else about the inn after this," Janice said. "At least not until we've enjoyed our breakfast and shopping. But it is a pretty quilt, and it would look absolutely stunning in the inn, don't you think?"

"Ask me later," Tess said. "When we're talking about the inn again."

Both LuAnn and Janice laughed. Finally Tess joined them. "Yes," she said. "It will look glorious and stunning and all of the other lovely adjectives. But first we have to finish what we started and get the inn up and running."

"And the café," LuAnn added. "I cannot wait to begin testing the soup recipes in the inn's kitchen. Winnie and I have so many ideas." She grinned. "And I will tell you all about them after our breakfast and shopping."

"Thank you," Tess said. "That will be lovely."

"And glorious," Janice added.

LuAnn giggled. "And stunning."

By the time Wendy returned, she surely must have wondered what had three women of a certain age laughing so hard in the middle of the quilt shop. While she and LuAnn completed their discussion, Tess wandered over to the window again.

Outside, the sun shone brightly with only a few cotton puff clouds hanging in the sky. From this vantage point she could see the river and, if she leaned just so, the inn.

The plumber's van, which had been parked outside when they left, was now absent. Likely he and his crew were taking another of their long breaks.

Tess sighed as she reached into her purse for her keys. She ought to return to the inn and see to this. While Tory "Thorn" Thornton, the friend and former shop teacher they'd hired to oversee the renovations, was an exceptionally good handyman, his skills did not extend to wiring and plumbing. Though she always made it a policy not to second-guess her contractors, it appeared the tradesmen Thorn hired had either been family members or people who owed him money.

When they took on the renovation, Thorn told them he would need the first week in July off to go out of town. She hadn't asked why, and he hadn't offered. Thorn was a private man whose personal life was his own business, or so she told herself as she tried to figure out where a man whose only interests seemed to be centered right there in Marietta would go.

In any case, if they hoped to get the work done in a reasonable amount of time, the workers had to be more closely supervised. Maybe she should fire the electrician and find someone who actually worked a full eight-hour day.

Or at least more than half of that.

Yes, that's what she would do. She would catch the lazy fellow in the act of abandoning the job site and fire him on the spot this evening. A few photos of what Tess found this morning would provide sufficient evidence that the arrangement was not working.

Her keys jangled in her hand. The trip would just take a few minutes, surely not long enough for Janice and LuAnn to miss her.

Tess had taken three steps toward the door when she stopped in her tracks and shook her head. *What am I thinking? This is not how the morning is supposed to go. Here I go thinking about the inn too. Maybe I do need a hobby.*

Despite the knowledge that Jeffrey would warn her against it, Tess snatched up a flyer about quilt classes and tucked it into her purse. Yes, a hobby would be great. Of course, finding time to do anything other than deal with contractors was unlikely, at least not for the foreseeable future.

There she went thinking about the inn again!

"Tess," LuAnn said as she smoothed the corner of the quilt back into place. "Is something wrong? Don't you like the quilt?"

Wendy gave her a disapproving look. "You don't like the red, white, and blue quilt?" she echoed.

"I love the quilt. Truly, it is beautiful. And so is the one for your bedroom. The problem is not the quilt."

"Then what's the problem?"

Tess shook her head. "At this rate, it will be Christmas before we can have visitors, so if you want a quilt for the parlor at the inn, I suggest you start looking for something in red and green. Or better yet, let's go next door and have breakfast. I'm starving. And remember the purpose for this outing was to get away from the renovations for a few hours."

"Tess is right," LuAnn said. "We have spent far too much time talking about the inn. And yet this quilt is so pretty and will be stunning no matter where it ends up, but I suggest we wait and see what we actually need before we buy anything for the public rooms of the inn. What do you say?"

"I agree," Janice said.

"I'll just get the one for my room today," LuAnn said, "and we can come back for the other if we decide on it. How's that?"

"I like that," Tess said.

"You two go on over and grab a table. I'll be right there after Wendy rings me up."

Wendy tucked the red, white, and blue quilt back onto the shelf where LuAnn found it and hurried off with the one for LuAnn's bedroom without a backward glance. LuAnn followed a step behind.

Janice grinned and nodded toward the door. "Come on, Tess. I'm starving too."

They left the quilt shop with LuAnn now clutching her beloved quilt while Wendy swiped her credit card, the bells on the shop door jangling as it closed behind them.

A few steps beyond the quilt shop was the new tearoom. Borrowing heavily from the quilt shop decor next door, the little space was filled to the rafters with fabric art, quilts of every size, and even a few antique sewing machines situated on shelves or as centerpieces on some of the larger tables.

Tess recognized the old black Singer machine with the pretty gold lettering like her grandmother used to own. A quilt piece in a red and white Jacob's ladder design had been placed under the foot, giving the old machine a new life as a piece of art.

Immediately she wanted to do the same in the little second-floor alcove at the inn. Tess groaned quietly. Would she ever stop thinking about the inn?

She and Janice were seated at a table near the large front windows and had just ordered iced teas for three when LuAnn came through the door, her quilt now wrapped in white paper and bundled into an oversized shopping bag.

"Girls, I just had the most interesting conversation with Wendy. She told me a fascinating story about General Lafayette's visit here. Did you know that when he died and was buried in Paris, his coffin was covered with American soil taken from Bunker Hill? Oh, and there's a connection between the general and the inn!"

"LuAnn," Tess warned, "we agreed not to talk about the inn until our morning out was over."

"This isn't technically about the inn," she said as she settled the bag on the empty fourth chair at the table. "It's about a quilt that was made at the inn, and it's famous."

"Do tell, right?" Janice said, looking to Tess for her approval.

"Yes, all right," Tess said. "Do tell."

LuAnn's eyes lit up. "As I said, we all know that General Lafayette paid a visit to Marietta in 1825."

"Who could miss the plaque down by the river marking the spot where he first stepped out of the boat?" Janice quipped.

"Or all the stories we learned in history class?" Tess added.

"Well, here's a story you never learned in history class." LuAnn continued. "The general was presented with a quilt called the River of Life commemorating his visit. It was commissioned by a group of wealthy businessmen, but unfortunately it was lost when the barge carrying some of the general's personal belongings sank."

"Fascinating," Tess said.

"Yes," LuAnn said. "But the story of a copy of that quilt is even more interesting."

"A copy? I don't understand."

"It was made by local ladies—not the fancy folk but farmers' wives—and for the man the abolitionists were hoping would be the next president. That would be Abraham Lincoln."

"Oh wow," Janice said. "I've never heard this story, and I have lived in Marietta all my life."

"It is a story that needs to be told. See, they created a pattern of intricate stitches and piecework that exactly detailed the Ohio and Muskingum Rivers as they flowed through Washington County, and rumor has it that the stitches were meant to show how many supporters the Underground Railroad had in this area. Or maybe it told the tale of how many lives had been saved. Or lost. We really don't know." She paused, her eyes wide and her smile broad. "But..."

"But?" Tess prompted.

"But they did all the quilting at the inn!"

Janice sat back and grinned. "Well how about that? One more reason to save the old building."

"What happened to the quilt?" Tess asked.

"That's the best part. The River of Life quilt was handed off to people who were charged with delivering it to Lincoln but since he was traveling all over the country before he was elected, he ordered it sent ahead to his home in Illinois. Only it didn't arrive for a very long time. Like years. And no one knew where it was. Then all of a sudden, the quilt showed up at the White House and ended up in the National Archives. Isn't that interesting?"

"Sounds like a few experiences I've had ordering things online," Tess said. At LuAnn's disappointed look, she amended her comment. "But I am very glad he got his quilt."

"Well," LuAnn said slowly, her grin returning, "there's more. Wendy just told me that the River of Life quilt is part of an exhibit of artifacts related to the Underground Railroad. The exhibit opens on the Fourth of July in Washington, DC and closes on Bastille Day."

"Bastille Day?" Janice asked.

"July 14," LuAnn said. "It's a national holiday in France, you know."

"Yes, my dear," Tess said with a wink. "Even we business majors had to learn a little about international history. Just seems a stretch to end the exhibit on Bastille Day when the quilt is honoring the Underground Railroad."

LuAnn grinned. "I guess they were going for a connection to the original quilt, which was made for General Lafayette, who was from France."

"That's nice," Tess said as she spied the waitress coming toward them with a tray of iced teas. "Should we try to arrange a trip to go and see it?"

"We don't have to," LuAnn said, her glee apparent. "The organizers of the exhibit are participating in a documentary about the quilt. You cannot say anything about this, but I have it on good authority that Art & Antiques Network is coming to Marietta to film the quilt returning home, even though it's just for Bastille Day. Isn't that great?"

"Returning home?" Janice shook her head. "You mean to the inn? There's not much to return to."

"Maybe so. Wendy told me she heard from her quilting friends in high places that all of this is very hush-hush."

Tess snorted. "Quilting friends in high places? What in the world does that even mean?"

"I don't know," LuAnn said as she reached for a sugar packet. "But if the Arts & Antiques Network is coming to Marietta, then I do believe we need to convince them to take a little tour of the home of the River of Life quilt, don't you think?"

"A tour?" Tess shook her head. "They'd have to wear hard hats."

"Who cares?" LuAnn said. "The inn was in uninhabitable shape. Now it's merely in need of renovation. If the producers like what they see, maybe they'll come back to follow up. And people who watch the Arts & Antiques Network like historical things."

"Like inns in old buildings," Janice supplied, her enthusiasm obvious.

Tess opened her mouth to respond but never got the chance. Instead, Wendy threw open the tearoom door, her face stricken. "It's the most terrible thing," she said as she hurried to their table. "Just the most terrible thing ever."

CHAPTER THREE

W hat's wrong?" LuAnn asked.

"The River of Life quilt!" Wendy was frantic. "I was just checking my Twitter feed and..." She gasped for air, shaking her head. "I just cannot believe it."

"Believe what?" Tess said. "Use your words, Wendy."

The quilt store owner nodded. "Okay. The River of Life quilt has disappeared."

LuAnn called the waitress over and ordered a glass of water for Wendy then moved her shopping bag off the chair so the girl could sit down. Tears welled in Wendy's eyes.

"It's just a quilt," Tess said in an attempt to comfort her.

Janice reached to pat her shoulder. "I'm sure they'll find it. And if it's the Arts & Antiques Network thing, don't fret. We've got some ideas to try to get them to come to Marietta for another reason. We'll see that your quilt store gets a mention."

Both LuAnn and Tess shot their friend warning glances. Of course, Janice ignored them.

Wendy drank half the water in the glass and placed it on the table with shaking hands. "You don't understand," she said. "That quilt was made by escaped slaves who put a curse on it. It was meant to point the way for the lost, and anyone who tries to keep it will lose it. I really wanted to see it in person."

"A curse?" Tess said. "That's ridiculous."

"Is it?" Wendy replied. "It's missing, isn't it? The whole exhibit had been packed up a few weeks ago and was under heavy guard and on its way to the museum. After they finished getting it set up yesterday, they found that the River of Life quilt wasn't there, and no one had seen it. It's the only quilt missing!"

Wendy's face grew serious. "The president supported the cause. That quilt was a map of all the stations on the railroad up and down the Ohio and Muskingum Rivers. In the right hands, it would have shown people in high places how many here were supporting the Underground Railroad. But in the wrong hands..."

"It could have incriminated a lot of people if the secret had been discovered," LuAnn said as Wendy nodded.

"The curse they put on it kept it from falling into the wrong hands. Whenever there was danger of discovery, the quilt disappeared."

"More likely people friendly to the cause of abolition saw to it that the quilt was removed to safety."

Wendy shrugged. "You can believe that if you want, but one of the ladies who sewed that quilt was my great-great-oh-a-bunch-of-greats grandmother, and I believe there was a curse." She rose. "Thank you for the water, ladies, but I've left the store alone so I'd better go. I'm so sorry to have disturbed you."

"Not at all," LuAnn said as they all said their goodbyes.

"Oh come on now," Janice said when the door had closed behind Wendy. "You don't believe in curses and that sort of thing, do you?"

"It does sound silly," Tess agreed. "Some poor admin probably packed the quilt in the wrong box and will be fired over the whole ordeal."

With that explanation agreed upon, the ladies enjoyed a wonderful breakfast and a morning of shopping where they kept their promise not to discuss the inn. Mostly. Although they did find an adorable set of bookends for the library and a rug that would be perfect in the upstairs hall.

They returned to the car exhausted but happy. "I'll be glad to get home and take my shoes off," LuAnn said.

"Agreed." Janice grimaced. "I need to get one of those fitness trackers so I can keep up with my walking. I bet we did three miles of shopping."

"Ladies," Tess said with trepidation, "would you mind if we make a brief stop at the inn? I noticed the plumber's truck was absent when we were at the quilt shop earlier. I'd like to see that he's returned and is working."

"Isn't that Thorn's job?" Janice reminded her. "I'm sure he's made the proper arrangements with the contractors."

"It is," Tess said as she chewed on the corner of her lip. "But I just thought…"

"You thought Thorn wasn't doing his job?" Janice asked.

"Oh, no that's not it at all. It's just that while he's out of town this week, I figure we're the ones responsible for making sure the work is being done. Time is money, you know."

Janice and LuAnn exchanged glances. "What?" Tess demanded. "Am I wrong?"

"You're not wrong," Janice said. "But don't you think you're worrying a bit too much? The work will get done."

"Of course it will," Tess said. "It's just going to get done with me watching what's happening while Thorn can't."

Neither LuAnn nor Janice offered a protest as LuAnn turned the car toward the inn. Soon they were parked at the curb in front. Just as Tess feared, the contractor was nowhere to be found.

Tess unbuckled her seat belt and reached for the door. "I'm just going to go see what he's accomplished today."

"You go ahead," Janice said. "My feet won't take me another step right now."

LuAnn nodded in agreement as she folded her sunglasses and placed them on her lap. "I'll stay with her, but just give us a shout if you need us."

"Hurry up, though," Janice called. "It is July, and I'm no spring chicken. I don't want to roast in here."

Tess giggled at the image as she closed the car door behind her. "I'll just be a minute."

She unlocked the inn door and stepped inside, immediately engulfed in silence and gray light broken here and there with streams of sunlight through windows that desperately needed a good cleaning. While it was indeed warm outside, the interior of the inn was at least ten degrees cooler.

Taking two more steps, her foot thudded against something on the floor and she nearly stumbled. Kneeling down, she found a small wooden trunk that looked as if it might belong to a child and not an adult.

On top of the trunk was a note.

Went to pick up a drain and a backflow preventer.
Found it in a wall inside the room below the basement.

She tucked the note into her pocket and picked up the trunk, carrying it and half the dust in Ohio to the bar. Though they had already found many interesting artifacts hidden in the old inn, Tess never tired of what Thorn called urban archeology.

To his definition, urban archeology was finding the past hidden in buildings that were being used in the present. To Tess's thoughts, it was just plain fun to see what the old building held.

And this looked to be their biggest treasure yet.

Tess went to the door and waved her hands to get the ladies' attention. "Girls, the contractor found something in the secret room. Come see!"

"How exciting," Janice said as she jumped out of the car, her sore feet and claims of advanced age obviously forgotten.

"Turn on some lights in here," LuAnn said as she followed Janice inside and began flipping switches to illuminate the room.

True to the contractor's questionable skills, the fan overhead sprung to life but the lights that had been recently added remained dark. Ignoring her irritation, Tess returned her attention to the box and the excitement of yet another urban archeology find.

"Open it," LuAnn said. "I bet there's something fabulous inside. I wonder what it could be."

"Only one way to know," Tess said as she toyed with the latch.

"Oh my goodness," Janice said, fanning herself. "Are you sure we shouldn't wait to open it? Anything could be in there."

"There's only one way to find out what's in there," LuAnn said as she grinned at Tess. "Open it."

Tess matched her grin as she lifted the lid. "Here goes nothing."

"Or something," LuAnn said.

"And that's what I'm afraid of," Janice added.

"Ladies, I thought I would find you here." The familiar voice of Bradley Grimes drifted toward them as the door swung open on hinges that definitely needed oiling. "I saw LuAnn's car outside and stopped by to see if you had changed your mind about featuring the inn in the Fourth of July parade." He glanced around the room and then allowed his gaze to settle on LuAnn. "It looks like I've interrupted something more important. Well now," he said as he examined the trunk, "that looks old."

"So does all the dust on it," Janice declared and then sneezed.

"God bless you," Tess, LuAnn, and Brad all said in unison.

"Tess was just about to open it," LuAnn said as she turned her attention from Brad back to Tess. "Go for it."

"Well, all right, then," Tess said. "Here goes nothing."

"You said that already," Janice told her. "Just open the thing. The suspense is killing me."

The trunk opened without a sound, its hinges in much better shape than the inn's front door. The light revealed a package wrapped in crisp white paper. Had she not just opened the trunk and found it there, Tess would have thought the package contained the quilt that LuAnn purchased this morning.

"Look at that," Brad said. "Unless I miss my guess, that is not old."

"I think you're right," LuAnn said as she leaned forward to touch the paper. "It's definitely modern."

"Yes but that dust isn't," Janice offered. "So what's inside?"

Tess carefully unfolded the paper to expose a quilt. And not just any quilt. The fabric was pale ivory and felt fragile to the touch.

Though it had been folded so only the corner was showing, the thread work was unlike anything she'd ever seen. Intricate tiny stitches traveled in a complicated pattern over the pale fabric. This was not the work of an amateur quilter.

"What in the world?" LuAnn said under her breath.

"Goodness gracious goat!" was Janice's reply.

"It's a quilt," Brad said, stating the obvious. "But where could it have come from?"

"The secret room," Janice told him. "The plumber found it in the wall."

He glanced over at Janice. "But where was it before someone put it in the wall? And why in the world would anyone go to all that trouble?"

Tess lifted the corner of the quilt and spied a message embroidered there. "To General Lafayette upon his visit to Marietta in 1825," she read aloud. "May the lost be found along the river of life." Tess gasped. "I think we've found the missing quilt."

"What missing quilt?" Brad asked.

"The missing quilt that the folks at the Arts & Antiques Network are filming a documentary about," Janice supplied. "It was lost but now it's found, apparently."

Tess gently settled the quilt back into the box, then took a step backward. She looked up at her friends who were all still staring at the open trunk on the bar.

"That is just not possible," LuAnn said. "How could a famous lost quilt end up inside a wall in our inn?"

Janice shook her head. "I don't like to think of the answer to that question, Lu. The only possible way it could end up here is if the thief hid it there."

"Wait just a minute," Brad said, holding his hands up. "Are you saying that quilt belonged to General Lafayette?"

"Well," LuAnn said, "that's what the inscription on the quilt says, but from what I've heard there are two of these. The original supposedly went down with a vessel on the river and then a second was made sometime just before President Lincoln was elected."

"I'm confused," Brad said.

"So were we," LuAnn agreed. "But my understanding is the second quilt was used to promote the abolitionist cause in this area. That quilt has been in the National Archives since the late 1800s, or thereabouts, and was about to be put on display for ten days this month. The Arts & Antiques Network is filming a documentary about it that Wendy had hoped would include Marietta."

"You know, I did hear some buzz about some filmmakers wanting permits to film at several places around the city, but I didn't pay much attention to the details," Brad said. "Where exactly was this trunk found?"

"I knew it," Janice said, ignoring the blue-eyed charmer's question. "The network is planning to come here. See, we need to get the inn ready for them."

"Or have a plan to convince them they need to feature us," LuAnn added.

"I think you're both jumping the gun," Tess told her friends. "They might have been planning to come when the quilt was part of an exhibit but now that it's lost, I think we can safely say there won't be any filming in Marietta. Why would there be?"

"Oh, I don't know," Brad said. "Background shots for the story they'll tell about how it's missing? Sort of like that television show that used to film reenactments of how people went missing and then asked viewers to call if they had seen them?"

"I remember that show," Janice said. "Once I could have sworn I saw a fugitive who'd been on the previous night's episode at a gas station in Kansas. We were on our way to Lawrence's sister's house, and he refused to stop and let me call the police. That was before cell phones or I would have called anyway." She grinned. "I still think that was him."

LuAnn giggled. "I don't know which is funnier, Janice catching bad guys or the story we were told about this quilt having a curse put on it."

"I don't think there's anything funny about it," Janice said. "Not that I believe in curses. Except for the ones in the Bible. I mean, if God says it, then I believe it. But a bunch of quilters putting a curse on a quilt to make it disappear any time there is danger? That's just silly." She paused. "And for the record, I am absolutely certain that was the fugitive from the television show, so I hope someone else saw him and called."

"Right, okay." Tess carefully lowered the paper back over the quilt and closed the lid on the box. Her mind reeling, she took a deep breath, then fell into a fit of coughing.

"It's dusty," LuAnn said as she took a step back. "That's our first clue. How could something that just went missing end up in a box that has such a thick layer of dust? That makes no sense."

"It makes no sense that it's here at all," Tess said.

"And yet here it is," Janice said. "Right here. In our inn."

"Isn't it exciting?" LuAnn said. "An artifact of that sort of age and importance hiding *here*."

"I wonder if the quilt was being held for ransom," Janice said. "That would explain why it was hidden."

"But not why there's so much dust," LuAnn offered.

The ladies continued to debate until a loud whistle cut through their discussion. Brad smiled. "Now that I have your attention, I will ask you again. Where exactly was it?"

"Tess found it," Janice said.

All eyes turned toward Tess. "Technically I nearly tripped over it by the door. However, there was a note on it from the plumber."

She reached into her pocket and pulled out the paper. Brad took it and read. He looked up.

"This isn't signed."

Tess looked again. "Well, no, it isn't, but since whoever wrote it was going to get some kind of valve and we've had a plumber here all week, I assume the author is the same person."

"You assume," LuAnn said. "But you don't know for sure."

"Well, no," Tess admitted. "I haven't exactly seen a writing sample so I...oh..." She grinned. "Actually, I have seen a sample of the electrician's handwriting. Before Thorn hired him, he required written estimates from everyone. It's in my files back in my home office."

"Then it should be easy to determine whether he wrote the note. Who is Thorn using, by the way?"

"I can't remember," Tess said, "but Thorn assured me he came highly recommended. I think he said the guy had a connection to the inn. I believe the name of the business was AAA Plumbing, but I could be wrong."

"AAA Plumbing?" Brad said. "And I thought I knew everyone who worked in the building trades in Marietta."

He met her gaze, and she could tell Brad was concerned. Tess shared that concern.

"Thorn vouched for him," was all she could offer.

"Then I'm sure he's fine," Brad said, although she couldn't tell if he meant it or was trying to convince them all.

"We should call someone," Janice blurted out. "People are looking for this thing, and I sure don't want to be the one who had it and didn't tell anyone. What will people think?"

"They will think we found it," Tess assured her fraidy-cat friend. "Which we did. And there's nothing wrong with that."

"But who do we call?" LuAnn countered. "The police? The FBI? The Arts & Antiques Network?"

Janice shook her head. "Just having this thing out here in the open makes me nervous. Anyone walking by on the street can see it. And us. Can't we take it somewhere less visible first?"

"Good idea," LuAnn said. "We need to put it somewhere safe."

"But where?" Janice demanded. "If the thief was able to get the quilt into the inn, then he or she will easily be able to get it out again. And I'm certainly not going to offer my house. I'd never get any sleep knowing something that valuable was under my roof. I doubt Tess would either."

"Relax, Janice," Tess said. "We're not taking this box any-where except away from the front of the building. The last thing we need is for someone to casually walk by and see what we've got. And we don't even know for sure there was a thief. This could be a copy, you know."

"That's true. It's mighty convenient to find a copy of that quilt on the same day the real one goes missing, don't you think?" LuAnn said.

"I can't think right now." Tess gathered up the box, being careful not to smudge the layer of dust on its top. "Follow me, ladies and gentleman," she said. "Brad, would you please lock the door?" she called as casually as she could manage.

It wouldn't do to get her friends overwrought, but Tess had a bad feeling about this. There was something very specific about the thief—if indeed this was the stolen quilt—choosing the inn as his or her hiding place.

Something creepy.

Tess shook off the thought as she headed toward the kitchen. The oversized room, once the hub of the inn, was so close to completion that LuAnn and Winnie would be testing soup recipes soon.

Because the painters were preparing the window trim for a fresh coat of white paint to match the cabinets, the windows had been covered in brown paper to protect the old panes from drips. Thus, the normally bright and airy kitchen was completely hidden from the outside world.

Lights blazed overhead as LuAnn flipped the switch. The room smelled of turpentine and oil-based paint. And best of all, only the tiniest amount of filtered sunlight filtered through the brown paper.

The highlight of the kitchen, however, was the authentic 1954 O'Keefe & Merritt Aristocrat stove that had been fully restored to her original glory and then wrapped in a coat of fire engine red paint. When Tess looked at the grand beauty, she saw perfect lines and a vintage appliance that could stand up to or best any modern commercial range. LuAnn, however, saw two baking ovens, two broiling ovens, six cooktop burners, and a whole host of other things that only a chef could figure out.

No matter who was looking at it, Big Red, as Tess had named her, was absolutely stunning. And practical.

But mostly stunning.

Returning her attention to the task at hand, Tess gently placed the box on the oversized island and then took a step backward. "Now what, people?"

"Now we pull that thing out and take a good look at it," Janice said. "I want to see just what we've got all wrapped up in there."

"I know you're curious, but what if it's fragile? I say now we call the authorities," Brad said.

A knock at the front door caused Janice to squeal and hide behind Brad while LuAnn gasped. "Who could that possibly be?" Tess asked.

"It's probably your plumber, Mr. Davis," Brad said as he made his way toward the door. "I'm going to go see."

Brad smiled and immediately LuAnn appeared to relax, reminding Tess of how good those two would be together. "Probably," she echoed.

Another series of knocks, this time more insistent. "I know you're in there," an unfamiliar but ominous male voice called. "Don't make me call the cops."

CHAPTER FOUR

"You have got to be kidding me," Brad said as he stormed toward the door.

"It sounds like Brad knows who that is," LuAnn said.

Janice nodded, her face pale. "And he doesn't sound pleased."

Tess's heart jumped to her throat. "No, he doesn't."

"What are we going to do?" Janice said in a loud whisper. "Goodness gracious goat!"

LuAnn glanced around the room. "Until we can figure out who to trust with this, we need to hide the trunk."

"Good idea," Janice agreed. "But where?"

Tess looked around the room and spied the perfect solution. Big Red.

Snatching up the trunk, she gestured to LuAnn, who was nearest to her target. With all those oven doors available for the choosing, even if someone wanted to look for the little trunk, the odds were extremely low that it would be found on the first try. Or even the second or third.

"Open one of those oven doors up," she said as she carefully but quickly moved toward the O'Keefe & Merritt.

"No," Janice said. "You absolutely cannot put that quilt in the oven. It is far too dangerous."

The front door opened on loud hinges. Men's voices rose.

Tess turned her attention to the former home economics teacher. "Unless you plan to bake a cake right now, I can't see a better alternative. Can you?"

The front door slammed shut as the sound of two men's voices drifted toward them. Though it was impossible to tell if their banter was friendly or argumentative, no one could miss the fact that the men were heading their way.

"That is a precious piece of history. We have a responsibility to take care of it until the mystery of where it came from is solved. Shoving it into an oven is not taking care of it!"

"Look," Brad said as he seemed to be just outside the closed kitchen door. "Can we do this another day? I'm kind of busy right now."

LuAnn pressed past Janice and pulled open Big Red's nearest oven door just in time for Tess to shove her treasure inside. The door slammed shut, and Tess leaned against it. She put on her best smile as Brad pressed open the kitchen door and stepped back inside.

On his heels was a man of similar age and build, but where Brad was dressed in business-casual khakis and button-down shirt, this fellow wore a brightly colored Hawaiian shirt with palm trees marching across the front and a pair of tan cargo shorts. His tan was hard to miss, as was the crossed drumsticks tattoo that climbed up his right forearm.

"Ladies," Brad said with very little enthusiasm, "may I introduce you to my younger brother Grant? Emphasis on young."

The man looked exactly how Brad would have looked twenty years ago, Tess decided, as she bypassed the matching broad smiles to see that the man's eyes were the same distinctive blue as Brad's. And where Brad kept his gray hair close-cropped and well-groomed, Grant was sporting a brown, shaggier hairstyle.

If Brad Grimes was *GQ*, then Grant Grimes was most definitely *Rolling Stone*.

"By seventeen years," Grant declared as his gaze scanned the room. "So you three must be the women my aunts call 'Brad's women.'" He elbowed his brother then made a motion like a drumstick crashing a cymbal and grinned. "You always had good taste, big brother, but this time you've outdone yourself. Rock on."

"And you have always managed to make a fool out of yourself in the first five minutes you meet a lady," Brad snapped.

Refusing to move away from the oven, Tess upped her smile. "It's very nice to meet you, Grant," she said. "But you've got the wrong impression about us. We're friends, and that's all. I'm sure if your aunts have spoken about us they have been very clear about that."

Grant shrugged. "My aunts are very clear about a lot of stuff. Doesn't mean I pay much attention. They're old and they talk a lot."

"Wonderful," Brad said under his breath. "Don't you have another vacation to take or something?"

Grant ignored him to turn his attention to Janice. "And who do we have here? Women with curls rock."

"Grant, I was your pastor's wife, but then, I am a little older than the last time I saw you, so I suppose I can understand how you wouldn't recognize me. Oh, and I count your brother as a friend. Period," she continued in an unmistakably teacher-like tone. "But thank you for the compliment about my curls. They're more of a bother than anything else."

Grant seemed unsure of what to say. Finally he smiled. "If anything you look younger, Mrs. Eastman. Please forgive my rudeness," he said before his attention moved on to LuAnn. "Which one of Bradley's angels are you?"

LuAnn extended her hand to greet the stranger. "LuAnn, and I am also a *friend* of your brother's, so I will take that comment as the joke I'm sure you meant and not a suggestion of anything else. Pleased to meet you all the same."

Grant accepted her hand but instead of shaking it, he turned her palm down to kiss the top of her hand. "Feisty, isn't she?" he said as he winked at Brad. "The pleasure is all mine."

"Uh, Grant," Brad said as he moved between his brother and LuAnn, "what brings you here to the inn?"

"You do, actually." He stepped back and allowed his gaze to move between LuAnn and Brad. Though he seemed to be assessing what the true situation was between the pair, he refrained from commenting further.

"Well," Brad said, "here I am. What did you need?"

Grant shrugged. "A minute of your time. But first, what did I interrupt? For a bunch of folks who are all claiming you're just friends, you sure look to be in cahoots about something."

Silence fell. Tess looked around the room and saw that no one appeared ready to respond.

"Fourth of July parade," she blurted out as she leaned back against the oven. "We were discussing the inn's float for the parade. It's just three days away, you know."

"Yes," Janice said, relief etching her expression. "We have much to plan. What to wear, how to decorate the float..."

Her words faded away. LuAnn nodded and took up the thread of conversation. "Yes, I was just saying that I thought it would be a great idea to use that red, white, and blue quilt for our design."

At the word *quilt*, Tess cringed and wrapped her fingers tighter around the oven door handle. Her fingers brushed something that felt like metal. It moved. She adjusted her fingers to move it back into place.

"Something wrong?" Grant asked her.

"Wrong?" She shook her head. "No. We're just debating how to accomplish the right theme for the inn, and Brad has such great ideas. Don't you, Brad?"

"Ideas," he echoed. "For the inn's float. Yes, well, there are lots of them. Ideas, I mean. We're just going to have to decide on one and stick to it."

"I say go with the quilt idea," Janice said. "Why don't we all close up the inn and head over to the Sassy Seamstress and get that red, white, and blue quilt?"

"I think that sounds like a great idea," LuAnn said. "Brad, how about you and your brother come with us over to the Sassy Seamstress?"

"Sassy Seamstress?" Grant said, shaking his head.

"You know," Brad said. "That building downtown that changed hands a few months ago in some kind of super secret cash sale."

"Oh yeah, I remember that. Weird how that all went down, man."

"It was," Brad told them. "One minute we had a promise of listing the building, and the next minute a representative of the family told us they'd had a buyer and completed the sale."

"We do know how real estate sales can go south here, don't we, Bradley?" Tess said. "But in our case we were meant to own the inn, so here we are."

"Yes," Brad said, his expression unreadable. "Here we are. I mean you. Anyway, let's get out of here and let these ladies do whatever it was they were doing before we interrupted them."

Unfortunately, Grant remained rooted in place. "You know, I heard about that little issue you ladies had in getting this building purchased, but our agency handled it, didn't we? I mean we are the best in town, aren't we, big brother?"

"Maybe we could all talk about this on the way to the shop," LuAnn offered as she moved toward the door.

Brad tried to follow LuAnn but quickly realized Grant wasn't going anywhere. "So what are your plans for the inn? I mean as far as renovations go?"

"Our LuAnn has a master list of everything we're going to be doing, so she's the one who could best answer that question," Janice said as she made eye contact with Tess.

When Grant turned away to look back at Brad, Janice mouthed a hasty, "Get him out of here" to LuAnn.

"Well, much as I wish we could have listed that building where the Snappy Stitcher is, I'm sure glad we were able to list this one," Grant said. "I was right about taking on that contact, wasn't I, Brad?"

"Sassy Seamstress," LuAnn corrected. "And truly, you just have to see what they have. I've been very impressed."

"LuAnn is right," Brad told him. "It's an impressive shop. But right now, I think we are keeping these ladies from getting some work done here. How about you and I go grab a late lunch, and we can talk about whatever it is you wanted to talk about?"

"And leave these ladies here to fend for themselves when there are two strong men who can help?" He shook his head. "Well, one strong man and my brother Brad," he told LuAnn and then added a grin.

"Very funny. Let's go, Grant," Brad said.

"All right but not until you admit that it's your turn to pay."

"Mine?" Brad protested. "I paid last time. And for that matter, I have paid every single time in recent memory."

Grant offered the ladies a smile. "He remembers things a little differently than I do."

"Conveniently," Brad snapped.

Tess listened to the men banter for as long as she could stand it. Finally she turned around and faced the oven, her temper boiling.

And that's when she felt the heat of the oven.

"Oh no!" she said as she looked down to see that she'd somehow turned the oven on. Quickly, she fiddled with the levers and knobs until she found which of the multiple ovens on the old stove had been lit.

Fortunately, it was not the oven where she'd put the trunk. Still, she needed to get that trunk out of there fast. Who knew whether that side of the oven might be heating up too?

Seeing her dilemma, Janice sprang into action. "Come on, Grant and Brad," she said as she linked arms with the surprised Grimes brothers and led them out of the kitchen. "There's no need to argue over who's going to pay for lunch. It's on me today."

"You two go on ahead. I'll catch up," Brad said as he stuck his head back into the kitchen. "What just happened?"

Tess couldn't stop giggling. "I have no idea, but it worked."

"Bradley, are you coming with us or not?" Grant called.

"Yeah, give me a second." He fixed his attention on Tess. "Get that box out of the oven. That was a close call."

"Speaking of calls," LuAnn said. "Who are we going to call?"

"Ghostbusters?" Tess offered.

"That goose will be the death of us all with her noise, Wife."
Jason gave Prudence a protective hug but she knew he was
distracted by Patience, who had just ceased a symphony of
noisy honks. The source of her alarm this time had been a
dead tree limb that had the audacity to fall within the range
of her hearing.

"As thou hast reminded me in the past, that goose just
may save us all with her noise, Husband," she said gently.
"Remember that what annoys thee most is also what draws
attention to anyone who might approach."

She let that thought settle between them. Gradually her
husband relaxed his expression.

"I suppose thee are correct." Jason looked down at the
log and then back up at Prudence. He now wore the smile
she so loved. "Now that we've been approached by this log, I
will do my best to remedy the situation by turning it into
firewood."

Prudence bit back a warning and let her concern over
the wisdom of a man with Jason's injuries swinging an ax
become a prayer. The Father had allowed her husband to
survive what he should not have survived. Who was she to
question what He would do with the man He had given
her?

She squeezed Jason's hand and then looked up past the
canopy of trees to the vast blue sky that was slowly fading to

purple as twilight moved closer. Each evening the Lord allowed her to see the sun set with this man by her side was a gift. A precious gift given by a loving Father.

Moses's cry interrupted her thoughts and caused her to turn back toward the house where her son would be wanting his next meal. Jason fell into step beside her, his gait not nearly as slow as it had been since the incident that led to his injuries.

Another reason to be thankful, Prudence reminded herself.

"Perhaps thee could wait until tomorrow to chop the limb?" Prudence suggested, though she knew she would return from the quilting tonight with a freshly cut stack of wood waiting by the door, even if that meant Jason had to complete the task by torchlight.

After seeing to both her son's and her husband's dinners, Prudence bundled up baby Moses and slung the handle of her sewing basket over her arm. Her hand trembled as she reached for the doorknob, but she quickly steadied herself lest her husband realize her concern.

Tonight's quilting was not the first she'd attended, but it was the first to be used for a purpose other than making bedcoverings. The last thing she needed to add to the anxiety already growing in her heart was the concern that Jason could harm himself while she was away.

A familiar Scripture rose to her mind. *It is better to trust in the* LORD *than to put confidence in man.*

That reminder of exactly Who was in control immediately soothed her worries. Jason would be fine. Or at least he would be under the Lord's watch and not hers.

And that was the best place for anyone to be.

"Yes, Lord," she whispered as she closed the door behind her. Prudence tucked Moses close to her as the comfort found in Psalm 118:8 followed her down the path toward the inn.

And so did Patience.

CHAPTER FIVE

By the time Janice returned from her surprise lunch with the Grimes brothers, Tess had given up on deciding which of the many law enforcement agencies should be called and had sent LuAnn to summon the ultimate authority on the quilt: Wendy at the Sassy Seamstress.

They decided they wouldn't let Wendy know the reason for their sudden interest in the missing quilt. Instead, they would have their expert clue them in on everything she knew about the artifact.

Or at least that was the plan.

Seated on a stool in the kitchen, Tess ran her finger along the edge of the painter's drop cloth she'd used to cover the trunk.

Janice settled her purse on the old butcher block and regarded her with a questioning look. "Where's LuAnn?"

"I sent her to get Wendy. We decided we could ask some questions about what we've got before we decide who to tell."

"So she wouldn't know we have it, then?" Janice said as the front door opened.

Tess moved to stand between the trunk and the door. "Who's that?" she called.

"It's just me. Wendy wasn't there." LuAnn stepped into the kitchen without their expert. "There's a sign on the door that said she'd be back tomorrow." She paused to look at Janice. "Well, I see you're back from your double date. That was impressive."

"I thought so too," Tess said as she returned to the stool. "I've known you since college and I cannot remember a single time you asked a man to go to lunch, much less two of them."

Janice laughed. "When I saw that oven light come on and knew there was a one in four chance that the oven Tess had accidentally turned on was heating up a national treasure, I had to do something. So I blurted out the first thing I could think of, other than goodness gracious goat, which was what I was thinking. Once I realized I would have to sit through an entire meal with those two, I just about had a panic attack."

"Well, I'm glad you didn't," Tess said. "You're our hero—or rather heroine. You definitely saved the day."

"You certainly did," LuAnn agreed. "I shudder to think what might have happened."

Janice smiled. "So the quilt wasn't harmed?"

Tess noted that Janice seemed to stand a little taller beneath the praise. "Not this time." She eyed the pile of painter's drop cloths on the kitchen counter. "But it could have been, so we really need to figure out how to keep it safe until we can decide what to do with it."

LuAnn pulled up a stool at the counter and gestured for Janice to join them. "Let's put our heads together and reason this out. Who besides Wendy at the Sassy Seamstress would know anything about a famous quilt with ties to Marietta going missing?"

"Maybelline Rector," all three said at once.

"But only two of us should go," Tess said. "Lu, you're the history buff so you should be the one to go for sure. If the conversation lags, you can always bring up something about Napoleon or Lafayette or one of those folks to keep Maybelline from throwing us out on our ears."

LuAnn laughed. "I'm glad my interest in history is going to finally get some use."

"Now, which of us goes and which of us stays?" Tess said to Janice.

"Can I do neither?" Janice asked. "I don't want to be responsible for watching over what could be a valuable international treasure, but I sure don't want to go over there and face Maybelline Rector and have to try to wrangle information out of her. She'd know for sure I was hiding something and just like I did when I invited the Grimes brothers to lunch, I will say or do something stupid."

Tess wrapped her arm around her friend. "That was a stroke of brilliance, Janice. You saved the quilt and got those two men out of here when neither LuAnn nor I could budge them."

"Well, budge Grant," LuAnn said. "But Tess is right. We tried, but you succeeded."

"Then maybe I should stay here?" she said, her tone doubtful.

"I agree," Tess said.

"But we can't just leave the quilt out on the counter," Janice protested. "It needs to be hidden somewhere."

"And not the oven," LuAnn added.

Tess looked around the room and then gathered up the trunk and the painter's cloth that covered it. "Janice, would you open that pantry door, please?"

Janice rose to cross the room and do as Tess asked. Inside the pantry, a shelf-lined room the size of a walk-in closet, were stacks of cleaning supplies, paint, and various other items. Tess stepped over the mess and situated the trunk in the corner and then backtracked to view her handiwork.

"With the mops and brooms and all the paint cans stacked as they are, no one will know there's anything behind them," Tess said.

"Much less a priceless quilt," LuAnn offered.

"Thanks," Janice said. "I didn't need that reminder."

Tess smiled as she ushered Janice out of the pantry. "Don't you worry," she said gently. "No one knows about that quilt but us."

"And the plumber," Janice reminded her.

"Yes, that's true," Tess said. "We'll need to investigate him further, but first I think we need to go see Maybelline."

"I agree," LuAnn said. "If that contractor had any idea what he found, he certainly wouldn't have left it on the floor with a note, would he?"

"No," Janice said thoughtfully. "I doubt he would have just left it there. He probably just thought it was something left over from previous owners that we might find interesting."

"It's definitely interesting, whether it's the lost quilt or just one that looks like it." Tess paused to close the pantry door and then returned her attention to Janice.

"And if the plumber returns?" Janice said.

"We've got questions for him, but I prefer all of us to be there when those questions are asked," Tess said. "I doubt you have to worry about that guy coming back today."

Janice's expression relaxed slightly. "Okay, then. I guess I can stay here for a little while by myself."

"Sure you can," LuAnn said. "It won't take long. We promise."

Tess nodded in unison with LuAnn. "It's just over to the museum and then we'll come right back." She gave Janice a look of what she hoped would be encouragement. "You'll be fine."

"I will," she said although Tess wasn't certain whether she meant the words as a statement or a question.

Having left a somewhat fearful Janice behind to guard the quilt—or to make sure the doors to the kitchen stayed locked and no one returned to try to get in—they elected to make an attempt to see Marietta's foremost authority on the history of the town without an appointment.

Emma, a woman in her twenties whom Tess recognized from the local vintage clothing shop, met them at the museum door. Tall and tanned with beautiful dark hair that she wore casually tied into a ponytail at the nape of her neck, she was dressed in denim shorts and a faded orange T-shirt.

"I didn't expect to find you here, Emma," Tess said. "Don't you work at Antoinette's Closet?"

"I do," she said, "but I also volunteer here at the museum one or two days a month as a docent."

Tess looked down at the young woman's clothing. She certainly wasn't dressed for the part of docent today. More like handyman or painter. Still, her outfit was a far cry from the usual polka-dot ensembles she wore.

"We're not officially open today," she said as she looked down at her clothes and then back up at Tess. "We're getting ready for the Fourth of July celebration. Not only are we doing a float, but the Marietta Underground Railroad Museum is also hosting an open house. Is there something I can help you with?"

"Actually," Tess said, "we were just wondering if Maybelline might be around. I've got a few questions that I think she may be able to answer."

"About the inn? Oh my goodness. I am so excited that you ladies are fixing up that old inn. It's such a fascinating piece of town history, and who doesn't love history?" Her broad smile and enthusiasm suggested that the Marietta High Cheerleader shirt she wore was likely earned and not borrowed.

Besides, as a former cheerleader herself, Tess could spot a kindred soul a mile away. There was just something about being handed pom-poms and told to wrangle a crowd into chanting encouragement to a bunch of sweaty football players that gave a girl special insight.

Or maybe it just took one to know one.

"I love history," LuAnn said.

"So do I." Tess slid LuAnn a sideways look. "And yes, actually, the questions are in regard to the inn."

Emma's expression softened as she nodded for them to follow her. "Oh, what a dreamy place it's going to be. I'm so excited to see what you're doing with the place. I always hoped one day to have a wedding there. Do you plan on hosting weddings?"

Tess smiled as she spied an old photograph of the inn in an exhibit called Marietta Responds to World War II. The parlor had been turned into a Red Cross staging area where local women rolled bandages.

"We will definitely be hosting weddings," Tess said. "The parlor on the first floor would be a lovely place for a reception, and we've got a full-sized caterer's kitchen being installed that would certainly allow for any sort of celebration."

Emma's enthusiasm returned. "That is so exciting. People will come from all over."

"We certainly hope so," Tess said as she thought of the budget required to restore the inn and how long she had projected before their investment would break even.

"For sure," Emma said.

They were now passing an exhibit dedicated to forms of transportation used along the river. Tess paused to admire a painting done in brilliant colors. A paddle steamer sat at the dock near where the park was now situated. Alongside the larger vessel were several smaller ones. Men ran up and down the river's edge, many carrying heavy burdens. What a difference when compared to the quiet riverside area that now existed there.

"Hey," Emma said, distracting Tess from her thoughts. "Did you know I come from one of the families who originally settled here? There are things in this museum that belonged to my ancestors. I guess that's why I love history so much."

"I didn't know that," Tess said, "but then I'm still learning about Marietta."

"So you'll be living in the inn too?" she asked, her blue eyes wide. "How exciting. All of you or just you?"

"All three of us. Another friend, Janice Eastman, is our third partner in the venture."

"Mrs. Eastman the home economics teacher? The one who was with you when you bought those outfits from the vintage store?" she asked as her eyes brightened. "She's such a nice lady. I still make the sugar cookie recipe she taught us every year for Christmas."

"The very same one," Tess said as she once again fell into step beside Emma.

"Well, you tell her that Emma from second period said hello, won't you? I should have said that when you came into the shop, but I had my mind on other things."

"I will," Tess said.

"Speaking of that," Emma said. "I heard you've hired Mr. Thornton as your handyman. That was really nice of you."

"He has been a godsend," LuAnn said as she wandered into the room adjacent to the foyer.

"Yes he has," Tess agreed. "We're blessed to have him working for us. Now, about that visit with Maybelline. Do you think we could see her for just a minute? You can tell her we promise we won't take up much of her time."

Emma nodded. "Sure thing. I'll just be a minute."

Tess looked around for LuAnn and found her standing in front of a glass case filled with what appeared to be the contents of an antique kitchen. "What did you find?" she asked her.

"Look at this," she said. "It's a display of Civil War era recipes and cookware. And here's a soup. This would be a great addition to the menu at the inn."

"I'm sure we can get a copy if you ask Maybelline nicely."

LuAnn grinned. "Or if I just try really hard to remember it."

Tess shrugged. "Surely she will give you less trouble about having a copy of a recipe than she did about us buying the inn. Remember, she did change her mind about us."

"True," LuAnn said as she gave the recipe card one last long look. "I think I can remember it. Remind me to look at it again before we leave." She shook her head. "Sorry, I didn't even ask. Did Maybelline agree to see us?"

She nodded toward the door where a beaming Emma was watching them. "We're about to find out."

"Come with me," Emma said. "Mrs. Rector said she would see you as soon as she can break away from her meeting."

A few minutes later, Tess and LuAnn were seated in the office of the woman herself awaiting their turn to speak with her. The room was a jumble of books spilling off shelves on two walls and ancient filing cabinets filling the spaces between them. Rolls of documents were stacked atop a small harvest table that sat beneath the room's only window, sharing space with a pair of African violets that appeared to be flourishing. Outside, the sights and sounds of the outdoors were muffled by thick green brocade curtains that looked as if they were left over from some genteel dining room of another era.

Minutes turned into what seemed like an hour. Finally the door opened. "She won't be but a minute longer," Emma said, her cheerleader-like demeanor still in place.

Another ten minutes passed, and LuAnn stood. "We've waited long enough," she said. "I say we go back to the inn and come up with another plan. She's obviously too busy to see us today, although it would have been nice if she—"

"I am so sorry," Maybelline said as she threw open the door and hurried inside.

With hair the color of the sauce at Bar-B-Cutie, the museum director would have been noticed wherever she went. But in this room full of subdued colors and scholarly materials, she stood out like the proverbial sore thumb. So did the lime green sandals, skirt, and matching top she had paired with a chunky necklace dotted with sunflowers.

"Please forgive me for making you wait so long," she said as she hurried to take the seat behind her desk. "We at the museum are committed to bringing all the best pieces of Marietta history to rest under our roof, and I was in the middle of an exciting conversation that just might bring a whole other..."

Maybelline paused and seemed to be reconsidering the direction her statement was going. "Well anyway, Emma said you had a question for me."

"We do." Tess offered LuAnn a tentative look before turning her attention to the woman who once tried to prevent them from buying the inn.

She sat back in her chair. "So ask away."

"Okay," Tess said, and took a breath for courage. "It's about a quilt. A special quilt that has ties to activities with the Underground Railroad in Marietta. It's called the River of Life quilt. We were wondering if you had heard the rumors about—"

"They're true!" Maybelline exclaimed and then grinned. "I don't know how the news has traveled so fast, but yes, the rumors are true. The Arts and Antiques Network is going to interview me about the missing River of Life quilt."

"Well, Tess, how about that?" LuAnn said.

"Yes," Tess managed. "How about that?"

"I just got off the phone with the producer, so I truly don't know how you found out so fast, but I'm just pleased as punch to be asked to take part in the filming."

"Filming?" Tess said. "Here in Marietta?"

"Well, here at the museum, but yes," she said. "Now that the River of Life quilt is missing, the plan for the documentary that was in progress has been adjusted to follow the course of the mystery until the quilt is found. Since the quilt was made in Marietta, *Quilt Mysteries* is coming here to investigate and I am the expert. Isn't it exciting?"

"It is," Tess said as she tried to process the news.

"Are you a fan too?"

"No, sorry," Tess said. LuAnn shook her head to indicate she had not seen the show either.

"Well, since you are renovating a property with historic value, you really should be. The premise is, there are all these fabulous antique quilts that have stories no one has told. The show investigates and tells the stories. The Lafayette quilt episode was already in progress when the River of Life quilt went missing. Those poor folks at the network are beside themselves."

"With excitement?" Tess quipped.

A crimson flush climbed up into Maybelline's cheeks as her eyes narrowed. "Why in the world would you say that?" she said, her expression aghast.

"Because a missing quilt has got to generate publicity," Tess said. "And publicity has to be good for business. That's certainly what I have learned over the years."

"I'm sure you have," Maybelline said, her tone haughty. "But the theft of a priceless artifact is hardly something that a lover of history would want to celebrate."

Suitably chastised, Tess simply nodded. Meanwhile, Maybelline continued to stare at her as if expecting a response of some sort.

"What can you tell us about the quilt?" LuAnn said.

When Maybelline glanced away, Tess sent LuAnn a look of thanks. Because the only response she could think of was to repeat that a quilt of that provenance and value would only go missing for one of two reasons: money or publicity. Or, possibly, for both.

The museum director seemed grateful to shift her attention to the former history teacher. "I can tell you that the women who created that quilt did so at the request of persons who were active on the Underground Railroad. These men planned to take advantage of the town's ties to the famous Lafayette quilt but with a twist. You see, this quilt would carry special information."

"You mean like signals to alert escapees to places that were friendly to the Underground Railroad?" Tess offered.

Maybelline returned another less-than-pleased look. "No," she said tersely. "Any stories regarding quilts being used as an Underground Railroad signal are likely pure fiction. But quilts as a way to safely tell others about the cause? Yes, that would be true."

"I don't follow," Tess said. "How would a quilt do that?"

"Well," Maybelline said slowly, "I've never actually seen the quilt in question, but history records that the River of Life quilt was meant as a gift for Abraham Lincoln."

"Do you think there's any truth to the rumor that there's a curse?" Tess asked.

"Curse?" Maybelline shook her head. "Whatever do you mean?"

"We were told that the curse the women who sewed the quilt put on it kept the artifact from falling into the wrong hands," LuAnn said. "Whenever there was danger of discovery, the quilt disappeared."

"And who told you that?" The museum director's smile was still in place, but all humor had left her face. "Because that's an interesting story."

"Wendy at Sassy Seamstress," Tess offered. "Have you met her yet? I'm sure you two would get along famously."

"She's that new girl, isn't she?" Maybelline shrugged. "I'm sorry to say I haven't had an opportunity to welcome her to the city, but I will certainly do that at my earliest opportunity."

"I think you'd enjoy talking quilts with her," LuAnn said. "But back to the River of Life quilt specifically. What would the gift of a quilt to a presidential candidate mean to the Underground Railroad?"

Maybelline looked at LuAnn with admiration. "That is exactly the mystery the show was trying to solve when the quilt disappeared. Some think the intricate pattern that matched our local rivers held the key to showing the future president exactly how many supporters the abolitionist movement had here in this part of the country. Others think the quilt was merely a cover for whatever else was going on at Riverfront House." She paused. "Oh, cover. Get it? That's quite a pun."

LuAnn grinned. "It is," she said as she slid a glance toward Tess as if encouraging her to respond with the appropriate humor.

"Okay," Tess said instead as she thought carefully of how she wanted to word her question. "Exactly how would someone go about authenticating this River of Life quilt? If it is ever found, that is. Are there pictures of it? Or, I suppose given the time period, are there drawings of it?"

"None known to exist, no." Maybelline shrugged. "We have mention of it in diary entries from that time but nothing else."

"Then how will anyone know when it is found?"

"Oh," Maybelline said with a gleam in her eyes, "there are ways."

CHAPTER SIX

"What do you mean she wouldn't tell you how the quilt could be authenticated?" Janice rested her elbows on the kitchen counter and shook her head. "That makes no sense."

"It does if you're worried that anyone other than you might be interviewed," Tess said. "My guess is she wants us to know as little as possible so she's the star. She didn't actually say she wouldn't tell us. It was sort of like she couldn't with a dash of she wouldn't."

"Well, whatever the reason, I would agree it makes no sense," LuAnn said. "She did give that passionate speech about true historians not being willing to use something like this for publicity."

Tess shrugged. "And maybe she meant that, but if she did, then why not tell as many people what you know about the missing quilt so it could possibly be found faster?" She shook her head. "I don't buy it. Maybelline Rector is hiding something."

"Hold that thought." LuAnn reached into her purse and grabbed her keys, then headed out of the kitchen.

"Where are you going?" Janice called.

"To get my notebook," she said over her shoulder. "We need to be writing these clues down."

"We?" Tess called. "Don't you mean *you*?"

The front door opened and closed as LuAnn's laughter followed her outside. Tess cast a quick glance at the pantry door and then turned her attention to Janice. "Until we know more about what we have and how that quilt came to be here, I don't think we need to tell anyone we have it. What do you think?"

"Including the police?"

"Yes," Tess said. "I've thought about this, and it makes no sense to report an old trunk our plumber found in a wall to the authorities. Now, if the contents of that old trunk turn out to be something valuable that was stolen, that's a different story. But we don't know that yet, do we?"

"No, we don't." Janice shook her head, her curls bouncing. "I think I wish we had never found that thing," she said. "But since that can't be changed, I guess you're right. But what are we going to do with it while we're trying to solve the mystery?"

"I've thought about that too, and I think the only reasonable thing to do is to lock it away where no one can get to it. The quilt is certainly not safe here, especially with construction going on. With the Fourth of July holiday just a couple of days away, the town will basically be shut down for the parade and celebrations anyway."

"All right," Janice said, "but please don't ask me to keep it at my house. I just don't think I could sleep knowing that thing was under the same roof as me. I mean, who knows who might be after it? And I certainly don't want to end up on television being questioned about something that I know almost nothing about."

Tess smiled gently. Her dear friend was bold when she needed to be, but oh how she could be fearful as well.

"There's nothing to worry about," she told her. "We'll keep it wrapped in the painter's cloth and carry it out to LuAnn's car when no one is looking. I'll have LuAnn park her car in my garage. From there, we can bring it into my house and lock it up in Jeffrey's gun safe. It's empty now that Jeff Jr. has the guns, so there's plenty of room for the trunk."

Janice appeared to be considering this. Finally she nodded. "Yes," she said. "I think that could work. No one would think there was anything odd about us taking a stack of painter's cloths out of the inn, and if anyone did go to the trouble of following you and LuAnn back to your house, once the garage doors shut, they wouldn't be able to see what you did with the contents of the trunk anyway." Janice paused to smile. "Yes, that's a good plan. Do you want me to follow you to be sure no one tries to waylay you on the way to your house?"

Tess tried to imagine her fearful friend stopping some imagined carjacking and could only giggle. "Thank you," she said, "but I don't think that's necessary. Besides, on an average day, we would go our separate ways, so let's just do what we always do."

"That does make sense." Janice shook her head again. "You know, Tess, when the In Crowd became the Inn Crowd, I didn't think we would also become sleuths, but it sure does look like it, doesn't it?"

Just last month they had to figure out who was behind a series of mysterious happenings at the inn.

"That's true, Janice," she said, "but we're pretty good sleuths, if I do say so myself. If we weren't, we wouldn't be standing in our kitchen planning for the opening of our inn."

"And apparently for the float we're putting into the Fourth of July parade," Janice said.

"What?" Tess shook her head. "We didn't enter a float in the parade."

Janice looked reluctant to respond. "Well," she managed, "I guess I should have already mentioned that while I was at lunch with Brad and Grant, Bart Sandman came over to our table to speak to the guys."

"And what does the owner of the town's Porsche dealership have to do with us entering a float in the parade?"

"That is a good question. You see, he was telling the Grimes brothers how he had just been offered an old fire truck in trade for one of his new vehicles, but he was a little hesitant to take the trade even though apparently the fire truck is a valuable antique."

"Okay," Tess said. "Again, what does that have to do with the parade? And, more specifically, with us putting a float in the parade?"

Janice shrugged. "Well, they were talking and I got drawn into the conversation. And it just sounded like so much fun when they were discussing all the great ideas for making use of the fire truck. Then Paul Townsend came in and he joined us at the table."

"That's nice," Tess said, again wondering what the chairman of the local bank had to do with the owners of the inn entering a float in the parade.

"He is very nice, actually," Janice said. "But then I knew him from church choir for all those years before he became a somebody in this town. He has such a lovely baritone voice. Truly, you cannot imagine how beautiful his rendition of 'O Holy Night' is. I wonder if the new pastor would be willing to ask him to sing it at Christmas this year. Oh, that would be lovely. I don't know why I hadn't thought of that before now. It's been years since—"

"Janice," Tess interrupted. "The parade float?"

"Oh, yes, that." She shrugged. "Well, so Paul was saying how great the fire truck would look all decorated up at Christmas and parked alongside the holiday decorations down at the riverfront park, and Brad said that he thought it would be a great idea for the city to buy the truck or maybe for a group of local business owners to get together and donate it so it could be used for local events. I said I thought that was a wonderful idea, which I still think it is."

"Yes," Tess said. "It does sound like a good idea. But again..."

"What does it have to do with us entering a float in the Fourth of July parade? I'm getting to that. So Grant said that we mentioned possibly doing a float that had something to do with the red, white, and blue quilt we saw at Sassy Seamstress."

Tess groaned. "Yes, that's true. But we were just trying to get Grant out of the kitchen. We didn't actually intend on entering a float."

"Well no one told Grant that," Janice said. "He thought our idea of a float based on that quilt was such a good idea that he told not only Paul and Brad but also Ed Baxter from Hilltop Auto Wrecking. Ed insisted on getting the fire truck ready for its big debut in the parade."

Again Tess groaned. "With us riding on it?"

"Not just us," Janice said. "Brad thought we should invite Wendy from Sassy Seamstress since she's a new business owner and our theme quilt came from her store."

"That Brad is brilliant," Tess said sarcastically. "So let me get this straight. In the course of the hour that you were gone today, you got the city of Marietta an antique fire truck and us a ride in the parade on the thing along with poor Wendy who may or may not agree to hang out with us along the parade route?"

"Yes," Janice said, "that's about the size of it. You know though, none of this would have happened if we'd just gone to breakfast at the tearoom like we planned instead of taking that detour into the quilt shop and letting Wendy get us all worked up about a missing quilt ruining some television network possibly coming to Marietta." She paused to let out a long breath. "So we're going to be the grand marshals. Sue me."

"Grand marshals?"

"Yes, didn't I tell you that?"

"No." Tess started giggling and couldn't stop. By the time Janice joined her, there were tears rolling down her cheeks.

"Janice, Tess!" LuAnn called. "Would you come out here, please?"

"Oh my goodness," Janice said. "I didn't even hear LuAnn come back in. I wonder what's going on?"

Tess wiped her cheeks and followed Janice out the kitchen door. They found LuAnn standing near the front entry with a man wearing jeans, work boots, and a navy shirt that bore the name Tom over the right pocket.

"Look who's back," LuAnn said with a smile. "The plumber."

"We sure are glad to see you," Janice said.

"And we're very glad to see that you're finally back," Tess said.

"I did say on that note that I was coming right back." Tom shrugged. "It just took a little longer than I expected because they were out at my usual supplier so I had to go to a couple of other places before I found what I needed." He lifted a paper sack as if proving what he was saying. "So I'll just go back down in the basement and finish what I started, and I promise it won't take long."

"Wait!" all three of them said in unison.

When Prudence arrived at Riverfront House, the quilting was already underway. Leaving the goose outside, she closed the inn's door behind her and hurried to her place at the quilting frame. Moses was quickly taken from her and began his path from lap to lap around the frame, each quilter taking her turn to shower love on the precious child.

Pretending had always been one of Prudence's more accomplished talents, so it took very little to manage a comfortable expression while stranger after stranger held her son. With guests coming in and out of the inn, true strangers all, it was vital that the group settled around the quilt frame in the corner of the room look as if they were close friends.

That fully half of those seated there had spent the night before this one in a slave cabin or hiding out until the boat found them could neither be spoken of or allowed to show. So Prudence managed a smile when a thin older woman with her gray hair tucked under a multicolored scarf teased a smile from the infant's lips.

"He likes thee," she said. "Thee has a way with babies."

"She don't speak," the younger woman seated beside her said without looking up from her work. "Can't anymore." She made a gesture that indicated the woman's tongue had been cut.

"Oh," Prudence said softly as tears threatened to fill her eyes. Meanwhile, the older woman appeared too enthralled with Moses to pay any attention to the discussion concerning her.

"That's what they do when you sass them," the girl continued. "They don't think we hurt, but we do."

Now the tears were in the younger woman's eyes. The woman holding Moses had moved her attention from the baby to the girl. Meanwhile, the door behind them opened as a new set of guests entered the inn.

Prudence rose and walked calmly around the table to kneel between the women. As she spoke, she kept a smile on her face and the tears carefully in check.

"Our lives depend on us looking like a regular group of church ladies working on a quilting. Please nod if thee understands?" When they both had nodded, Prudence continued, her voice soft and her expression friendly. "What are thy names?"

"Sally," the younger woman said. "She's Liberty."

The older woman's eyes narrowed as if to protest. Sally shook her head.

"No, Mama," she said softly. "I promised you if we got out of there we'd both be free and changed, and that includes our names. Before they done what they done to you, you said you'd be called Liberty if the Lord ever set you free. Well, Liberty you are and Liberty you'll be."

The woman's voice rose as she spoke, causing the other ladies at the frame to look up.

"Thee are breathing free air here, but thee are not yet free. Please keep in mind this is only temporary, and there is a permanent home far north of this place."

Prudence looked across the frame to a farmer's wife she knew fairly well and nodded. Amity nodded in return as the door closed behind the new guests.

"'There is a balm in Gilead,'" she began to sing, her clear and sweet voice cutting through the tension.

"'To make the wounded whole,'" the others sang as they joined in the familiar hymn.

"Sing along," she told Sally. "Please," she whispered. "I do not want thee caught. And I'd really like to see my husband at the end of the evening." She nodded to Moses. "That child was born free. Don't cause him to lose that freedom with thy anger."

Sally looked over at Moses who was grinning again. Reaching over to touch the boy's fat cheek, she smiled. Prudence looked away from the scars on the girl's hand to focus on her son as she joined in singing.

Leaving Moses happily in Liberty's arms, she returned to her spot at the frame and picked up her needle. Fresh tears sprang to her eyes when she realized Liberty was singing along though not a sound came from her mouth.

When the song ended, Amity started another, and so it went while the needles worked thread through fabric and below them in the room where even the innkeeper never went, men were saving lives and protecting souls who were no different than those born free save the accident of geography on the day of their birth.

Moses fell happily asleep on Liberty's shoulder, though Prudence knew soon enough the baby would be fussing for his next feeding. Praying while she worked, she never noticed the white soldier and his green-eyed woman moving toward her until it was too late.

The woman touched Prudence's shoulder, causing her to stab her finger with the needle. Crying out in pain, she jerked her hand away and then looked up to see who had touched her. All the breath went out of her as she looked up into the face of a woman from a past she thought long hidden.

A woman who knew Prudence as a child before she went to live with the Friends and who shared her Melungeon heritage.

And who could ruin everything.

CHAPTER SEVEN

W e have a few questions," LuAnn said.

"Just one, really," Tess added. "Tell us about the trunk. Where exactly did you find it?"

"And did you look inside before you brought it up here?" Janice said.

"So we have more than one question," LuAnn amended. "But we really would like to know more about the trunk."

The puzzled look on his face prompted Tess to clarify. "You know. The trunk you left for us right here. You left a note too."

"Oh, the note," he said as he nodded. "Yes, I wanted you to know where I went."

"We do appreciate that," Janice said. "But what about the trunk?"

"Trunk?" He looked at each of them and then shook his head. "What trunk?"

Tess gave the others a look as she retrieved the note from her pocket and unfolded it. "Right here it says, 'Went to pick up a drain and a backflow preventer. Found it in a wall inside the room below the basement.'"

Tom looked down at the note and then back at Tess. "Yeah, I wrote that. What about it?"

"What do you mean 'what about it'?" LuAnn said. "You say right here that you found it in the wall inside the room below the basement."

Tom nodded and reached into the paper sack to retrieve something that looked like a piece of plumbing. "Exactly. This is what I was talking about. I'd show you the one I took out of the wall, but I left it at the plumbing supply. It wasn't worth salvaging."

LuAnn shook her head. "So you're saying the 'it' to which you refer is that thingamajig there and not a trunk?"

The plumber's eyes narrowed. "Ma'am, I truly do not know what trunk you're referring to, but yes, when I wrote that note, I was trying to tell you I found a faulty drain and backflow pre-venter in the wall down there. As you can see, I've got the new one ready to put in. Do you want me to put it in now or wait until another time?"

"Now, please," Tess said.

"All right, then." Tom shook his head as he walked past them toward the stairs leading to the basement. As he descended to the floor below, he was muttering something that sounded an awful lot like he thought they were crazy females.

Not that Tess blamed him. If he didn't put that trunk out there, then they must have truly sounded certifiable questioning him. Still, a thought occurred and she hurried to follow him.

"Tom," she called down the stairs, "may I ask you just one more question?"

"Sure," the plumber said as he returned to the stairwell. "What's up?"

"When you left the inn to go get the backflow drain thing-amajig, where exactly did you leave the note?"

"On the front door, of course," he said.

"Our front door?" She gestured toward the entrance of the inn. "That one?"

"Unless you have another, yeah," he said, his tone short. "With all due respect, I'm going to have to shut off your water for about half an hour to install these parts. I'd prefer to go ahead and do that and let you ladies get on about your business. But if you've got more questions, I can do this tomorrow. I've got three more calls to make before I can go home today."

"No, you go ahead and finish, and thank you. We promise we won't disturb you," Tess said as she stepped away from the basement entrance to face the girls.

Nodding toward the kitchen, she led them back into the place that was quickly becoming the base of operations for the Wayfarers Inn sleuths.

Janice remained by the kitchen door as Tess and LuAnn settled onto stools. LuAnn placed a turquoise notebook with silver lettering that spelled "Notes" on the counter in front of her. A matching silver pen fitted nicely into the spiral rings binding the notebook.

"That's pretty," Tess said.

"Thank you. I thought if we were going to be sleuths, I would need a notebook just for clues." She gave Tess a sideways look. "What? There's nothing wrong with making lists and jotting down clues."

"Of course not," Tess said. "Janice and I are grateful that you're so organized. And in awe," she said as Janice nodded. "I helped Jeffrey with his business holdings for decades and never managed the amount of organization you have just in the process of getting this inn up and running."

"Well thank you. I guess making lists is my spiritual gift," LuAnn said with a chuckle as she turned toward Janice who was still standing at the kitchen door. "Come sit with us so we can write down the clues we have so far."

"One of us needs to listen for the plumber, don't you think?" Janice asked.

"Good idea," Tess said. "The front door should probably be locked too."

"I'll do that."

When Janice had left the kitchen, LuAnn swiveled toward Tess. "What has gotten into her? First she takes the Grimes brothers to lunch to get them out of the kitchen, and now she's standing lookout and locking the door?"

"About that lunch," Tess said, stifling a giggle. "There's more to it than you would expect. You should ask her what happened at Bar-B-Cutie."

"What do you mean?" LuAnn asked. "You mean romantically, because I just can't see her having an interest in either of them. Although Brad is quite a nice man and quite handsome."

"And yours if you were to say the word," Tess said and then held up her hands as if fending off LuAnn's next statement. "I know. Just friends. I'm joking. I will keep all my serious comments to myself as long as I know you two are not interested in dating." Tess paused. "Yet," she said under her breath.

"I heard that," LuAnn said as she opened her notebook to a blank page.

"Heard what?" Janice said as she returned to the kitchen.

"Never mind." LuAnn glanced up at Janice. "Tess says I should ask you what happened at lunch today."

"The long version or the short version?" Janice asked.

"Short," Tess said.

Janice nodded. "The short version is the city is getting an antique fire truck; we're riding on that truck along with Wendy from the Sassy Seamstress and that red, white, and blue quilt; and we're the grand marshals. Oh, and someone is getting a new Porsche. I didn't ask who."

LuAnn raised an eyebrow. Tess gave her an I'll-tell-you-later look while Janice prattled on.

Finally LuAnn shook her head and held up both hands. "I'm sorry. Did I just hear that we're riding on a fire truck in the Fourth of July parade?"

"As grand marshals," Tess added. "And yes, you did."

"Well," LuAnn said, "that is not at all what I thought you were going to tell me, although I cannot for the life of me recall what I had expected you'd say."

"I had a similar reaction," Tess said. "So I guess we're buying the quilt, and we're riding in the parade. Although I really think we need to handle the issue of the quilt before we concern ourselves with being grand marshals."

"Agreed," LuAnn said, "but at some point you have got to tell me the long version of that story."

Janice shrugged as if there was nothing unusual about what had transpired during the meal. "Sure."

"All right," Tess said, steering the conversation back to the quilt. "Let's start with what we know. There is a famous quilt missing, and it may or may not be in our pantry."

"In a dusty trunk wrapped in paper that looks very much like it is not old," LuAnn said as she recorded the fact in the notebook.

Janice nodded. "Yes, and let's talk about how that trunk got where it was when Tess found it. Tom says he left us a note on the door. We didn't ask if he locked the door before he left."

"But he probably didn't," Tess said, "because if he did, how would he get back in?"

"And if Tom thought he was coming right back, he would need to get in," LuAnn supplied.

"Exactly." Tess shifted positions on the stool. "Which means anyone could have come in and left that trunk where I found it. With Tom's note on the door and no cars parked outside, it would have been obvious no one was here."

"I don't like that the door was left unlocked," Janice said. "The person who left the trunk could have been here when you walked in, Tess. That just scares me."

"Me too," LuAnn agreed. "When he gets back, we need to talk to Thorn about keeping this place locked up now that the renovation is progressing."

"Agreed," Tess said, "but let's get back to what we know. Maybelline Rector is going to be interviewed by someone from a show about quilt mysteries. The River of Life quilt has a connection to Marietta because local women made it, and its purpose was to be given as a gift to Abraham Lincoln. That's pretty much all she would say, but I felt like she knew a whole lot more."

"So did I," LuAnn said as she continued to write. "Okay, what else?"

"Since Wendy was the first one to talk about the quilt, she's definitely going to be on the list of suspects," Tess said.

"But she was so upset when she heard the quilt was missing," Janice said. "I tend to believe that was genuine and not acting."

Of course her sweet friend would believe a total stranger's reaction was genuine. There wasn't a more loving soul than Janice Eastman. But sometimes that meant she was a tiny bit gullible.

"Just for argument's sake," Tess said, "let's see if we can come up with any reason why Wendy might have something to do with the quilt showing up at the inn, okay?"

Placated, Janice nodded. "Okay, well, if we're just speculating, I suppose she would be happy that the producers of that show would be coming here after all. Didn't she say before she knew it was missing that she hoped they would? To me that says she wasn't sure it would happen."

"Oh," LuAnn said. "Yes, she did. She has a new shop, and the publicity would be helpful to her. Of course, we said the same thing about the inn."

"We did," Janice said. "But I doubt any of us considered breaking the law to make that happen."

"True," Tess said. "I'll spare you what Maybelline said about publicity and historical artifacts, because I still think that's a powerful motive for making the quilt conveniently disappear only to be found in Marietta. It certainly would guarantee the film crew would come to the city, don't you think?"

"That does make sense." LuAnn made a note as she spoke. "But Wendy wouldn't be the only one to benefit from that film crew coming to town. Obviously Maybelline would as well."

"She's already benefiting," Tess added. "Remember, she's already got her interview set up."

Janice fixed her attention on Tess. "Did she say when the interview would be?"

Tess and LuAnn exchanged glances. "No," LuAnn said. "Now that I think about it, I don't remember her being specific about a time or date. Why?"

"Just curious," Janice said. "Whether we have the real quilt or not, it's apparently a known fact that the River of Life quilt was sewn right here under this roof. Wouldn't that be enough to get those television cameras over here for a little mention of our new B&B?"

Tess laughed. "Spoken like a true businesswoman."

"No, I'm just a retired home economics teacher," Janice replied. "Which is why we need to get this place up and running so I can use the actual skills I have." She grinned. "And so LuAnn can start making all that soup. Just reading the recipes she leaves lying around makes me hungry."

"Speaking of hungry," Tess said. "I never did get lunch. What say we all head back to my place after the plumber leaves to continue this discussion there over a gourmet meal?"

"Gourmet meal?" LuAnn said. "Do tell."

"Okay, I was thinking omelets and ice cream."

"Sounds gourmet to me," Janice said. "But remember we had a schedule for our exit that doesn't include me following you guys home."

LuAnn looked up from her notes. "Janice Eastman," she said with a grin. "We are all retired women of a certain age and thus are not bound by schedules. When the schedule changes, we go with it."

Tess regarded her by-the-rules, keep-to-a-schedule friend with surprise. "What has happened to you?"

She shrugged. "If Janice can ask a man to lunch, then I can deal with the occasional change of schedule."

"Technically I asked two men," Janice said. "But who's counting? Oh! I think I hear our plumber coming up the basement stairs."

"Tom," Tess said when he stepped into the parlor, "do you have a minute?"

He shrugged. "Sure."

"How is it you're getting in and out of the inn? I mean, with Thorn gone this week, what arrangements has he made for the work to continue?"

"It's just me this week," he said. "When he needs any of us to do work while he's not around, he gives us a code."

"A code?" Janice said. "To what?"

"The key lock on the service entrance." He nodded in the direction of the area Brad had referred to as a loading dock. "The code changes, so if we have an old one, it won't work. Keeps us honest, I guess."

A few minutes later, Tom had gathered up his tools and left with a promise to return with some other sort of plumbing object the following day. Once the van had left the premises, it was time for Operation Remove the Quilt.

But first Tess went to the back entrance to confirm Tom's story. Thorn had indeed added a keypad lock to the back entrance. She returned to the kitchen to report this to the girls.

"I don't know why I never noticed it," Tess said.

"Because we don't use that entrance," LuAnn offered. "But I'm glad it's there."

"So am I. And I'm very happy he's not just leaving the place unlocked for the workers to come in and out," Janice said with a shudder. "Otherwise who knows who could get in?"

"Well," LuAnn said, "anyone who has a working code can, so let's not forget that."

"True," Tess said. "So make a note in your notebook, and then let's get the quilt out of here."

Janice once again acted as lookout to guard the quilt while LuAnn went out the front door and drove the car as near to the service entrance as she could. Once the car was in place, Tess went back into the kitchen to retrieve the quilt.

And found Winnie Washington sitting on the stool LuAnn had just vacated. Tall and willowy, the former cook at Butter Beans Restaurant had been hired to be the inn's chef de cuisine.

Of course, until the chef had a kitchen to cook in and a restaurant to serve those dishes, Winnie was not considered an employee.

Today she wore a sundress in shades of gold and brown with a pair of gold hoop earrings and matching gold sandals and handbag. The effect was both regal and elegant.

"Winnie," Tess said as she clutched her throat, "you gave me a terrible fright! How did you get in here?"

"Through the front door," she said as if she thought Tess had lost her mind. "I came to see LuAnn. Is she here? I promised her I would bring her copies of the recipes we discussed."

"We really don't need recipes until there are people to cook them for. How about I tell her you'll be back another day?"

"I'm already here," she said. "Seems silly to have to come back if LuAnn is still here."

"Well," Tess said slowly as her heart slowed its furious rhythm, "she is still here, but she was just leaving. I believe she's already in her car waiting for me."

"Then how about I walk out with you?" Winnie retrieved her purse and stood. "Want me to lock up?"

"Oh no, don't bother," Tess said. "You go on out and talk to LuAnn, and I'll check the doors. She's parked at the loading dock."

Winnie lifted one dark brow. "Isn't that a little inconvenient?"

"Locking doors? No, I do it every time I leave here."

"No, parking at the loading dock. It's all the way around the side of the building." She shook her head. "If you two are unloading heavy things, you need to hire someone to do that. I could name a good half-dozen kids from the college who would be glad for the extra work. A few from Butter Beans too, since it closed."

Tess moved to hold open the kitchen door and then smiled as Winnie walked past her. "I'll keep that in mind," she said. "With all the work going on here, you never know when there's going to be heavy lifting involved."

Winnie strolled toward the service entrance and then stopped short and turned around. "Tess, I wonder if I could ask a favor of you."

"Certainly," she said. "Ask away."

"Do you mind if I take a look at that kitchen one more time? I just can't believe I'll be cooking in it soon. I couldn't help noticing you got that new range in. The Aristocrat model, isn't it?"

"It is. Had it delivered and installed. It just went in last week."

"All those ovens and burners!" Winnie clapped her hands like a child at Christmas. "Oh my, am I going to have a good time cooking on that thing."

"Good luck figuring out what all those knobs and buttons are for."

Winnie paused and then turned back toward the kitchen, the decision made. "I won't be a minute, I promise. I just have to at least take another look at that stove I'm going to be making magic on."

Had she not been so desperate to get Winnie out of the inn, Tess might have laughed. Instead, she followed their soon-to-be cook into the kitchen and watched as she exclaimed about all of Big Red's ovens and burners and assorted other features. She even pulled out her cell phone and snapped photos of the stove as if she were photographing a favored grandchild.

"We call her Big Red," Tess said.

"And a beauty she is," Winnie said softly. "I always wanted a stove like this. My mama, rest her soul, would have loved cooking on this." She returned her cell phone to her purse and then stood back to give the appliance one last long look. "Thank you," she said. "I'll just see myself out."

Winnie was halfway to the front door when Tess realized what was happening. "I thought you wanted to leave some recipes for LuAnn," she called.

"I can do that another time," Winnie said over her shoulder as she tugged on the front door. "We don't need recipes until there's people to cook them for."

Tess stood there, flabbergasted. "That's what I said," she muttered, her hands resting on her hips.

"What is taking you so long?" LuAnn demanded as she rounded the corner. "I thought you were just grabbing the quilt and coming right out."

"I was, but then we had a visitor." She nodded toward the front door. "Winnie."

LuAnn's eyes narrowed. "What did she want?"

"She said she was here to deliver the recipes you and she discussed. Her family recipes for the inn's restaurant, I think."

"That's interesting," LuAnn said. "Other than briefly when we discussed her coming to work for us, we didn't talk about recipes at all."

"That is strange." Tess went to check that the front door was locked and then turned back toward the kitchen. "She certainly was impressed with Big Red. I thought she'd never stop taking pictures of it."

"It is impressive." LuAnn fell in behind her as they walked into the kitchen.

"Well, it's pretty. And apparently complicated enough to keep me from incinerating what could be a valuable missing antique quilt."

"Thank you for allowing me that extravagance," LuAnn said. "I don't think you'll ever know how much it means to me to cook on such a beautiful appliance."

Tears glistened in LuAnn's eyes as she walked over and traced her palm across the shiny silver shelf that spanned the distance over the cooktops. Big Red was obviously much more than just a stove to LuAnn.

Tess stopped just shy of the pantry door and glanced back at her friend, a woman who allowed very few extravagances for herself but freely lavished them on others. Without saying a word, Tess walked over and hugged LuAnn.

"Hey," Janice called from the kitchen door. "Can I get in on that hug too?"

"Sure, come on," LuAnn said as she held out her free arm and gathered the third member of the Inn Crowd into a group hug.

"Well, ladies," Tess said. "I think we're living up to our motto. Nothing about the process of getting this inn up and running has been boring, has it?"

"It sure hasn't," LuAnn said, stepping back to wipe her eyes.

And then the smoke alarm went off.

CHAPTER EIGHT

I don't smell smoke," Janice shouted over the din. "Do either of you?"

Both shook their heads.

"Divide and conquer, then," Tess said.

While Tess frantically tried punching in the code to turn off the new commercial fire deterrent system and Janice ran around looking for what might have triggered the alarm, LuAnn calmly walked outside. A few minutes later, flashing lights danced through the windows announcing the arrival of the Marietta Fire Department.

"Not boring at all," Tess said as she looked up at the kitchen ceiling just in time for the sprinklers to go off.

Hurrying away from the spraying water, Tess joined the others in front of the inn. Only then did she realize exactly what she'd left behind in the kitchen. Unfortunately, the fireman guarding the door did not care what was left inside.

"It'll either keep or burn, ma'am," he'd told her. "Either way, you're safer out here."

She stalked away from the fireman and grabbed Janice, who was standing nearest to her, and leaned close. "I left the quilt in the pantry," she said. "I have to go back and get it."

Janice's eyes widened. "But what if there's a fire?"

"Did you find any evidence of one?"

"Well, no," Janice said, "but there could be a slow smoldering fire in the walls somewhere. I saw that once on *Investigation Fire*. There were two wires in the wall of a house that had somehow gotten crossed, and they sat like that for years until finally they started smoking. It took weeks to figure out where the smoke was coming from. Finally, it blossomed into a real fire, and poof! Everything was gone."

"Poof?" Tess said as she shook her head. "If everything was gone, how did *Investigation Fire* know what happened? Or anyone else for that matter?"

Janice looked disappointed. "I hadn't thought of that."

"And why are you watching shows about fires? You know that sort of thing keeps you up at night fretting." Tess rested her hand on Janice's shoulder. "Now listen carefully. Those firemen will not let me just walk right in and get what I need to get. They're going to try to stop me. So, I'm going to need a diversion."

"A diversion?" Janice said. "Like what?"

"Oh no," Winnie shouted from the back of the crowd that had gathered to watch the excitement. "I hope that beautiful stove doesn't burn up before I can cook on it!"

Winnie went running for the door only to be stopped by the same burly fireman who'd refused Tess entrance.

"Like that," Tess said as she hurried toward the edge of the building and then slipped inside while the fireman was busy coaxing Winnie out of her distress.

The alarms had been silenced, but Tess's ears still rang as she hurried into the kitchen and promptly went sailing across the wet floor. Before she could scramble to her feet, a fireman swooped in and gathered her into his arms.

"Gonna need an EMT," he said into that talkie thing firemen wear on their uniforms.

"I'm fine," Tess said. "Just put me down."

"Can't do that, ma'am," he told her as he marched toward the front door. "You could have a head injury. Best not take a chance."

The fireman used his boot to open the door wide enough to carry Tess outside. "Hey watch it," she said. "We just had that wood refinished."

Later she would likely wonder whether she imagined it, but at that moment it seemed as though the fireman paused to pose in the door so the news channels could capture his heroic efforts to rescue a damsel in distress. Whether it was accidental or intentional, the smiling fireman sure took his sweet time allowing her to put her feet back down on solid ground.

"And don't even think about calling the EMTs," she told him. "It's a waste of time."

He nodded toward the ambulance screaming its way down the street toward them. "Too late."

LuAnn pressed past the fireman who was now more interested in speaking with reporters. "What happened?"

Tess shook her head. "I knew we should have replaced the original tile with something nonskid. But I just loved the look of it, and it was original, which also fit the budget."

"You're not making sense," LuAnn said.

"I'm making perfect sense," Tess countered. "The sprinklers went off causing the kitchen floor to become wet. Because wet tile is slick, I fell and slid halfway across the room before Captain America over there decided I needed saving. I couldn't talk my way out of being forcibly removed from the kitchen, so the trunk is still in the pantry."

"Still in the pantry?" Janice echoed, eyes wide. "I thought you put it in the trunk of LuAnn's car."

"No," Tess said. "First there was Winnie and then the fire alarm and that dude over there talking to the television cameras."

"Oh, he's a cutie," Janice said.

"Cutie or not, he kept me from my mission so he is not on my Good Fireman List. The good news is there are no sprinklers in the pantry, so the trunk should be dry."

"There she is," someone called as the crowd parted ways to allow two men in uniforms through. The older one led the way while a younger fellow trailed behind. Both wore looks of purpose on their faces, and no one seemed willing to stand in their way.

Until they reached her, Tess didn't notice they carried medical bags.

Tess glared at the fireman who was still happily sharing the spotlight with no one and then returned her attention to the medics. "Thank you," she said, "but I am fine."

"You don't sound fine, ma'am."

"I suspect I sound like I want you to leave me alone. Am I right?"

"O'Hara said he found you prone on the kitchen floor. He said you may have a head injury."

"I've thought that a time or two," Brad said from somewhere behind her, "but unfortunately, sometimes she's just cranky like that."

"Still we need to check her. Please, just let us take a look at your eyes, ma'am."

"If you don't stop calling me ma'am, I'm going to scream," Tess said. "I am fine. I promise if at any point in the foreseeable future I become anything less than fine, I will call my doctor or present myself to an emergency room. In the meantime, I am fine."

The older of the two exchanged looks with Brad. "She's fine," Brad told him.

"All right, then." He nodded to the younger of the two. "Have her sign the forms, and we're out of here."

Tess dutifully signed a paper stating she refused treatment and then turned to face Brad. "I guess you're here because of all the excitement with the fire trucks?"

"Actually I'm here because I wondered whether you were able to get a better look at that thing we were all so interested in earlier today."

"Not yet," she told him. "But it wasn't for lack of trying. We had a plan, but it was interrupted by a cook and a fire alarm."

Tess glanced around and saw many faces she knew in the crowd. From across the distance, Maybelline Rector offered a smile. Standing near her was Saffron Navratilova, Brad's niece, deep in conversation with two other young women. Ed Baxter from Hilltop Auto Wrecking stood waiting a short distance away, no doubt making sure all vehicles that had been driven to the excitement would be able to be driven away from it as well.

In all, half the town must have come out to see what the fuss was about. Not exactly the situation she'd hoped for when she planned how to get the quilt out of the inn unseen.

"So apparently there was a short in the electrical system that sent a false reading to the fire alarm," her hero was telling some cute little reporter from the local television station. "Luckily there was no fire, so the old inn was not damaged in any way."

"No, but the old innkeeper will have bruises where the sun doesn't shine," Tess muttered as she hobbled inside with Brad on her heels.

This time no one attempted to stop her as she wound her way around fire hoses—which had never been needed or used but were making an awful mess on the hardwood floors—to reach the kitchen.

"Watch your step," she told Brad. "Wet tile is slick."

"So I heard," he said with a half smile as he picked his way across the tile to open the pantry door.

"It's wrapped in painter's cloth," she told him. "Look in the back behind everything."

Brad disappeared inside and then came back out empty-handed. "It's not there."

She was a Gibson, this woman, born and raised into a family of Melungeon men and women like Prudence. Prudence had chased adventure where it could be found, but Violet Gibson was very much the opposite.

Mama had encouraged a friendship with the lovely Violet. Likely Mrs. Gibson had done the opposite in regard to the occasionally reckless pastor's daughter.

Violet had changed little in the years that had passed between them, but there was no mistaking eyes the pale green of the creek that ran behind the parsonage. And there was also no mistaking the fear Prudence found in those memorable eyes.

Much as Prudence was terrified at this moment, so Violet also seemed. The thought only offered the slightest of comforts.

"Welcome to the Riverfront House, travelers," Prudence said as she rose and offered a smile. "Might I assist in making thy stay more comfortable?"

The white man stepped between Prudence and Violet, his expression unreadable as he grasped Violet's arm. He nodded toward the women pretending to ignore him while covertly watching his every move.

Finally he spoke. "What is this? Are you ladies making a quilt?"

His voice was a rich baritone, thick with culture and woven through with the timbre of a man raised somewhere other than this part of the country. He appeared to be quite possessive of the woman at his side.

His uniform consisted of a dark frock coat with stripes and epaulets indicating an advanced rank. His gray wool trousers were spotless, showing no evidence of the sort of travel normal folks would have endured. The dress sword he carried at his hip looked both menacing and elegant.

Though much older than Violet, his attention continued to stray to her. Prudence guessed he was smitten. Perhaps more.

Prudence had seen his sort in Marietta before. Generally men like this one were just passing through on their way to somewhere important. Never, however, had she seen one who brought his woman with him.

"It's a quilting, sir," she said, her gaze meeting his directly so that he might believe she had no reason to fear him.

The man's pale eyes moved slowly around the circle and then stalled on Liberty. "And who is this?"

Prudence's heart lurched. The hand that had been patting Moses's back as he slept stalled. Slowly Liberty looked up, eyes wide. Sally's fingers continued to move as she sewed tiny stitches along the part of the quilt meant to represent the junction of the Ohio and Muskingum Rivers, but her eyes were now clearly on her mother.

Whether the man spoke of the escaped slaves or her son, Prudence could not say. Fear coursed through her even stronger now. As did the knowledge that lives were held in the balance and could fall as easily as that limb she and Jason had squabbled over only a short while earlier.

"He is a beautiful child," Violet said, breaking the silence. "Might I hold him?"

Prudence relaxed her breath and put on a smile. "Thee have given a great compliment," she said. "Moses is my only son, and his father and I are quite proud of him."

Not an answer but a distraction. To allow her child into the hands of either of these two was unthinkable. Having lost babies to death, Prudence had no doubt she would follow them to the grave rather than see her son taken.

And as much as she knew what Violet Gibson was like as a child, she was unwilling to be certain the woman had not changed since then. The fact that she now traveled with a white man in uniform surely belied the possibility.

"A fine-looking lad," the white man said as he tore his attention from Moses to settle his gaze on Violet. "Would that we had a son as sturdy of body and fair of face as he. Do you not agree, Victoria?"

Victoria? Despite herself, Prudence openly stared. Surely Violet Gibson had no twin. God would not create such beauty twice, would He?

Whatever her name, the woman's smile did not quite reach her eyes. "Indeed, Captain. Would that we did."

CHAPTER NINE

"Of course the trunk isn't there," LuAnn said from the door. "The eagle has landed. It's in the trunk of my car. Janice is standing guard. Can you believe it?"

"Again?" Tess said. "I repeat, what has gotten into her?"

"Oh, don't be too proud of her bravery. She's hiding under the extra painter's cloth. She'll let us know if anyone gets near the car, but I guarantee it will be because she's screaming her head off."

Tess and Brad chuckled together, and then Brad shook his head. "Wait. The eagle has landed?" he said. "Was that movie terminology part of your plan? It sounds very secret agent."

LuAnn grinned. "No, I just made it up. Sounded pretty good though, don't you think?"

"Very secret agent," Tess said. "But now that the eagle has landed in your trunk, what do we do with it? There's no way we can leave the inn like this. The fire department has made a mess of everything, and there's a crowd on our lawn that doesn't appear to be in a hurry to leave."

"I solved that too," LuAnn said. "Look who I found. Thorn is back early."

"Am I glad to see you," Tess declared as the other two echoed a similar sentiment. "We have had quite a day. First the plumber and then, well, some other stuff, and now this."

Dressed in camo as usual, the former shop teacher turned construction supervisor seemed completely nonplussed at the fact there were fire hoses scratching floors he'd just had refinished and a sheen of water covering most of the kitchen that would be painted tomorrow. He looked around and retrieved a small notebook from his shirt pocket.

"I've got a team of cleaners who can get the dirt off the floors out there and dry up this kitchen. It'll cost extra, but I think if we get them in here tonight we may find the wood won't have to be refinished again after all."

"Then call them," Tess said. "At this point, I'll pay whatever it costs. As long as it costs less than refinishing those floors."

Thorn tipped his camo-patterned hat. "I guarantee it will. Now, what do you want me to do about all those folks trampling the lawn?"

"Could you get rid of them? Nicely," Tess added. "Maybe add a word of thanks on behalf of the innkeepers?"

He nodded. "I can do that."

"Oh, and Thorn," Tess said, "do you really think the fire alarm had an electrical short? That's what I heard the fireman say, but I'm skeptical. We just had that put in and tested. My ears are still ringing from that day last week when the technician insisted on multiple tests. Emphasis on multiple."

"I'm skeptical too. Seems more like kids playing a prank by pulling an alarm," he said, "but I'll have them back out to check. You never know with contractors."

"Speaking of contractors," LuAnn said, "your plumbing guy was here today. He did some work down in the basement."

"Davis?" At Tess's nod, he continued. "He's ahead of schedule, then. He told me he wouldn't be able to get to the job until next week. I'll go down and check his work before I lock up. Anything else?"

"That's interesting," Tess said. "Because he had the code to get in the service entrance."

Thorn shrugged. "I thought I had changed it, but maybe I forgot. I do apologize."

"Okay good," she said. "And just one more thing."

"What's that?"

Tess gave him a tired smile. "Never go on another vacation again."

"You're kidding, right?" Thorn said. "Because I was supposed to be off the rest of the week, you know. If the weather forecast hadn't called for rain later in the week, I would have gone camping as planned. Instead, I decided to put off my vacation and come back to work."

"We're glad you did, and I'm pretty sure she's kidding," Brad said with a grin as he led Tess and LuAnn out of the kitchen. "But if I were you, I'd ask her next week, not today."

Thorn nodded. "Or the week after."

"Indeed," Brad said as he followed LuAnn and Tess out to the loading dock. "Why are you parked out here?"

"So no one would see us leave."

Brad waved at two reporters from the *Marietta Times* who were deep in conversation with Paul Townsend. "So much for that part of the plan," he said.

"True." LuAnn clicked the unlock button on her key fob. Instead of a beep, there was a muffled scream from inside the car. "It's just us, Janice."

A head shrouded in pale fabric popped up out of the front seat. "Is that you, LuAnn?"

"And Tess."

"And your favorite Realtor," Brad added as he helped Tess into the back seat and then closed the door. "Take the eagle and go. I'll hang out here with Thorn until the crowds leave, but one of you needs to call me tomorrow and give me the update."

"LuAnn will," Tess said innocently as she ignored her friend's glare in the rearview mirror. "What?" she said after they had driven away, leaving the inn behind them.

"You know that Brad and I are just friends. Nothing more, and neither of us wants anything more," LuAnn said as she eased the car down the alley.

"Oh, I know, but which of us has appointed herself note-taker for the Wayfarers Inn Sleuth Society? It's only logical that you should be the one to contact him."

"Is that who we are now?" Janice said with a frown. "Because that just sounds silly."

"It was supposed to be silly. Can't a woman recently accused of having a head injury be allowed a bad joke?"

"You have a head injury?" Janice asked, eyes wide. "Lu, we need to get her to the ER."

"She told the EMTs she was fine," LuAnn said. "But I promised Brad I would watch her for signs of a concussion."

Janice picked up her phone and started typing.

"What are you doing?" Tess asked.

"Looking for signs of a concussion. I used to know them, due to our mandatory first aid training at school, but I'm rusty on concussions." She paused. "Okay, here we go," she said as she began to read from whatever medical website she'd found.

"Not you too, Janice. I'm fine."

"I don't know," Janice said. "Let me see your eyes."

Tess leaned forward to allow Janice to look into her eyes, and then she crossed them and stuck out her tongue. "That's all you get, Dr. Eastman. I am fine. LuAnn, please drive to my house. We're having gourmet meals and then a slumber party. I hope you're happy borrowing pajamas, Janice, because you're stuck with us tonight."

Janice looked more happy than doubtful. Likely she was looking forward to another round of investigation now that the quilt was safely stowed in LuAnn's car.

"I suppose I can get my car tomorrow," she said as the other two cheered. "Besides, Tess, ever since LuAnn moved to town and started living in your house I've been jealous that you two get to spend evenings together."

Later that evening after dining on omelets and ice cream, the girls removed the trunk they had stashed in Jeffrey's gun safe before their meal. The safe had long been emptied of its previous contents, and Jeff Jr. always promised to take the safe the next time he visited. But each time he conveniently forgot to bring the proper equipment to move such a monster.

Tess could once again feel her husband's presence as she punched in the code and pulled the door open. Perhaps that's why she had sent LuAnn and Janice up to tuck the trunk into the safe. She'd only opened it once since Jeff Jr. removed its contents, and that had caused a wave of tears that lasted the remainder of the day.

She would do better this time. After answering a whole barrage of questions regarding her supposed head injury and her fitness to carry the silly box a few feet to the coffee table, she managed to retrieve the trunk and walk out of the closet-sized safe without a single tear. Not that she wouldn't allow a few later.

But none for now. She had another purpose that was more important than feeling sorry for herself and mourning what she had lost. For whatever aches her heart had suffered, the women and men whose lives were represented in this quilt had certainly endured much more.

Carrying the trunk into the upstairs sitting room, Tess deposited it on the coffee table and then pulled the curtains shut and waited for Janice and LuAnn to join her. Silence fell between them as Tess once again opened the latch.

Though the trunk's time wrapped in painter's cloth had removed most of the layer of dust, enough remained to cause Tess to fall into another fit of sneezing. "Okay," she said when she could manage to speak, "here we go."

LuAnn and Janice grinned. "Hurry up," Janice said. "I want to see this quilt."

"We saw it," Tess said. "Are you thinking we should try unfolding it to see the entire design?"

"I think so," Janice said. "Otherwise how will we know if this is truly the River of Life or just some copy? What we saw was beautiful, but what if the rest of it isn't? Or is ruined?"

Tess looked to LuAnn. "What do you think, history teacher?"

"I'm divided," she said. "I agree with everything Janice said, but I worry that we'll harm fragile fabric if we handle it too roughly."

Tess grinned. "Then it's settled. We will handle it gently, but we do need to see what we have. Agreed?"

"Agreed," Janice and LuAnn said together.

"Okay," Tess said as she let out a long breath. "Here we go. I'm opening it. Hello, River of Life quilt!"

She pulled up the lid of the trunk and the three friends leaned in as she peeled away the paper that covered the quilt. Three pairs of eyes opened wide and three mouths dropped open.

"It's gone!" all three of them said in unison.

CHAPTER TEN

Tess sat back and stared at the trunk and the length of painter's cloth that had fooled them into believing the River of Life was still safely hidden inside. Finally she found the words to speak.

"All right," she said slowly. "We all agree it was there earlier today, right?"

"We do," Janice said as LuAnn nodded.

"And we agree that besides us, Brad also saw it." Again they nodded. "So, we also agree that there is considerable discussion about a missing famous quilt that looked very much like the one in this trunk."

LuAnn held up her hand. "Hold on now. We never actually saw the entire thing, so we can't say for sure if this is even a copy of that one."

"That's true," Janice added. "We only saw the corner of it. But what we saw certainly looked impressive."

"It did. And although the fabric did have an old feel to it, sort of like it might be too fragile to handle, it was wrapped in paper that looked fairly new."

"Paper similar to what my new quilt from Sassy Seamstress was wrapped in," LuAnn said.

"That did seem odd, didn't it?" Janice said. "I wonder if someone wanted to confuse us or just made a mistake wrapping something old in something new."

Tess sat back and let out a long breath. "It's all so frustrating, isn't it?"

"That's another thing," LuAnn said as she continued to write in her notebook. "Maybelline says there are no photographs of the River of Life. How can that be if it has been in the National Archives for the last century? Surely they record everything that goes in and keep very careful records."

"Records which would very likely include photographs," Tess supplied. "So all we have to do is make a call, and we should be able to find out about this quilt we thought we had."

"Or look on The Googles," Janice said.

Tess and LuAnn shared a giggle.

"What?" Janice said. "Are you making fun of me?"

"We love you," Tess said.

"Just the way you are," LuAnn added. "So about the River of Life, or whatever used to be in that box. Let's not mention we had it, okay?"

"Because we don't know for sure if we did," Janice added.

"And we certainly don't have it now," Tess said.

Janice's phone rang, and all three of them jumped. "I don't recognize the number. Should I answer it?"

"Probably a junk call," LuAnn said. "Ever since I signed up for that contest to win an all-expense-paid vacation in London, I get them all the time. Maybe you signed up for something too."

Another ring. Janice held the phone out at arm's length. "I didn't, and I'm certain of it. No one knows my cell phone number except a few family members and you two." She tossed the ringing phone to Tess. "Here, you answer it."

Skills learned way back when she was a shortstop in college softball kicked in as Tess caught the phone and pressed the button to connect the call. Imagine being afraid of answering a simple phone call.

"Hello," she said as she shook her head at Janice.

"Mrs. Eastman? This is Wendy from Sassy Seamstress. I'm sorry to call so late, but I got your message and you asked that I call you immediately."

"Wendy, this is Tessa Wallace. I'm with Mrs. Eastman and our friend LuAnn Sherrill. You might remember she's the one who bought a quilt from you this morning. I'm going to put you on speaker so you can hear all of us."

"Hello, Wendy," Janice said. "Thank you for calling me back."

"Is this about the parade? I'm thrilled to be asked, but I'm going to have to decline the opportunity to ride on the fire truck with you."

"Oh," Tess said, "that's a shame. We were counting on you joining us along with that beautiful red, white, and blue quilt LuAnn wanted this morning. We're ready to buy it and use it in the inn."

"I'm flattered that you want to put it in the parade, but I can't ride with you," Wendy said.

"Well, if there's any way to change your mind, you'll have to let us know," Tess said.

"Thank you," Wendy said.

"Say," LuAnn said, "since we have you on the phone, I wonder if you've heard any updates on that missing quilt you were so upset about this morning."

"Oh," Wendy said softly, "I really shouldn't have overreacted about something as silly as that."

After a few more minutes of polite conversation, Wendy said her goodbyes and hung up.

Tess frowned. "That was odd."

Janice nodded. "Very."

"I, for one, don't believe her," LuAnn said. "Remember I stayed behind while you two went to get a table for breakfast. Wendy absolutely couldn't stop talking about the River of Life and the Arts & Antiques Network. She was positively giddy."

"And then she was positively distraught," Janice added. "The poor girl was beside herself when she came through the door."

Tess yawned. "Something doesn't add up, that's for sure. Ladies, I say we continue this discussion over breakfast tomorrow morning."

"I agree," Janice said as she rose and stretched. "Much as I love a good slumber party, this has been a tiring day. I'm looking forward to Tess's comfortable guest room and a solid night's sleep."

LuAnn scooped up her notebook. "I'll look over my notes to be sure we have a full record of this day."

"I'm not sure I want a full record of this day," Tess said as she watched her two best friends disappear up the stairs to their respective rooms. "Nor do I want to repeat it."

As she sat in the quiet with the events of the day swirling around in her mind, Tess closed her eyes and gave thanks for all her blessings. For even when an antique quilt appeared and then disappeared, an inn purchase funded a plumbing venture, and faulty fire alarms brought the entire town to their lawn, every day she was given to live on this earth was a blessing.

"I miss you, Jeffrey," she said as she climbed to her feet and reached over to turn off the lamp. "You'll never be replaced, but I am thankful for family and friends who will fill the time until we are together again."

As if bidden by her thought, Tess's cell phone buzzed with a text from Lizzie. *Why didn't you tell me you were on TV today?*

Before she could fumble her fingers over the keys to respond, another text came through. This one was a link to a local news story.

Tess groaned. *Oh no.* Of all the photos they could have used and film they shot, why in the world would the television station choose to use that silly photo of her being carried out of the inn in the arms of that obnoxious fireman?

CHAPTER ELEVEN

Janice and LuAnn had been busy out on the patio comparing notes regarding the events at the inn yesterday, but Tess was not ready to join them yet. They had just solved one mystery, and now another had found them.

Since when did retirement not mean sitting quietly in a chair and aging gracefully while sipping a nice iced latte and reading a good book?

"Since you signed up for this adventure at the inn," she said as her phone rang and Thorn's name appeared.

"Good morning," Tess said. "Tell me something positive, please."

"All right," he said. "My crew did their magic and the floors are just fine."

"That is good news." She paused. "Is that why you were calling?"

"That was one of the things I wanted to tell you." He cleared his throat. "But there's another that you won't like as well."

Tess groaned. "Okay. What now? Trouble with the plumber?"

"No. Tom's a good guy. He told me to thank you for your part in opening his business. He'll work extra hard for you ladies, I promise."

"Well, that's encouraging."

"Yes, well hold on to that encouragement, because I got an email from one of the inspectors this morning and there's a little trouble with a permit."

Thorn went on to tell her the details of the current issue—something about something not up to code or some nonsense like that—while Tess leaned against the cabinet and did the unthinkable. She prayed for patience.

Mama always warned her that prayers for patience were the sort of prayers the Lord liked to answer. Just as soon as you ask Him for patience, He will give you a chance to use it.

Tess listened politely until Thorn was finished. "We've had several of these permit issues come up. I want the inn to be safe and up to code, but as a businesswoman I am beginning to wonder how much more of this our budget can stand. What do we need to do?"

"I do understand, Tess," he said. "But those are the hoops you jump through when you're opening a business. Nothing we can do about it but follow whatever instructions we're given."

"I wonder if Janice's brother-in-law Marv might be of some help. Or his friend, Joe. Marv's a retired architect, and Joe is a building inspector." Her chuckle held no humor. "Too bad he's not one of ours."

"I'll give Marv a call. He's come around a few times since I took over the project and given me a lot of help. As for Joe, he's a good guy. I've known him for years, but when it comes to inspectors, it wouldn't matter whether he is a friend or a stranger when he's charged with inspecting a property."

"I know," she said. "He's there to do a job, and we certainly don't want to open an unsafe building to the public."

"You asked what we need to do. My advice is we do what the inspector asks of us," he said. "Simple as that."

"Simple as that," she echoed. "I wonder if we'll ever be done with inspectors, Thorn. It seems like we've dealt with an endless parade of them."

"Sure we will," he said, his enthusiasm evident but not quite contagious. "And speaking of parade, the fire truck is here."

She gripped the edge of the counter. "Oh no. Did the fire alarm go off again?"

"No, but I do have a call in to our alarm guys. I expect he'll call back later in the day. No, Ed Baxter from Hilltop Wrecking just dropped off an antique fire truck. Said you ladies would know what it was for."

"Oh," Tess said. "Yes, that fire truck. Just leave it wherever he parked it." She sighed. "Please thank Ed for us."

Tess ended the call and then reached into the pantry for a coffee mug and filled it with her favorite flavor of dark roast blend. Janice and LuAnn were deep into a conversation about something on LuAnn's computer. She took a seat across the table from them and set her mug down.

"What's up?"

"Look what I found," LuAnn said as she passed her laptop over to Tess. "The National Archives are online. I haven't found the River of Life quilt specifically, but there are so many others that it just has to be there."

Tess glanced down at the screen. "You're not kidding. Four hundred sixty-three archival descriptions with digital object, two hundred twenty-six presidential libraries..." She looked up at Janice. "And the list goes on. There are pictures, stories, and even a few movies."

"And that's just with a search of the keyword *quilt*," LuAnn said. "I tried to be more specific but didn't get any hits using River of Life quilt. My guess is it's there but under a different name. Using the key words *Ohio* and *quilt*, the search becomes more manageable, but there is still a lot to sift through." She shrugged. "It'll take time to find it, but I'm sure I will."

Janice looked over at Tess. "So why would Maybelline say there was no photo of it?"

"Maybe she didn't want us to go looking for one." Tess shrugged as she handed the laptop back to LuAnn. "Or it could be that she wants to be the only expert when the cameras start rolling."

"That is very possible," Janice said. "That Maybelline always has liked being the expert. I can't tell you the number of times I've turned on the television or picked up a newspaper over the years and seen her giving some interview, claiming to be an expert on something."

"I guess that's just what she likes to do. I mean, she is the person who runs the Marietta Underground Railroad Museum, so that does make her an expert, at least in that area." Tess paused. "So, slight change of subject. About that fire truck, Janice."

"What about it?" Janice said.

"According to Thorn, it's parked in front of the inn right now. He asked me what we were going to do with it."

"We're going to decorate it and ride on it in the parade." Janice grinned. "There's actually more to it than that, and

I guess I should have told you last night, but you were so irritated with that nice fireman named O'Hara."

Tess's eyes narrowed as she thought of the photograph now posted on the television news site. "Tell me what, Janice?"

Her friend looked only slightly sheepish, and then she began to smile. "Well, you see, the fire department has the cutest little fund-raiser going, and I thought it would be great to take part in it."

"Fund-raiser?" Tess managed.

"Yes, it's a calendar and—"

"A calendar!" Tess burst out laughing. "Oh, Janice, truly? Do you know what those calendars look like? They're full of muscled firemen wearing spray tans and not much more than is necessary to be legal. Are you nuts?"

"Obviously I would never agree to anything like that." Janice shrugged. "Actually, the calendar will feature local firemen going about their duties. All funds raised go to local charities. And they are fully clothed, Tess."

"That's a relief."

"If you're in agreement that we should lend our support to the cause, then I would like to propose that we ask the firemen to ride on that truck in our place." She toyed with her mug. "I just don't know if I like the idea of being a grand marshal." Her eyes lifted to meet Tess's. "I was trying to be really brave when the men offered that honor to us, but the truth of the matter is the thought of riding at the front of the parade with everyone staring at me is terrifying."

Tess looked over at LuAnn who was absorbed in something on her laptop. "What do you say, LuAnn? Are you willing to give up the spotlight in favor of the local firemen?"

"Yes, sure. Fine."

Tess shook her head. "Lu, are you listening?"

She looked up and grinned. "Yes, I heard you. And I figure any man who looks this good despite saving a woman who obviously doesn't want to be saved deserves to be honored."

LuAnn swiveled the computer to show that same awful photo of Tess in the fireman's arms. Only this one had been posted to...she leaned in to be sure she was reading the name of the media outlet correctly.

"The *Chicago Tribune*?"

"And the *Houston Chronicle*," LuAnn said. "Apparently your fireman is a Texan."

Tess shook her head. "This is ridiculous. Who in the world would want to see something as silly as that?"

Janice nodded toward the computer and then looked back up at Tess. "Apparently there are two hundred and twelve thousand people who would." She grinned. "In the kids' vernacular, you've gone viral."

"Wonderful," Tess groaned as she took another look at the photograph. Then something caught her eye. "Hey, look there behind us. There's someone else in that picture, and it's not a fireman. Who is that?"

Janice moved closer to the computer. "Can you make that bigger, LuAnn?"

"Let me see," she said as she clicked a few keys. "If I make this any bigger than it already is, then it's too blurry."

"Okay," Tess said, "then what can we see of what he or she is wearing? Maybe that will help."

"It looks like some kind of uniform," Janice said. "Not like fireman or police. Maybe like a worker's uniform of some sort."

"Is that black, blue, or dark brown?" Tess said. "I really can't tell. The shadows blur too much of it out. And they keep us from seeing the face or hair color too."

"If you look closely, there's a white circle on that shirt just about where a pocket would go," LuAnn said. "Or maybe it's just a trick of the light."

"No," Janice said. "I think that's a patch. Could it be our plumber, Tom?"

"Possibly," Tess said. "But why would he be inside the building while the smoke alarms are going off and firemen are everywhere? And is he carrying something?"

Janice leaned in.

"Hard to tell, but I don't think so. Looks like we've got something else to add to the notebook," LuAnn said.

Tess reached for her mug and took a sip of coffee. "Before we go any further," she said. "I have to ask, girls. Do we bother about this quilt thing or just figure that whatever we found in that trunk wasn't ours and it isn't any of our business where it went?"

LuAnn looked surprised. She closed her computer and seemed to be considering a response. Or maybe Tess had finally managed to make the history teacher mad.

"The quilt wasn't ours, but I think it does matter how it got into the inn." Janice looked over at LuAnn and then returned her attention to Tess.

"I agree," LuAnn said. "Yesterday someone put that trunk in the parlor with the note Tom left on the door. We don't know why but someone obviously wanted us to find that trunk, and I don't think it was Tom."

"No, probably not. He has no motive, at least that I can see. He's building a business, and I just can't see a plumber trafficking in stolen antiques." Tess shifted positions and ran her finger around the rim of her mug. "But who knows? And why bother to set us up to find the thing only to take it back again?"

Janice shook her head. "You did a great job of hiding the trunk. It wouldn't have been easy to find unless…"

"Unless someone was watching us," LuAnn said. "Which is just creepy."

"Then there's the guy behind you in the picture. If he's trespassing instead of being a first responder, that's worse than creepy," Janice said.

"So is it agreed that we continue to investigate the matter of the missing quilt?" LuAnn said. "Starting with the case of the creepy peeper?"

"Agreed," Tess said as she set the mug on the table in front of her. "So I suppose we need to get to work."

Prudence made her way around the quilting frame on shaking legs. All but one or two of the dozen or more women at the frame had given up their pretense of sewing to openly stare at the strangers.

Fear was not of God. This she recalled hearing from her place in the front pew at church and then later when she hid behind the skirts of the woman who took her in and became her second mama.

The Lord had also bestowed the gift of pretending upon her in great measure, an ability that had served her well in fooling not only the occasional slave owner but also passing as one of the community in situations where a woman with her background would not be welcome.

Calling on this gift, she straightened her backbone and offered Liberty an encouraging smile. The older woman looked past her, the fear in her eyes evident. Beside her, Sally sat trembling.

"He does love thee," she told Liberty. "But he'll be needing his mama, and you'll both be wanted at the meeting house soon. Please tell the reverend the cause for your tardiness is mine alone."

She looked over at Violet and then to her captain. "If thee will excuse these two ladies, I've caused them to be away from the meeting house far longer than promised. The reverend is tolerant of my requests for them to attend the quiltings, and I wish to not abuse his kindness."

Prudence turned her back on the strangers and leaned down as if to reach for Moses. "Go," she mouthed silently to Liberty. A glance at Sally told Prudence she understood.

Liberty nuzzled Moses for a moment longer and then handed him to Prudence. Beside her, Sally's trembling had become a more noticeable shake.

Accustomed to such fearful intrusions, Amity rose. "I'll just take the lantern lest the moon is insufficient to light thy path back to the meeting hall." She turned to the strangers and offered a smile. "If you'll excuse us."

She smiled at Prudence and ushered the women out into the night. Though Moses squirmed in her arms, Prudence could only stand and stare until the door closed.

Until Liberty and Sally had safely escaped for the second time.

CHAPTER TWELVE

The girls wasted no time in getting to work adding clues to their already growing collection of notes in LuAnn's book. After a while, their chief scribe stopped writing and put her pretty silver pen down.

"I've been thinking about our list of suspects," she said. "I hate to say it, but even though we've got the creepy peeper in this picture, I think we really need to consider that Winnie might be the one who made the switch and not this guy."

"You told us last night that she was in the kitchen alone when you found her, so that makes her the only one with the opportunity to access the trunk. And there certainly was extra painter's cloth in the pantry."

"I agree she had the opportunity," Tess said, "but where did she put it? Her purse wasn't big enough to hide a quilt. And she was sitting there at the counter looking as cool as a cucumber. I don't know about you two, but if it was me trying to pull that switch and then ditch the evidence, I'm pretty sure I would have broken a sweat."

LuAnn chuckled. "Me too, but one thing about her story doesn't ring true. She said she was there to drop off some recipes, but she didn't leave any. Why not?"

Tess shrugged. "Maybe you should ask her."

"That's a great idea." LuAnn gathered up her laptop and stood. "I'll pay Winnie a visit this morning. After that, we can meet back at the inn and see what we're going to do about that fire truck."

"We're going to let the firemen ride on it," Tess said.

Janice nodded, sending her curls dancing. "I'm with Tess. Leave the truck to the professionals."

LuAnn gave them one of her patented exasperated teacher expressions. "Come on, ladies. Get in the spirit. We're celebrating our nation's freedom. It'll be fun. Besides, think of the publicity we can get for the inn."

"Now you're sounding like me," Tess said grudgingly.

"You've already done your part for publicity with that viral fireman photo."

Ducking the pillow Tess threw at her, LuAnn turned to Janice. "Want a ride home?"

"Sure," she said as she picked up her coffee mug and LuAnn's and headed toward the kitchen. "Are you coming, Tess?"

"No, I've got an errand to run. I'll meet you at the inn."

A short while later, Tess pulled up in front of the Sassy Seamstress. Wendy was standing on a ladder stuffing a box into the topmost cabinet behind the counter when Tess stepped inside.

"Be right with you." Wendy closed the latch on the cabinet and then glanced over her shoulder. Her face registered surprise as she climbed down the ladder.

"Mrs. Wallace. Are you here to get the quilt?"

Tess paused as if unsure what to say. Today Wendy's T-shirt, which she wore over a white denim skirt, was a lovely robin's egg blue. Across the front in white letters spelled out *It's All Fun and Games Until the Bobbin Runs Out.*

"I am," she said.

Wendy smiled. "Give me just a second, and I'll get it for you."

"Thank you," Tess called as the young woman scurried into the back room.

Taking advantage of Wendy's absence, Tess wandered toward the glass-front display case and counter. Original to the building, it spanned the rear of the store and hosted not only an antique cash register but also a sleek silver iPad with a credit card attachment.

Behind the counter, a wall of cabinets climbed each side of a massive antique mirror. Someone had cleverly installed glass shelves across the mirror, spanning the space between the cabinets. On these shelves were various sewing related items interspersed with silver-framed photographs of quilts and various trophies and awards.

The only oddity in the entire place was an ugly frog made from seashells and wearing a hat and sunglasses. The thing looked as if it was purchased at one of those cheesy souvenir shops in Florida. A small card rested against the atrocity with Wendy's name printed across the center in green ink.

Despite the frog, Wendy had definitely achieved the goal that Tess taught in her hospitality and business classes. She had defined her audience and catered to them not only in the products offered but also in the ambience that surrounded those products.

Though Tess hadn't noticed any of this on her last visit, she had been distracted. With no one else in the store, and neither of her friends distracting her with quilt purchases, she could look and learn.

Because another thing she taught in her classes was that stepping into a public space told the customer a lot about the owner. In this case, Wendy's store was shouting homey and vintage. But was that who she was?

"Sorry it took so long," Wendy said as she emerged from the back with a large shopping bag. "Here it is."

"Thank you," Tess said as she took the bag and then glanced inside. "You've wrapped it up. That was nice of you. Did LuAnn give you the credit card information?"

Wendy shook her head as she leaned back against the counter. "She did, but would you consider accepting it as a welcome to the neighborhood gift?"

"Really?" Tess said. "That's very generous. But we couldn't possibly do that."

"Sure you can," Wendy said. "I insist."

Tess smiled. "Thank you. I hope you'll come and visit the inn and allow us to properly welcome you to the neighborhood too."

Wendy gave Tess a grateful smile. "I don't have many friends here yet, so I'm looking forward to getting to know you and your friends better."

"I expect you'll be seeing Janice in here frequently. She does love her crafts."

"What about you?"

"Me? Oh, I'm terrible at crafts. A hopeless cause. But I'll come by and say hello when I can. Remember, you prayed we would be friends, so I intend to be a friend." She lifted the bag to set it on the counter. "So, can I ask you a question?" At Wendy's nod, Tess continued. "Why the sudden change of heart about the missing quilt? You were completely distraught yesterday morning, and then last night you acted like it didn't matter at all."

Wendy pressed her palms against the counter and shrugged. "When I heard the River of Life was missing, I thought any chance of having *Quilt Mysteries* come to Marietta was gone. I love that show."

Tess looked past her to the stack of discs on the counter beside the television. Each of them was neatly labeled with the name *Quilt Mysteries* and a season and episode number. "So I see."

"So," she said slowly as she leaned toward Tess, "you cannot tell a soul, but I found out yesterday that *Quilt Mysteries* is still coming to Marietta. So, while I am disappointed that I won't get to see the River of Life in person on Bastille Day, my favorite show is still going to be filmed here."

And with Maybelline Rector in a starring role. Of course, there was no need to mention that right now. The entire town would find out soon enough. Maybelline would see to that.

"I see your point. So, one more question. What's up with the frog?"

"Frog?" When Tess pointed toward the center of the shelf, Wendy turned to look in that direction. Then she paled. "I'm sorry, Mrs. Wallace, but I'm going to have to ask you to go now."

"Are you all right?" Tess asked even though it was apparent the girl was anything but. "Why don't you come sit down and tell me what's wrong?"

"Nothing is wrong," she said. "I-I-I've just got something to do, and I need to lock up now."

Tess looked back at the frog and then returned her attention to Wendy. "I don't want to leave you like this. Can I drive you somewhere or stay with you while you call someone to be with you? You don't need to be alone if you're upset about something."

Wendy let out a deep breath and then mustered a smile. "You really would do that for me, wouldn't you?"

"Of course I would." Tess paused. "I can also keep a confidence. Care to tell me why the frog has you so upset, other than the fact it's absolutely hideous and doesn't go with any of the lovely decor you've put into the shop?"

Wendy's lips turned up into a smile, and she chuckled under her breath. "It is awful, isn't it?"

Tess reached over to place her hand atop Wendy's. "But that's not what's upsetting you," she said.

"It's from my father," she said.

"I see," she said. "Well, it's nice that your father wanted to do something for you."

Wendy nodded. "I suppose."

"That doesn't sound very positive. Are you and your father estranged?" She paused. "Just tell me if I'm asking too much."

"Recently reconnected, actually," Wendy said.

"Ah, well, then a gift from a recently reconnected father sounds like something positive." Tess glanced back up at the item in question and then returned her attention to Wendy. "But I understand it isn't always. So I'll just leave you and your little green friend, but only if you promise you'll stop by the inn later to let me know you're all right. Or text me. I'll give you my number."

"I can do that." Tess gave Wendy her phone number, and then Wendy wrote hers on the back of a Sassy Seamstress business card.

"One more thing," Wendy said. "Thanks for not insisting I ride in the parade. Despite the fact that I own this store, I can be kind of an introvert."

"I understand." Tess retrieved the bag, then pulled her car keys out of her purse. "Janice isn't too keen on riding on the fire truck either. For that matter, neither am I. I'm trying to convince them we need to leave the truck to the firemen."

"Speaking of firemen, congratulations on that mention on *Good Morning America*."

"You're kidding, right?"

Wendy grinned. "Remember me when you're famous."

"You just remember to let me know you're okay later."

Tess left the store smiling and with at least one question answered. However much Wendy wished to see the River of Life quilt, she wanted to see her favorites at the Arts & Antiques Network even more. Thus, the likelihood of sweet Wendy being involved in any shenanigans related to the famous quilt was low at best.

"Now I sound like Janice," she said as she shook her head.

A few minutes later, Tess parked her car beside LuAnn's and found her friend in deep discussion about the parade float with a familiar fireman bearing the name O'Hara on his uniform. Rather than join the conversation, Tess waited until it ended.

"May I speak to you for a second?" she asked him.

"Sure, Mrs. Wallace. Justin O'Hara, by the way." He reached out to shake her hand. "How's your head?"

"Fine, Justin," she said. "About our photo."

He grinned. "Pretty cool, huh? I hear they're talking about using it for the cover of the calendar this year. I mean, it did go viral, so it ought to beat out the picture of Jerry saving that dog from the river."

Tess pulled up a copy of the dreaded photograph on her phone and showed it to Justin. "Actually I'm more interested in figuring out who the third person is."

The fireman squinted at the photo. "How about that? I never noticed there was anyone else there."

LuAnn joined them and nodded toward the phone. "He's not wearing a fire or EMS uniform as far as we can tell, but I think there's a name patch on his shirt. If it's a he, that is. With the poor lighting and the shadows around the face, it could be a she."

"Could be," he said. "If that person wasn't fire or EMS, he shouldn't have been in the building. As Mrs. Wallace knows, we have rules about who can enter a structure under these conditions."

Tess grimaced as she thought of the bruises she spied this morning. Still, she let his comment go unanswered.

"I have a buddy who might be able to help. How about I send it to him and see what he can come up with?"

"Thank you," they both said.

"Okay, well I guess now that Miss Sherrill has our float planned out, I'll get the guys working on it. We've got to be down at the beginning of the parade route with this thing at 0600 hours day after tomorrow, so we're going to have to hustle."

"So early?" Tess groaned. "The parade doesn't start until ten."

LuAnn laughed. "Trust me. No one will be looking at us. Those guys will steal the show on the fire truck float. In fact, my plan doesn't even call for us to ride on the thing. Isn't that brilliant?"

Tess hugged her. "So I can sleep late?"

"Not exactly, but you can do what you promised in the Sassy Seamstress yesterday."

She gave LuAnn a sideways look. "Which was?"

"I'll give you a hint. Jeff Jr. was happy to have his red truck featured in the Marietta Fourth of July parade." She smiled. "Is it coming back to you now?"

"Vaguely. Remind me of the details."

"I'll do better than that. I'll show you." LuAnn opened her notebook to a drawing that featured the three of them standing in the back of Jeff Jr.'s truck with the quilt draped over the tailgate along with a sign that said Wayfarers Inn. Beneath, in smaller words, was written: Janice Eastman, LuAnn Sherrill, and Tess Wallace, innkeepers.

LuAnn grinned. "I went with alphabetical. I hope that's okay."

"Oh Lu, I love it." She shook her head. "Is Jeff Jr. really going to drive us in the parade?"

"He is," she said. "And even Janice is okay with that, although she asked if she could sit inside and enjoy the air-conditioning."

"I'm guessing she doesn't realize Jeff Jr.'s truck is vintage and has no air-conditioning."

"Oh, you know that's not why. She just doesn't want everyone looking at her. Or something like that."

Tess shrugged. "Whatever made her so fearful? I just don't get it."

"I don't know," LuAnn said. "But, before I forget, there's more to add to the notebook." She glanced around, then nodded toward her car. "Thorn and his crew are working inside, and our firemen and their truck have attracted a crowd out here. I don't want to be overheard."

Tess followed LuAnn to the car and climbed in. LuAnn went around to her side and did the same and then reached into her pocket to pull out a silver key. "Winnie was glad I stopped by. She said she'd been carrying this around for several days."

Tess raised her eyebrows. "A key?"

"A portable USB drive shaped like a key." LuAnn dangled the device by the loop at the end. "Apparently she's filled this with family recipes, some of them dating back to when the inn was new. Isn't that great? And it does explain how she could have been bringing me all of those recipes without carrying around a stack of papers."

"Yes, that makes sense. Slight change of topic. I was thinking this morning in the shower that we've been so focused on the quilt that we've missed an important clue."

"What's that?"

"The trunk," she said. "I know whoever took the quilt apparently didn't feel the trunk was worth taking too, but maybe if we research the trunk we'll find out a clue that will lead us to the quilt."

"It's worth a shot," LuAnn said. "I did wonder why someone wouldn't want that beautiful box. I think it would look lovely on the bar or maybe somewhere in the parlor, don't you?"

"Wherever you put it, it will look great," Tess said.

"Considering the trunk was free, it fits right into our budget," LuAnn said with a grin.

Laughter floated toward them, male and female, although mostly female. Tess repositioned the rearview mirror until she could see the source of the merriment. Saffron Navratilova and two of her friends were "helping" Justin O'Hara and a few of his fellow firemen wrap strands of red, white, and blue lights around the ladders on each side of the truck.

"Looks like Justin has a fan club," LuAnn said, forgoing Tess's covert observation technique to turn around and openly stare.

Tess returned the rearview mirror to its former position and joined her. Although the other two young ladies were quite pretty, Justin seemed to only have eyes for Saffron. From the broad smile on the young lady's face, the feeling appeared to be mutual.

LuAnn smiled. "I wonder if Brad knows where his office assistant is right now."

"I wonder if her father knows."

The inn's front door opened, and Thorn stepped out into the morning sunshine. "There you are," he called. "I just heard from the inspector."

"Step into my office," Tess said as she nodded toward the back seat of LuAnn's sedan.

"Sure, why not." Once Thorn was situated, he smiled. "So the building inspector who was giving us trouble a few hours ago has been pacified."

"That's great news," Tess said.

"It is," Thorn agreed. "But don't celebrate yet. I just got off the phone with the guy who has to sign off at the next level. He's not happy that the alarms went off last night and has put that permit on hold until he can come out and see for himself that we're up to code."

Tess frowned. "We are up to code, aren't we?"

"Sure," Thorn said. "But these inspector types tend to red flag permits when the fire department has to come out."

"But it was a false alarm," LuAnn said.

"Doesn't matter."

"Okay," Tess said. "When will he be out here?"

"His exact words?" At Tess's nod, he continued. "Mid-September."

"That's two months from now!" Tess exclaimed.

"Technically two and a half," LuAnn said.

Tess's heart sank. Every day the inn did not have paying guests or rental income on the public spaces was another day the three of them were not getting paid back for their investment.

"You've got to do something about that, Thorn," she said. "We need the permits approved so we can open the inn well before then. Ideally we get the kitchen up and running in a week or two and then have the downstairs operational and ready for rental after that."

"That's a tall order, Tess. The kitchen is close to ready as far as the cosmetic work. But a kitchen has to have plumbing and electrical that passes code. And—" Thorn's phone rang, and he pulled it out of his pocket. "Got to take this. It's our flooring guy." He slid out and closed the door as he put the phone to his ear. "Yeah, Mack, give me some good news."

Tess turned back around and rested her head on the seat. Out of the corner of her eye, she saw LuAnn watching her. "The middle of September," she said on an exhale of breath. "I would ask what next but considering how we spent yesterday, I don't want to know."

LuAnn reached for her purse and opened her notebook. Without a word, she started writing. A few minutes later, she looked up.

"What did you write?"

"A note about Winnie's key and a reminder to myself that when things like this happen, we shouldn't get discouraged."

"Ha," Tess said. "I'm not sure a reminder is going to fix how I'm feeling right now."

"'For I know the plans I have for you,'" LuAnn said. "Remember that one?"

Tess recited the remainder of Jeremiah 29:11 and then managed a smile. "Yes, I do. But sometimes it's just hard."

"We'll get through this. The permits will come through, and in no time we'll be sharing the top floor of the inn and wondering why we were so worried that it would never happen. We'll laugh about it, I promise." At Tess's skeptical expression, LuAnn shrugged. "Okay, maybe not all of it but most of it."

CHAPTER THIRTEEN

The next morning, Tess steered the car down the street and parked in front of the Antique and Salvage Mall. This place was one of her favorites, and Harry had been instrumental in returning not one but two valuable pieces of Wayfarers Inn back to their rightful places.

Thanks to him, there was a lamp that would once again shine light on the guests as they came and went from the inn. And over in the museum, a treasure trove of memorabilia from Prudence Willard, a nineteenth-century woman who was instrumental in securing the escape and safety of an untold number of slaves, would be preserved for future generations to see.

Today she hoped Harry could help with the origin of the trunk that held the mysterious disappearing quilt. If anyone could tell her whether this box was of the same era as the River of Life quilt, it was him.

Tess hefted the trunk out of the back of her five-year-old Honda and wedged it under her arm to make her way inside. Harry took one look at the trunk and shook his head. "Oh, no you don't. I don't want that back."

"You've seen this before?"

"Of course I have," he said. "Just last week. No returns."

"I didn't buy this," Tess said as she placed the trunk on the counter.

"I don't know if you did or you didn't," he said. "But I know I sold it, and the money has been deposited."

Tess leaned against the counter and shook her head. "First, I'm not trying to return it so don't worry about the money. It can stay wherever you put it. Second, I just want to try to figure out how this trunk got from your store to my inn. That's why I'm here."

He shrugged. "All I can tell you is that I sold that trunk to an online buyer who paid me through PayPal and gave me a shipping address."

"Now we're getting somewhere. Just give me the shipping address, and I'll take it from there."

He pushed his glasses up his nose. "You're a business-woman, Tess. You know I'd be breaking the law if I gave out that information."

Tess stared at him, thinking hard. "So if you can't tell me who you sold it to, can you tell me who you bought it from in the first place?"

Harry frowned. "Now, that's kind of a crazy thing. A couple of weeks ago I got an email from someone at an antique store in New Jersey telling me they had this strongbox that they thought had maybe come from our neck of the woods, and they offered it to me for a song. I usually don't do my deals like this, but I thought I could hardly lose much, with the little they were asking, even if the sale went south. So I sent the money, and this came last week. I listed it online, and a couple of days later it sold and I sent it off. Now here you are with it, and I'm telling you, I can't tell you who I sold it to unless a crime has been committed."

"That is what we're trying to determine."

Harry grinned. "So you ladies are solving a mystery again?"

It was her turn to play coy. "More like trying to figure out where things came from and where they went."

"Oh, in that case, I can tell you that you've got yourself a nice example of a mid-1800s strongbox."

"So it's not a trunk?"

"Technically, no," he said as he turned the item around as if to examine it again. "See these hinges? That puts your box at about 1850–1870. Back then these were used to transport documents and other valuables safely on long journeys or as decoration in homes." He opened the lid. "What sets this one apart is its size. These are usually much smaller. Document size, basically."

"Why do you think this one was made so big?"

He closed the lid and peered at her a moment. "My answer would just be a guess."

"Guess away," Tess said. "Because I have no idea."

"All right." He shrugged. "Strongboxes were made to order. A customer ordered this from a carpenter or, more likely, a furniture maker for a specific purpose or to hold a specific item."

An item like a quilt destined to make a long journey from Ohio to Washington, DC. Possibly with many stops along the route.

"Was it empty when you sold it?" she asked.

"Don't know," Harry said. "The latch was jammed when I got it, and like that box I found for you ladies, I couldn't get the thing open so I sold it as it was. Have I helped you with your mystery?"

"You have," she said with a grin as she picked up what she now knew was a mid-1800s strongbox. "Although it would help even more if you'd let me have a peek at that address."

"Go on now," he said good-naturedly. "And don't come back until you're ready to furnish your inn. By then I'll probably have found a dozen or more items that came from it."

"It's a deal," she said. "You gather those things up, and we'll come and see what you've found."

"How much time do I have?" He looked around the shop filled to the brim with all sorts of antiques and then back at Tess. "This is a big place, and I've got two warehouses that look just like it."

She sighed. "Thanks to a certain inspector and who knows what other delays, you've got plenty of time."

"Sorry to hear that."

Tess shrugged as she cradled the strongbox. "Me too. But at least we'll have a mystery to keep us busy while we're waiting to open the inn to guests."

She stepped out onto the sidewalk and nearly collided with Margaret Ashworth, president of the local historical society. Practically as old as some of the objects she collected for the museum, Margaret had been a valuable source of information in the past.

"Oh my goodness, so you're the one who bought the strongbox," Margaret exclaimed. "I had my eyes on it but just couldn't manage to make myself pay what Harry wanted for it." Her eyes ran the length of Tess then returned to the antique in her hands. "I suppose you'll be putting it on display at the inn. All those strangers handling such a..." She shrugged as her bony fingers curled. "Pay no attention to me. You do what you want with it."

"We haven't decided yet," Tess said. "But since you've had your eye on it, do you mind telling me what you found so special about it?"

Margaret's hand-drawn brows rose. "You mean you don't know?" She glanced around. "There is so much to tell, but I'm late to meet Thelma and Irene to go over the final details for tomorrow's Fourth of July ribbon cutting on the renovations to the gazebo. Without the generous contributions of the civic-minded citizens of Marietta, we would never have been able to make it structurally sound. A proper thank-you needs to be given in the form of a party the town will never forget."

Tess stifled a grin. The fact that the three women planning this party were all above the age of seventy indicated the sort of party the town might expect. Likely everyone in attendance would be home before dark. "Then I won't keep you," she said.

"Oh, please come along. I'm sure the ladies would love to give their opinions about the strongbox, especially given its ties to local history."

"I'm listening," Tess said.

Margaret shook her head. "Not another word out of me until you agree to join us over at Jeremiah's Coffee Shop."

"Why not?" Tess said. "I'll just put the strongbox in my trunk and—"

"No! You couldn't possibly be considering putting something that valuable in the trunk of your car and walking away?"

She didn't dare tell Margaret that she'd tripped over the thing on the dusty floor of her unlocked inn. Or that she'd been keeping it in her trunk since yesterday.

"I suppose I could bring it in."

"Of course you can, Tess. Now come along. Those two are notoriously punctual, and I know I'll never hear the end of them wondering where I was."

Tess hurried to catch up with Margaret. Sure enough, as soon as Margaret opened the door of the coffee shop, the two older women voiced their concern over her whereabouts.

"Blame Tess," Margaret said. "When I saw what she was carrying out of Harry's place, I had to stop and invite her to join us."

All three sets of eyes turned toward Tess as she set the strongbox on the seat beside her then dropped her purse on top of it.

Thelma Bickerton and Irene Bickerton Martin lived together in the palatial Bickerton home in the best part of Marietta. Aunts to the Grimes brothers, the sisters had only recently survived the discovery of a family secret that meant Brad and Grant were the rightful owners of the Bickerton fortune, not them.

As far as Tess knew, the only other ones who knew of this were Brad, the ladies of the Inn Crowd, Winnie, and Brad's cousins, Charlotte and Leo. Grant hadn't been there to find out he was suddenly a wealthy man. Having met the younger Grimes brother, she wouldn't blame Brad if he'd failed to mention to his brother that the fortune the elderly ladies were sitting on was rightfully half his. Nice as he seemed to be, though, Brad had probably told him the whole sordid story.

Irene, the younger of the two by six years, was close to ninety. Thelma was spry for a woman whose centennial was in the not-too-distant future.

"So you're the one who stole Margaret's trunk," Irene said, her eyes twinkling. "We wondered who would dare do such a thing."

"'Stole' is such a harsh word," Margaret said as she slanted Tess a look. "More like 'beat me to it.' It's my fault for trying to wait until that stubborn man came down on his price. Who in the world would pay three thousand dollars, no matter the historical significance?"

"Three thousand dollars?" Tess gulped. To think it had been sitting on the floor covered in dust. And that she'd practically tripped over it.

"Yes, dear." Thelma toyed with the gold locket she always wore. "Personally, I felt that was a reasonable price. I have asked Margaret several times if she was just using the strongbox as an excuse to go flirt with Harry."

"That's enough, Thelma." Margaret shook her head but did not deny the allegation.

"What can you ladies tell me about the strongbox?" Tess asked. "Harry dated it from the mid-1800s and said the size of it meant it was made to order for a specific purpose."

"For the purpose of holding something very valuable to those who supported the abolitionist movement," Margaret said.

"The River of Life quilt?" Tess offered.

Three sets of eyes widened. Only Irene nodded. "So you know, then."

"About the quilt? Yes. Wendy over at the Sassy Seamstress told us about it."

The sisters exchanged looks. "What did she tell you?"

At Prudence's nod, the other women went back to sewing. Each who sat at the frame had been told what to do. For some, that knowledge was as fresh as the Ohio mud on their hemlines. For others, their survival in this place so close to the river had depended on taking this knowledge in and recalling it time and again.

Each of them would understand why Prudence had sent Liberty and Sally away. One false move, one small sign that this was something more than an innocent quilting, and their very lives would be in jeopardy.

As Prudence held her son tightly against her shoulder, she couldn't help but look around the table at the faces there—dark and light and shades in between—who would never be recalled with such glory as Mrs. Tubman. And yet to those they saved, however few or plentiful the number, these women's value could not be measured.

She turned around and found the captain blocking her path. A slave would be afraid. A woman not of this man's stature would as well.

So Prudence put on her most confident expression and looked the man directly in his eyes. "There is no finer child than this one," she said. "I stand in testament to that."

Silence fell between them. Still Prudence held his gaze. In her arms, Moses began to awaken.

Finally the man's expression softened. "And I stand in agreement. To whom do I have the pleasure of speaking?"

"Prudence Willard," she told him. "Wife of Mr. Willard who owns a farm in the vicinity. Perhaps thee have had business with my husband?"

"I have not," he said as Victoria came to stand beside him. "Though I will recall the name once we have settled in so that I might seek him out for such business. Wife," he said as he looked down at Victoria with great tenderness, "this is Mrs. Willard, wife of a farmer." He nodded toward the frame. "And quilter as well."

Prudence shifted her attention to her former friend. The fear she thought she saw earlier was gone. Rather, Violet Gibson was gone and Victoria, wife of a white army captain, stood in her place.

In this moment, Victoria held sway over Prudence's life. A word from her and the white man could order her hauled across the river. Surely no one would stop such a thing.

And Moses would go with her. Jason too.

In an act of supreme desperation and trust, Prudence thrust her son toward the captain's wife. "Keep him a moment, then," she said, her tone even. "A finer child there is not."

"Captain Markham," the innkeeper called. "A word, please."

"I'll be only a moment," he told his wife.

Her husband no longer at her side, the woman who had once played alongside her in the forest before either of them knew a thing about the world outside their safe homes took Moses. She held him as he softly fussed, just as Prudence would have done.

And then Violet began to cry.

CHAPTER FOURTEEN

Tess shifted positions. "Wendy told us there were two River of Life quilts, one made for General Lafayette that was lost and another made by church ladies at our inn. That one had a connection to the Underground Railroad."

"But not because there were signals sewn into it," Margaret said. "That is a popular misconception."

"She is right," Irene told her. "But so are you. That quilt was made for a purpose, but it wasn't just the quilting that went on at the inn. There were other things happening."

"I saw the tunnel connecting the inn with the river," Tess said. "So I do know about the history with the Underground Railroad and housing escapees. Is that what you mean?"

Irene nodded and then took a sip of her tea. "While the ladies were meeting for their quiltings, others were downstairs caring for the folks who had not yet made their way to the next stop on the railroad. Sometimes that involved just feeding or clothing, but other times that meant nursing wounds or, on occasion, a discreet burial."

Tess sat back. "What do you mean, Irene?"

"Oh come now," she said. "You must know those who arrived at the inn were rarely in good health. Some lived to move on to the next stop. Some stayed and hid in plain sight."

"And some did not survive," Tess supplied. "What did they do with them?"

"What could they do?" Thelma said. "They buried the poor souls."

"At the inn?"

"Heavens no," Margaret said. "They were taken to consecrated ground and buried properly, possibly at the Harmar Cemetery—although most experts say that did not happen."

"Where is Harmar? I only know about the Mound Cemetery."

"Everyone in town knows that one," Margaret said. "So many famous souls resting there. Oh, but the Harmar is older and some say more historically important. Sadly, it has been known to flood and isn't much visited anymore. Of course the historical society would like to remedy that, but there just aren't enough funds to do everything we want to do."

"How very sad to get all the way to Ohio and freedom only to die here," Irene said.

"And be buried in the dead of night, I've been told."

"Officially, no slave burials took place in our local cemeteries, in daylight or dark," Margaret said. "Although it is well known the Harmar contains the remains of many children of freed slaves. Burying black and white in the same ground caused quite a fuss in some circles back then."

Irene and Thelma nodded in unison.

"And remember, many of those who participated in helping slaves escape were of the Quaker denomination. Their markers were simple—a small stone rather than an elaborate headstone—so these were easily lost to flooding or crumbled over the years. And they didn't keep careful records of where they buried anyone. If a stone wasn't placed, they went from memory as to where the next body was put. So maybe they're there, and maybe they're not. But somewhere in our area there is a cemetery that welcomed those poor souls who barely found their freedom before they lost their lives."

The three women fell silent. Finally Irene spoke. "Oh, but we've strayed from talking about this lovely strongbox you stole from Margaret."

"I didn't steal it," Tess protested. "I found it."

Margaret's brows rose again. "What's this? You didn't tell me you found my box. Where was it?"

She shrugged. "On the floor in the inn. I nearly broke my neck tripping over it."

"How can that be?" Margaret said. "Who would leave a valuable antique just sitting on the floor of an abandoned building?"

"The inn is a mess right now but it's hardly abandoned," Tess said. "But I would love to know too."

"Margaret," Thelma said, "if anyone can pry the information out of Harry about who bought that strongbox, it's you. Why don't you go see if you can get the old codger to talk?"

The idea of a woman nearing a century of life calling someone an old codger was enough to make Tess stifle a giggle. Then Irene winked at her, and the giggle escaped.

"Oh, you don't think I can do it?" Margaret said.

"I think you couldn't get him to sell it to you at a cut-rate price," Irene said. "So I'm skeptical. We'll just leave it at that."

"Then watch this." The challenge made, Margaret reapplied her lipstick and marched out of the coffee shop without a backward glance.

"I thought she'd never leave," Irene said.

Thelma stirred another lump of sugar into her cup of Earl Grey. "Once we saw you walk through the door with Margaret we knew we had to get you alone."

"We have questions," Irene said.

"All right." Tess picked up her coffee mug. "Fire away."

Once again the ladies exchanged glances. "Well," Thelma said, "you said you went to the Sassy Seamstress. We wondered what you thought of it."

Tess shook her head. "Considering I am not a seamstress, I can only tell you that I thought the shop was well laid out, the inventory was impressive, and Wendy, the owner, was very nice."

"About Wendy," Irene said. "What is your impression of her?"

"As I said, she's nice."

"Nice," Thelma echoed.

Tess placed her mug back down on the table without taking a sip. There was something these ladies weren't saying, and Tess got the impression it had everything to do with Wendy.

"Stay away from her, dear," Irene said. "She's bad news. Someone we care very much about is being blackmailed by that woman, and we are furious about the whole thing."

"Blackmail? Not Wendy. She's adorable. I cannot imagine she'd be involved in blackmail."

"Have you ever seen pictures of serial killers, Tess?" Irene said. "Being ugly has never been a requirement. Look at that Dahmer fellow. Good-looking man. They say people really liked him too. And that doll that went around killing people on that movie? Charlie or whatever his name was? He was cute before people started dying."

"He was never cute, and that is enough, Irene," Thelma snapped. "We promised not to say anything."

"Then I should have kept my big mouth shut," Irene said although she didn't look a bit sorry. "But Tess and her friends are our only hope. We've talked about this, and neither of us can come up with any other answer."

Thelma seemed to be considering the statement. Finally she nodded. "Yes, I think you're right." The door opened, and a trio of giggling high-school-age girls stepped inside. "But let's not have this conversation here," she said.

Irene turned to Tess. "Would you and the other two ladies mind paying us a visit next week after the big Fourth of July to-do is over? I believe we could benefit from your wisdom."

"Of course," Tess said. "Now maybe I can benefit from yours. What exactly is it about the strongbox that makes it so special? I think I know, but I would love to have that confirmed."

Thelma and Irene giggled. "Nothing that we know of, but we've had great fun making Margaret think so."

Tess sat back in her chair and rested her hand on the antique beneath her purse. "You're serious. There's nothing special about this?"

"Oh, I'm sure it's special enough," Thelma said. "I mean it *is* old, and the wood is pretty. But as to somehow being connected to Marietta history?"

Both ladies shook their heads.

"So this has been an elaborate joke?

"And a good one, don't you think?" Thelma said. "We had no idea the story of that old strongbox being the one made for the River of Life quilt would sound believable enough to fool the president of the historical society."

Tess lifted her coffee mug as she tried to hide her disappointment. "Well done, ladies. Does this apply to the fake River of Life quilt that was inside of it when I found it?"

Their smiles fell. Then Thelma shook her head, a grin beginning. "Oh, I get it. She's joking with us, Irene."

"No, I'm serious." Tess shrugged. "When we opened the strongbox, there was a quilt folded inside."

"What did it look like?" Irene asked.

"It looked old," she said. "The fabric almost felt like it would fall apart if I unfolded it. But the part we saw was beautiful. The handwork was so intricate. It almost looked like..."

"A river flowing down the fabric?" Thelma supplied.

"Yes, exactly, with all these beautiful decorative stitches and tiny quilt pieces. So I assumed it was the famous quilt. Or at least a copy of it." Tess shrugged. "But now that I know about your joke, I have to ask how you managed to find something so close to the original. I'm assuming you opened it somehow, because Harry said he couldn't get it to open."

"We never tried to open it," Irene said. "We've never even touched it. We just told Margaret it was the box that once held the River of Life quilt."

Tess shook her head. "So you didn't put a fake River of Life quilt in the strongbox?"

Irene jabbed Thelma with her elbow. "She's joking again."

"No," Thelma said slowly. "I don't think she is."

"I'm not," Tess said.

Both ladies leaned conspiratorially forward. "When you opened the strongbox, was the River of Life inside of it?" Irene said.

"We think so, but it went missing before we saw the whole thing. There was definitely a quilt of some kind in it."

Irene shook her head. "How could it be missing when you still have the strongbox?"

"Someone removed the quilt and filled the strongbox with painter's cloth. Best we can tell, it happened during that episode with the fire alarms. It was a false alarm, by the way."

"So someone sets the fire alarm off and the next thing you know, the quilt is gone?" Thelma shrugged. "I say once you find out who was in the inn during that time, you'll find out who took that quilt."

"The ladies and I are investigating, but at this point half the town had access to the inn. Plus, we've never seen a picture of the real one, so we don't even know if what we lost is worth looking for." Tess paused. "Anyway, we haven't told anyone else about the quilt, so please don't say anything."

"We promise," Thelma said as Irene nodded in agreement.

"Have you called the National Archives?" Irene asked.

"No, but LuAnn has been searching their collection online."

Thelma shrugged. "Short of showing up at someone's front door, I have found that making a phone call sure beats poking around online to get an answer to something."

Irene nodded. "Call us old-school—Brad does—but we like the direct approach. If you want to know what the 1850s version of the River of Life quilt looks like, make the call and see if someone at the archives can help."

"You know, that sounds like a great idea."

The door opened again, and Grant Grimes stood back to let Margaret press past him. Today his Hawaiian shirt was a subdued tan color with lines of orange surfboards marching across the front. His khaki shorts and sandals gave him the look of a tourist in search of a beach. All he needed was a camera.

"Excuse me, sweetheart," Margaret told him. "I need to have a word with your aunties."

Grant met Tess's gaze across the space between them and then chuckled. "You first and then me," he told the older woman.

She returned to her chair and offered the sisters a broad smile. "For your information, I have a date with Harry tomorrow night for the fireworks."

"Well, isn't that nice?" Thelma asked Irene.

"Very nice," Irene said. "But did he tell you who bought the strongbox?"

"He will," she snapped. "Now if you'll excuse me, I have things to do."

After they said their goodbyes, the sisters motioned for Grant to join them. "No doubt she's gone to go redraw those eyebrows," Irene said.

"Be nice," Thelma warned.

Irene offered her a sideways look. "Oh hush. You wish you'd thought to say it." Then she moved her attention to her nephew. "How are you, Grant? I haven't seen you since you returned from Mexico."

"Grand, now that I'm with three lovely ladies."

"Oh, stow it, child," Thelma said. "Your charm hasn't worked on Irene and me in nigh on five decades, and I doubt it'll work now."

Stunned at Thelma's harsh tone, Tess decided to make a quick getaway. "If you ladies will excuse me, I need to get back to the inn."

"We will call you next week," Irene said.

"And see you at the parade," Thelma added.

Grant rose when Tess did and managed a smile. "Let me help you with that," he said.

"Thank you, but I've got it."

Ignoring her, Brad's younger brother retrieved the strongbox and nodded to the door. "After you."

"All right. Thank you." She turned to smile at the sisters. "I look forward to seeing you at the parade."

"And next week," Thelma reminded her.

Tess left with Grant and the strongbox in tow. When she reached her car and pressed the button on her key, the trunk opened. Grant settled the box inside and closed the trunk.

"Again," she said, "thank you."

He nodded. "I think we might have gotten off to a bad start yesterday," he said. "Brad told me later that I came off as a little obnoxious. I do that sometimes."

Tess shrugged. "Obnoxious is in the eye of the beholder."

"Touché." He shrugged. "Then in that case, going forward I will try not to be so obnoxious."

She laughed. "While I appreciate your apology, I really think you're wasting it on me. I tend to say things myself I shouldn't on occasion."

He stepped back to watch her get into the Honda. "See you at the parade, then," he told her before heading back into the coffee shop.

Tess was still thinking about the change in Grant Grimes when she pulled into her garage and parked next to LuAnn's car. She found her friend sipping a cup of almond pecan roast coffee at the breakfast room table.

"Want a cup?" LuAnn asked as Tess dropped her purse onto the credenza beside the door.

"No, I just had coffee with Thelma and Irene. I think I'll get a bottle of water and tell you about it. I've had an interesting day so far."

"I bet," she said. "Those two are characters."

"They are, but that's not where my story starts. I actually began the day by stopping by the Antique and Salvage Mall to ask about our trunk." Tess returned to the table and opened her water bottle. Then between sips she filled LuAnn in on everything Harry told her.

"That is interesting," LuAnn said.

"Yes, but until he agrees to give me that address, we're kind of stuck." She took another sip. "Well, there is the possibility that Margaret Ashworth will convince him, but I'm not holding my breath."

"The historical society president?"

Tess nodded. "That's a story for another time. Let's stick to the strongbox and our mystery, shall we?"

"Okay, I understand Harry has to follow the law," LuAnn said. "It just seems like there ought to be some loophole that could get us that address."

Tess looked over at the line of photographs in silver frames that marched across the breakfront, her eyes coming to rest on a picture of her only son and his father taken while working on the red truck that had meant so much to both of them. The same red truck she and her friends would be riding in as grand marshals of the Fourth of July parade in the morning.

"It's at times like this I wish Jeff Jr. had gone to law school. At least now we know that strongbox was built for a specific purpose."

"Given the fact that the quilt fit nicely in there, I'm guessing we know what that purpose was." LuAnn shrugged. "I sure wish we had unfolded the quilt while we had a chance. I still wonder if the rest of it was as beautiful as that one corner we saw."

"As my mother used to say, if wishes were horses, then beggars would ride." Tess grinned. "Anyway, I left Harry's place and ran into Margaret—literally. She asked me to join Irene and Thelma at Jeremiah's Coffee shop."

LuAnn giggled. "That must have been fun."

"It was interesting." She paused to consider how best to explain the odd goings-on at the coffee shop. "They want to talk to the three of us next week. Wendy from the Sassy Seamstress is allegedly blackmailing someone they care about."

"Another mystery?" LuAnn shook her head. "Do we need more to try to figure out?"

"It's Thelma and Irene," Tess reminded them. "They're very sweet and very elderly. How can we not help them?"

"True," LuAnn said.

"Oh," Tess added, "and I got an apology from Grant Grimes for being obnoxious. He was really nice about it."

"Really?" LuAnn shook her head. "You did have an interesting morning."

"I did," she said. "Hey, did you ever find anything in your online search of the National Archives?"

"Nothing that would help us identify the River of Life."

Tess returned the top to her water bottle and sat back in the chair. "Then remind me to call them next week, please. I think it's time to go old-school."

LuAnn grinned. "Why wait? They're still open."

"How do you know?"

She turned the notebook around to face Tess. There on the bottom of the page beneath the words National Archives was a phone number and business hours.

"I was going to call next week, but maybe right now is a better time."

Tess pulled her phone out of her pocket. "Given the day I've had, I agree."

CHAPTER FIFTEEN

The morning dawned early, but true to his word, Jeff, Jr. had them all packed into his vintage red 1953 Chevrolet 3100 pickup truck with the shiny whitewall tires and the custom wood rails along the bed. Every time she saw this truck, Tess thought about how much Jeffrey would have loved how it turned out.

Of course, every time she saw Jeff Jr., she thought the same thing.

All around them participants were gathering, some dressed in patriotic garb and others who wore costumes more suited to Halloween. A woman wearing what appeared to be a fairy costume complete with blue mask, white wings sprinkled in red and blue glitter over a matching leotard and long flowing red vest strolled past. She waved a flag in one hand as she smiled up at the ladies.

"What in the world does a red, white, and blue fairy have to do with our nation's birthday?" Janice asked after she returned the wave.

"This year's theme is 'It's a Red, White & Blue World,'" LuAnn said. "The rules specify that each entrant follows the theme."

Jeff Jr. had moved the truck into position at the beginning of the parade, just behind a half-dozen motorcycle policemen.

Bunting draped the front of the truck and announced to the citizens of Marietta that the grand marshals had arrived while the Sassy Seamstress quilt and the Wayfarers Inn sign LuAnn designed decorated the back.

As a transplant to Marietta, Tess had never attended one of its annual Fourth of July parades. Given the level of interest from the citizens and the number of floats and marching bands, she shouldn't have waited so long.

After the parade a barbeque cook-off would be held at the park and then, once the sun set, fireworks would light the sky over the river. Given the fact she'd been awake since well before dawn, staying up to see the festivities might require an afternoon nap.

"Everyone okay out there?" Janice called.

LuAnn grinned. "You're missing the fun."

"Janice, are you sure you don't want to ride out here with us?" Tess called.

"Thank you, but no. I am perfectly happy where I am."

Jeff Jr. beamed at his mother through the back window. "I'll see that she doesn't get into any trouble."

"You'd better see that you pay attention to the road and not the passenger," Tess said.

Jeff Jr. rolled his eyes. "Thirty-six years old and my mother is still telling me how to drive."

"Mimi!" Tess turned around to see three of the most precious children on the planet hurrying toward her with their mama and daddy trying their best to keep up.

"Hey, Mom." Lizzie handed Tess the triplets one by one. "It's like herding chickens. But we wouldn't miss this for the world."

"Come see your Mimi, you precious darlings," Tess said as she knelt down and embraced all three at once. "My arms are full of love," she told the wiggling trio as their father closed the truck's tailgate.

It was what Jeffrey used to say when he held her. They were now the words she used to remind these precious babies how much they were adored.

"Where are your kids, Janice?" LuAnn asked.

"They're meeting me at the picnic," she said, "although I'm sure Larry won't be pleased when he hears he missed out on riding in the parade."

Her five-year-old grandson was her husband's namesake and absolutely adorable. Janice loved to give the little boy extra cuddles and Nana time.

Lizzie nudged Tess. "Mom, who is that man taking videos?"

She looked over the little ones' heads to see a dark-haired man aiming a long lens in their direction. "Probably someone from the newspaper," she told her. "Apparently this parade is a very big deal."

"Apparently you and Ms. LuAnn and Ms. Janice are very big deals too," Lizzie said. "Because I've been watching him ever since we arrived, and you're the only ones he's filming."

Tess stood and gave the fellow another look. Something about him seemed familiar. "Maybe he's a fan of antique trucks."

"Or antique women," Lizzie said with a giggle. "Just kidding, Mom. He's young, but if he's interested in you, then that's great. You're still young enough, you know."

"Interested in me?" Tess tried not to gape. "Whatever for? I don't cook or clean and the last time I dated, I was still cheering on the weekends. Thank you, but no. Besides, he's just a baby."

Lizzie nudged her. "Don't rule it out, Mom. Jeff and I have talked about it, and we're okay if you wanted to start seeing people."

"I see lots of people right now." Her hand swept the horizon. "Just look. They're all over the place."

"You're making a joke of this," her daughter said. "You always do. But when you're ready—if you ever are—then just know that Jeff and I support you, okay?"

"Okay." Tess pulled Lizzie into a hug. "Have I told you lately that I love you?"

"Every day. But I never get tired of hearing it." She stiffened. "Mom, that guy. He's heading this way, and he's still snapping pictures. This is just weird."

Tess's son-in-law touched her arm. "You and Lizzie watch the kids. I'm going to go see what he wants."

"That's not necessary," Tess said even as she knew her daughter's husband would go anyway. Michael might have left the military, but the instincts that kept him alive through deployments also made him very good at protecting his family.

She watched as Michael confronted the man with the camera, who immediately appeared to show an ID. A moment later, the men were laughing. Then Michael escorted him toward the truck.

"Innkeepers Tessa Wallace and LuAnn Sherrill," Michael said, "this is Barrett George. Oh, and Ms. Janice, I didn't see you in the truck. Barrett, this is the third member of the innkeeper group." He nodded to Jeff. "And my brother-in-law, Jeff."

"Not an innkeeper. Just a lowly CPA," Jeff Jr. said as he shook his hand. "I'm driving Miss Daisy today. Or rather Miss Daisies."

"Pleased to meet you, Barrett," Janice said through the open window. "You look so familiar. Were you one of my students?"

"No, ma'am," he said before turning his attention to Tess and LuAnn. "I'm not from around here. Ladies, it is a pleasure."

Tess shook his hand and then stepped back to allow LuAnn to do the same. Barrett looked younger up close than he looked from a distance, somewhere in the seven-year age gap between Jeff Jr. and Lizzie.

"Why are you filming us?" she asked him as she studied his dark eyes and curls and tried to place him.

"Barrett is undercover this morning, Tess," Michael told her. "He's posing as a part of the press but he's really here for another purpose." He nodded at Barrett. "Tell them."

"Yes, tell us," Tess said.

A bullhorn sounded, and Tess jumped. Bart Sandman stepped in front of the police escort and raised his hand.

"All right, folks. It's almost showtime. Everyone ready to go?"

"Why don't you join us?" LuAnn asked.

Barrett grinned. "I hoped you would ask." He secured his camera on his shoulder and climbed up. "As to your question, Mrs. Wallace, I am—"

The horn blew again and then the police motorcycle engines roared to life. Sirens screamed, both in front of them on the motorcycles and behind them in the old fire truck.

LuAnn nudged Tess and placed something in her hand. "Earplugs. Janice brought them."

Tess mouthed a silent word of thanks as the ear-splitting noise became tolerable. Now that conversation was impossible, Barrett retrieved his camera and turned it toward the crowd.

Tess watched as Barrett took shots that panned the crowd. Then he turned the camera on her and LuAnn.

Instinctively, Tess covered her face with her hands. When she peeked, Barrett was laughing and shaking his head. Throughout the length of the parade, he kept up his filming and his attempts to get shots of the innkeepers. Finally she managed to ignore him and enjoy herself.

Faces she knew and some that she'd only just met appeared in the crowd as the truck rolled slowly past. Pastor Ben Murphey waved, as did his darling wife, Paige. Tess returned the greeting with a smile.

A young minister taking on his first pastoral assignment, Ben had big shoes to fill following Janice's husband Lawrence's death. While someday he would be as eloquent a speaker as Reverend Eastman was, Tess sensed that Ben still had much to learn. Just last Sunday he had illustrated his sermon's main point with a Peanuts cartoon. And he'd even added a song. That he sang himself. That had caused a buzz among the older parishioners, especially those prone to linger over the coffeepot after church.

Charlotte Lane caught her attention from the opposite side of the road. How she'd ever thought that Charlotte was interested in Brad or the inn was beyond Tess now. Seeing Charlotte with Paul Townsend, CEO of the bank, it was obvious both were smitten.

Rumor had it that Paul turned down a chance to be grand marshal in favor of standing on the sideline and watching the parade with Charlotte. As the truck passed them by, she caught the pair sneaking a quick kiss and grinned.

The truck rolled on, and with each turn of the tires, the day grew warmer. By the time the parade reached the end of the route, which was very near to the inn, Tess was in dire need of air-conditioning and cold water. She found both in the inn's kitchen.

"Thank You, Lord, and thank you electrician, whoever you are," Tess said as she handed out bottles of cold water to everyone who had ridden the length of the parade route in the truck with her. "And special thanks to our driver, Jeff Jr.," she said as her son walked in.

"There's someone outside asking for you, Mom," he said as he intercepted one of the triplets before he could escape the kitchen.

Barrett George had made his apologies and taken off just as soon as the parade ended. "I'll be back, I promise," he had told her. "Don't give away my secret," he had said to Michael.

Likely he'd returned but was reluctant to interrupt family time.

"That's just the camera guy. Tell him to come in."

"No," he said slowly, concern etching his features. "It's not him."

"Oh," Tess said lightly. "Well, then, you all enjoy yourselves. There are snacks in the fridge, so help yourselves. I'll be right back."

She walked out of the kitchen into the parlor with Jeff Jr. a step behind. "What's wrong?" she asked him.

He nodded rather than responding, and Tess looked over in that direction. A man in a dark suit and white shirt with Ray-Bans watched her from near the door. Though Jeff Jr. seemed intimidated, the man reminded Tess of one of the characters in a Wallace family favorite, *The Blues Brothers*.

Jeff Jr. grasped her arm and leaned close. "He's a Fed, Mom," he whispered. "What have you done?"

Tears slid a silent path down pale cheeks. Behind them on the opposite end of the parlor, the captain and the innkeeper appeared to be having a companionable discussion.

Prudence reached into her sleeve and found the square of cloth she kept there. Carefully she wiped away her old friend's tears.

Violet's expression spoke of the gratitude her trembling lips seemed unable to convey. "So you are a farmer's wife?" she finally managed.

"Proudly so. And thee are a captain's wife," Prudence said.

Violet looked down at Moses then back up at her. "Your son is beautiful." She touched the top of his head with her lips, still trembling. "He is the color of…"

She did not complete the thought, but there was no need. Moses was safe because the secret of his lineage was not evident in his pale skin and eyes.

"I so fear a child would give me away." Tears fell in earnest now as she settled onto the chair Prudence had vacated. "The captain, he loves me so. I could not bear—"

"What is this?" Captain Markham's heavy strides closed the distance between them. "What has come to cause this, my darling?" The captain rested his hand on Violet's shoulder as he focused on Prudence. "Tell me what has caused this."

"Thy wife is distraught," Prudence told him and lowered her voice. "Might I now have a word?"

Though each step away from her son tore at her heart, still Prudence took those steps until she found some measure of privacy near the staircase. Once again she called on her ability to pretend to hide fear at what she was about to say.

"Forgive any impertinence," she told him. "I mean no such offense. But have there been children of this marriage? Perhaps thy wife grieves for them?"

He looked away. "Despite our fondest wishes, there have been none."

"I had despaired of a son," she told him. "The remedy is to accept what has already been decided."

"That no son or daughter will fill our cradle?" he snapped.

"No, Captain," she said gently. "That no cradle will fill thy home."

His face immediately reddened. She'd gone too far. Spoken too freely. Mama did say she knew not the place and time beyond which talking should cease.

"You have a son," he bellowed. "What sense does it make to do as you say?"

"Please, sir, do forgive me," she hastened to add. "My husband often tells me I am too bold. I fear him correct."

Captain Markham shook his head. "Your husband is correct, yet I require a response."

Prudence ducked her head, aware that they had captured the attention of the quilters once more. Without Amity to assist, the women would quickly grow fearful. She must attend to the situation.

"The sense, sir," she said gently, "is not in the result of what might be but in the accepting of what is." Moses wailed, relieving her of any further obligation to remain in conversation with the captain. "Might I see to the boy?"

"Do so, please."

She walked briskly back to where Violet stood. "The choice to bear a child is thine alone now," she said softly as she gathered up her son. "Choose wisely for thy husband does love thee so."

"He does," she said, tears falling freely. "But he loves the woman he believes me to be. What man of his position would wish for a wife who could easily be put up for sale on the other side of the river? He has been sent to Marietta to rid this place of people like me and those who would support us."

What Violet left unsaid also meant he was sent to rid Marietta of people like Prudence and Jason as well. Prudence curled her little finger to provide an alternate for Moses's noisy demands. The ploy generally worked but rarely for long.

"Then, again," Prudence said. "I urge thee to choose wisely."

"He will know someday."

"Not from me," she told Violet. "The tale is thine alone to tell."

"Thank you." Violet reached between them to place her hand on Prudence's arm. "I am in your debt," she said. "And you will receive the same consideration from me. Only say the word, and I will do whatever you ask."

CHAPTER SIXTEEN

D on't be ridiculous. I haven't done anything," Tess said over her shoulder as she walked toward the stranger.

The Fed, as Jeff Jr. referred to him, was of average height with an athletic build and hair cut so short it was almost military style. He looked like one of those crazy marathon runners who breezed past her on her morning walks by the river. The ones who wore neon and spandex and probably changed out running shoes more often than she changed her mind.

"Hello," she told the man. "I'm Tessa Wallace. May I help you?"

"Mrs. Wallace, is there a place we can speak in private?" He looked past her to give whoever was standing there—probably Jeff Jr.—a pointed stare. "That would mean just the two of us."

"Well that depends," she said. "Who are you and what do you want to talk about?"

He reached into his pocket and retrieved what looked like a wallet. With a flip of his hand, the wallet opened to reveal a badge on one side and a card identifying the man standing in front of her as Charles D. Butler, FBI agent.

"FBI?" She shook her head as her heart leaped into her throat. "What in the world would an FBI agent want with me?"

"I will need to discuss that with you in private, ma'am." He once again turned his humorless gaze to a spot behind her. Tess glanced over her shoulder at Jeff Jr.

"It's fine," she told her son. "I'm just going to speak to this man for a minute. Tell the others I'll be right there. And save some strawberries and whipped cream for me. You know how your sister always takes more whipped cream than she should."

He looked skeptical. "Are you sure, Mom?"

"I'm certain," she said, biting her lip. "Lizzie has always loved strawberries and whipped cream."

"No, Mom." He nodded toward Agent Butler. "About him."

Even as a child, her husband's namesake had appointed himself her chief protector. Little had changed over the years. "Yes, dear, it's fine."

Jeff Jr. seemed to consider whether to stay or go for a moment, and then he nodded. "All right, but Michael and I are on the other side of the door. You'll let us know if you need us?"

"I promise," she said. "Now go. If I don't get any strawberries, it's all your fault."

He waved away her attempt at lightening the mood and disappeared into the kitchen. Tess gave herself a moment to compose her thoughts and then returned her attention to the man in black.

"You know," she said lightly, "I don't think I've ever been visited by an FBI agent. To what do I owe the privilege?"

"According to your file, you have not," he said. "Now if you'll just come with me."

He held out his arm as if to escort her, but Tess resisted. "I have a file? With the FBI?"

"You do now."

"Whatever for?" she asked, her voice elevated.

"Mom?" Jeff Jr. called as the kitchen door opened. "Are you okay?"

"I'm fine, son," she said. "But I would be much better if you and Michael moved away from the kitchen door."

She returned her attention to the federal agent. "We can talk right where we are. If I let you take me off somewhere, how do I know you won't arrest me or turn out to have fake credentials and nefarious intentions?"

"We never have nefarious intentions," Agent Butler said with absolutely no humor in his voice. "But I'll comply with your request to remain here, at least for now." He paused to retrieve a small notebook from his pocket. "What can you tell me about the theft of an article identified by number 466753-q from the National Archives Domestic Textile identifier HQZ43 Women of History?"

The only part of that question Tess understood was National Archives. Which meant she knew exactly what this was about.

"That was fast," she said with a grin. "I just called last night. Too bad you don't work in construction. I've got an inspector who put me on his waiting list for September."

"Is that a joke, Mrs. Wallace?"

She sobered. "It was an attempt at a joke, yes."

"The issue I am investigating is no joke, ma'am," he said in the I-am-in-charge monotone they must have taught at the academy. "In fact, theft of an item of such patriotic and financial value is a felony as are several other possible offenses committed during and after this theft. Do you find multiple felonies funny, Mrs. Wallace?"

"Well," Tess amended, now flustered, "of course I don't find multiple felonies funny, but you have to admit you sure got here quick."

He lifted one dark brow, his expression unreadable. "Expedience is a virtue, ma'am."

She almost laughed. "Did you just make a joke, Agent Butler?"

The FBI agent ignored Tess's question to continue referring to his notes. "You indicated in your call that you had an interest in finding a photographic image of a quilt known as the River of Life, circa 1859 or 1860. Is that correct?"

"It is."

"When asked the purpose of this interest, you declined to comment." His attention snapped back to her face. "Why is that, Mrs. Wallace?"

"The River of Life was sewn here at the inn, but I was told there are no pictures of it. Since the quilt has supposedly been in the archives until recently, I figured it had to have been photographed at some point."

He nodded as he retrieved a silver pen that looked very much like LuAnn's. "And you wanted a copy of that photograph."

A statement not a question. "I did."

Agent Butler began writing. "For what purpose?" he asked without looking up or ceasing his scribbling.

Several answers occurred to her. She could offer him some response about being interested in its connection to the inn or even admit she had heard it was stolen and knew a film crew would be interested.

Instead, she decided to go with the truth. The answer that might end up getting her thrown in jail.

"Okay." She took a deep breath and let it out slowly. "So, I wanted to see a picture of this quilt because I'm pretty sure I had it the day before yesterday."

"Had?" He paused writing to look up at her. "As in past tense?" At her nod, he continued, pen poised just above the paper. "What did you do with the quilt, Mrs. Wallace?"

"I didn't do anything with it," she said. "Actually, that's not completely true. After I nearly tripped over it and set it on fire in Big Red, I hid it in the pantry until we could decide who to call. Ghostbusters was briefly considered." Tess paused. "That was a joke."

"Go on," he said as his pen continued to move across the page.

"Our cook showed up in the kitchen; the fire alarm went off; half the town traipsed through here; I met Brad's brother, Grant; and then we took the strongbox home. When we opened it after a gourmet meal of omelets and ice cream sundaes because only Janice had eaten since she went to lunch and helped Bart sell a Porsche and the city gain an antique fire truck, the quilt was gone and someone had stuffed painter's cloth in its place."

Tess stopped talking, suddenly exhausted. The agent had stopped writing and was now openly staring at her.

What was it about this Fed that made her tell him everything she knew without pausing to think of how ridiculous it sounded? They must teach that interrogation skill at the academy too.

"All of that happened yesterday?"

"The day before when the director of the Marietta Underground Railroad Museum told me there was no picture," she corrected. "Yesterday Harry identified the box and Margaret tried to get him to give her an address that would have been illegal to get. As an aside, I tried too but when I realized it was illegal, I gave up. Margaret didn't appear to care about this."

"And Margaret's last name is?"

"Rector. R-E-C-T-O-R. Wait, that's Maybelline. Margaret's last name is Ashworth. A-S-H-W-O-R-T-H. But she didn't care about the quilt. She wanted that box because of its value to the city and her being the expert of all things historical in this town. Other than Maybelline who thinks the same way, now that I consider it. Actually, that isn't completely true. See the Bickerton sisters—they're an institution in Marietta so even the president of the historical society listens to them—decided to play a joke on Margaret and make her think the strongbox for sale at Harry's place was the one that had contained the River of Life. She wanted it but refused to pay the three grand he was asking, and he refused to succumb to her womanly wiles and give her a discount. Oh, and there's someone blackmailing someone they love, but they won't tell me about that until next week. Probably Tuesday since I know Irene gets her hair done on Monday because that's when it's cheapest down at the Curl Up and Dye."

What in the world just happened?

Spots danced in front of Tess's eyes as she paused to take a breath. Her nerves were shot, her heart was beating rapid-fire, and she'd just spoken a full day's worth of words in the span of about a minute. She inhaled and then had to remind herself to exhale.

"Mrs. Wallace?"

"Yes," she managed as she took another gulp of fresh air.

"Do you normally talk like this?"

"Never," she said. "When they taught interrogation, you must have earned extra credit. No joke intended, I promise. You see, I was a teacher in the field of hospitality and hotel management at the community college level for many years up in Stow. My fellow innkeepers, Janice Eastman and LuAnn Sherrill, were teachers too. Janice taught home economics here in Marietta for decades and cooking classes at the community center. From what I understand, she's practically a legend here in the city for her sugar cookies. I know that sweet Emma at Antoinette's Closet thinks so. And LuAnn taught English and history in Clarksburg, West Virginia, for thirty-five years before she retired, so there's that. She's here now living in my guest room while we renovate the inn, then we plan to open for guests and—"

"Mrs. Wallace!" He shook his head. "I repeat, do you always respond to simple questions like this?"

"Well, first the question was not simple. When a federal agent is interrogating you, that is anything but normal, especially since there are felonies being mentioned, and my fingerprints are on that strongbox and probably the quilt too, if fabric can show fingerprints, that is, but anyway, it implies a level of..." Tess placed her hand over her mouth to keep any more words from escaping. "No," she whispered through her fingers.

To her surprise, his expression softened. He tucked the pen into his notebook and slid it back into his pocket. Either she was about to be free to go or she would soon see handcuffs and a ride back to wherever the FBI took their prisoners.

"My friend LuAnn—the one I told you about who taught English and history in West Virginia—has a notebook similar to yours. Her notebook is prettier, not that yours is ugly, and she has a silver pen that slides in just like that. She makes notes and lists and..." Tess paused. "I'm doing it again, aren't I?"

He nodded.

"Sorry about that. I just don't want to get arrested."

"It happens," he said.

"Getting arrested?" she squeaked.

"Well that, yes, but you might be surprised to know that innocent people tend to talk more than guilty ones."

She managed a trembling smile. "And that's why you put your notebook away?"

Agent Butler shook his head. "It is not."

"Oh. So you haven't decided if I'm guilty or not?"

Again she contemplated her near future. Out of the corner of her eye, Tess spied the camera guy from this morning covertly filming through the open window on the front of the building.

Wonderful. Another image to go viral, and this time without benefit of using it to raise money for local charities.

"No," Agent Butler said slowly as he nodded to a spot behind her. "I'm trying to decide how to write up a report on a missing quilt to show it was found when I spied a child of approximately three years wearing it."

Tess turned around just in time to see one of the triplets—she could never tell which from a distance when Lizzie dressed them alike—bundled up in something that looked like stained muslin and standing at the top of the staircase on the second floor.

What happened next seemed to occur in slow motion. Tess bolted for the stairs while her grandbaby grinned and called out, "Look at me, Mimi. I a catty-piller like Mama showed me on the 'puter. I'm gonna be butterfly and fly away."

And then he jumped as she screamed his name.

Agent Butler was a blur as he passed Tess and scaled the staircase. Somehow the Fed caught the little fellow and handed him into Tess's arms before she knew what was happening.

"I was right," she said as she cradled her grandson in her arms. "You are a runner."

"No, ma'am. A father of twins, a boy and a girl." He paused to let out a long breath. "You'd be surprised, but the girl is the worst. She's a jumper too. And what she gets into at the age of three is—"

"Hey, I'm free," the little one said as he stuck his hand out of the blanket and held up three fingers. "So's my bubba and sissy. We're all free."

"Am I free, Agent Butler?" Tess said as her family and friends came pouring out of the kitchen.

"Goodness gracious goat!" Janice called. "Is he okay?"

"First let's get this butterfly out of his cocoon," the agent said. "Then I'll need to conduct an investigation. But if the quilt is positively identified and unharmed, then it's possible."

She nodded at her grandson who was now being carried back to the kitchen on his father's shoulder while his mother spoke sternly to the child. "Thank you for saving my grandson. That could have been bad. And for believing I am not a felon."

"Multiple felon," he corrected as he retrieved the quilt and walked over to the bar to gently place it there. "And I haven't said I believe that yet. I just said it was possible."

"May I look at the quilt?" Tess asked. "My friends and I have only seen one corner of it, and I'm dying to see the rest of it."

"Oh yes, please," Janice said, and LuAnn nodded.

"Be careful," he told them. "I'm the one responsible for getting it back to the archives in one piece."

Fabric the color of faded muslin greeted Tess as she and the ladies unfolded the quilt. Here and there she spied stains that were likely the result of age. In other places it almost appeared a baby might have spit up on it, or worse.

With care, she flipped the quilt over. The exact same thing greeted her there. Stitches had been placed at random and with nearly no skill. In places it was apparent that stitches had been removed. In others, there might be a line of beautiful handwork next to an awful array of knots.

The exception to the wide expanse of muslin with stitches that had been placed seemingly at random was one corner, apparently the corner they'd seen when they opened the trunk.

There the stitching was intricate and appeared to indicate a river that would lead down the center of the piece.

"This makes no sense," LuAnn said.

"I taught home economics for decades and came across a few students who couldn't sew to save their lives. This, however, is worse than anything I ever encountered," Janice said. "If I were giving whoever created this a grade, I would have to give it an F."

"This is worse than the pot holder I gave my mother for Christmas when I was a child." Tess looked the quilt over once more and then shook her head. "Who in their right mind would give this as a gift when it looks like this? It's truly a quilt that even a mother couldn't love. Except for the corner over there."

"I have no idea," Agent Butler said. "You'd have to take that up with the archives staff expert in the textiles department."

"Oh, you mean the one who ratted on me and called the Feds? No telling what else she'll get me for." Tess grinned. "It's a joke, Agent Butler."

"Right." He shook his head. "Now, I will need a statement from the little guy. Think we can get that?"

Tess called to Lizzie who then was able to extract a story from little Liam that involved dinosaurs, castles, and a caterpillar that built a cocoon. "I'm a middle school science teacher, and we've been studying how a caterpillar becomes a butterfly. Liam and his brother and sister love to watch the videos I'm using for the lesson. I assume that's what's behind this."

"Liam," the agent said, "do you think you can show me where you found your cocoon?"

"Sure." He hesitated. "But I'm not supposed to go up there a-cause it's dangerous."

"That didn't stop you before," his father snapped.

Just as Liam appeared ready to burst into tears, Michael knelt down and gathered the little fellow into his arms. "Remember how I told you we are supposed to listen to police officers and teachers and be on our best behavior if they tell us to do something?" At Liam's nod, Michael continued. "This nice man here is like a police officer. He's trying to solve a crime, and he needs your help. So I want you to stop pretending and show him where you found the blanket you wrapped around yourself. Do that now, please."

"Okay, Daddy."

The little boy led the group upstairs to the third floor where construction equipment littered the floor and plastic hung in sheets from the walls. Agent Butler indicated for the adults and the other two children to remain at the edge of the large open space.

"What do you want us to do, Agent Butler?" Michael asked.

"Keep your distance and try not to touch anything. I don't want anyone accidentally tampering with the crime scene."

"Oh, LuAnn," Janice exclaimed, "he said this is a crime scene. That sounds just awful."

"Let's wait and see what happens," LuAnn told her. "Nothing illegal has happened at the inn. The agent is just here to confirm that."

Agent Butler nodded to Tess. "I'll need you to help me with the boy, please."

"Sure, but crime scene?" Tess said softly to the agent. "What does that mean, exactly? That sounds pretty ominous since we're trying to get a business up and running."

He spared her a brief but meaningful look. "That means until this investigation is complete, this entire inn is now under the jurisdiction and control of the FBI. Every inch of it will have to be processed."

"Then I shall ask it now. Swear to protect this child of mine no matter the cost to you."

"I so swear, my old friend." Violet wrapped her arms around Prudence. "And we are frightfully old, are we not?"

"Much older than we ever thought to be," she agreed as they shared a smile.

"Well done, Mrs. Willard." The captain's approach made her cringe despite his obvious good humor. "My wife is once again smiling. I owe you a great debt."

"That debt has already been well paid."

The door opened, and Amity stepped inside. With an almost imperceptible nod, she returned to her chair and took up her needle.

Prudence might never see Liberty or Sally again, but she would never forget them. And she would always remember the night the captain and his wife arrived at Riverfront House.

The quiltings continued at the inn, although there was no set day or time for them. Those who knew of these things decreed it better to keep the gatherings from a regular schedule.

Most who arrived at the inn departed safely, but some did not. To stop and consider anything other than the next arrivals and departures was a waste of time.

And time was something in short supply.

For the quilt they were making had a special purpose. There would be a new president elected next year, and friends to the cause of the abolition of slavery wished to make a gift of this quilt. And to make the quilt a symbol of the lives affected by the horrors of men enslaving other men.

With the warm weather, Jason's aching leg improved. Though he felt himself fit enough to row the boats that crossed the river in the dead of night, his job was more often to patrol the tunnel that traveled between the inn and the shore or to help as the doctor did what he could to ease the suffering of those who awaited transport to the next stop on the Railroad.

Then came the night when a man met Jason at the tunnel with news he was needed elsewhere. "Come with me," the stranger said. "Your wife bids you to assist her."

"Who are thee?" Jason asked. "What need has my wife of me?"

"The child is ill."

"Why send thee? I do not know you," Jason asked.

The man told a tale of bringing two men and a woman across the river and then being chased off the bank by a goose. The woman came running and said they were an answer to prayer. "Come and I will take you to her."

The night was dark, and what little there was of the moon had been hidden behind thick clouds. Fog covered everything and provided a blanket from which anyone or anything might hide.

It also provided sufficient covering for men intent on stealing Prudence husband's freedom and selling him to the highest bidder.

Prudence was home that night caring for Moses whose teeth were coming in, and thus nowhere near the river where Jason was lured. Word spread quickly that Jason had left his post at the inn, and men went out looking while Amity hurried to Prudence.

"Bar the door," she told Amity. "And should there be a threat, thee will take Moses to the captain. Should thee be detained, insist Captain Markham be called, understand?"

"But he prosecutes us, Prudence. The captain will have me jailed or worse."

"He is friend to me. His wife even more so. It is there I will go if I cannot find my husband." Amity remained reluctant, so Prudence finally grasped her by her shoulders. "Listen and thee will save lives. Ignore me…"

"I understand," she said.

Prudence went out into the night with a prayer that the goose would remain behind. Perhaps owing to the fog and perhaps to some strange knowledge only another goose would have, Patience remained at the farmhouse door with only a squawk of goodbye.

Or perhaps it was a warning.

She treaded slowly once she arrived at the river, for the fog hugged so low that she almost wished she was taller so as to see over it. No deliveries were expected so the night was silent save for the lap of water against the shore.

Prudence hugged her arms across her chest and listened. If Jason was near, if he had been near, she prayed she would know. But nothing came to her. Though she searched, there was no sign of her husband. When dawn came and she knew her son would be beside himself wanting to feed, Prudence headed for home.

Her tears stained the trail that led from the river to the farmhouse. Though God was sovereign, she prayed she might sway Him so that He would not take her husband.

Not now.

Not yet.

Not ever.

CHAPTER SEVENTEEN

Ignoring Tess's groan, Agent Butler turned to Liam. "Okay, young man. Show me where you found your cocoon."

Picking his way around the mess, Liam pointed to a mound of painter's cloth. "I got the pretty one," he declared.

The agent squatted down in front of Liam. "You did a good job. Can you tell me how you knew where that pretty cocoon was going to be?"

He considered the question a minute, and then he shrugged. "Because I saw the butterfly."

Tess sat down beside her grandson. "There are no butterflies inside the inn," Tess told him. "Remember how Mommy talked to you about the difference in truth and make-believe? Maybe there's another reason you came up here."

"No," he said stubbornly. "The butterfly was here."

"Where did it go?" Tess asked.

"That way." He pointed to the room where they had found the secret exit to the basement.

"All right," Agent Butler said. "Then I'll check for butterflies. Everyone other than Mrs. Wallace, please go back downstairs and try not to touch anything. Waiting in the kitchen will be fine."

"Why Tess?" LuAnn asked. "Is she in trouble? Because all three of us were here when the quilt was found, and we all saw her open the strongbox."

"Brad Grimes too," Janice added. "So please don't arrest her."

"I'm not ready to make any arrests right now, but if I did, I promise it won't be just Mrs. Wallace."

"Oh," Janice squeaked. "Well I don't want it to be any of us!"

"He's making a joke, Janice." Tess shot the agent a look. "Please tell my friend you're joking."

"Just please do as you were told and reconvene in the kitchen," he told everyone instead.

Tess shook her head. "I'll be down in a few minutes, I promise." Once the two of them were alone, Tess turned back to the agent. "There's a feature of the room where Liam said the butterfly disappeared that you need to see."

She opened the panel in the closet and showed him the tunnel that led down to the basement. Agent Butler braced himself on the wall and then leaned over the dark hole to look down.

"I can't see where this goes."

"That's because it goes all the way down to the basement. There's an opening in the corresponding closet of all four floors."

"Interesting," he said. "I've seen similar things in places where proprietors were trying to keep their booze from being found during Prohibition, but this one is new to me."

"This building dates from 1826, and the owners were involved in the activities of the Underground Railroad. There is also a tunnel that leads out to the river."

"That's going to make for an interesting crime scene," he muttered as he stood back and assessed the room. "Guess I better call in reinforcements. Before I do, walk me through the process of finding and losing the quilt again, would you?"

He took out his notebook and wrote while she spoke, this time sounding more like the levelheaded businesswoman she was instead of the fool who couldn't stop blabbering. When she was done, she waited for him to cease his scribbling.

"So when the boy said the butterfly came through here," Agent Butler said, "it's possible someone went down that tunnel and left through any one of the floors of this home?"

"I'm no professional, but I would limit that to the first floor or basement since we know we're probably not dealing with a real butterfly," she said. "I think the catch is that the person would have to know about the tunnel and how to get out. And why bother coming in here at all when the cars outside would make it obvious that people were here?"

"That is just one of the questions that need answers," Agent Butler said as he nodded toward the stairs to indicate she should follow him. "My team and I will be back. I assume I can trust you not to come back up here in our absence."

"Yes, of course," she said. "And I will make sure no one else does."

"Thank you," he said and then descended the stairs to head out the front door.

A thought nagged at her all the way downstairs. Butterfly. That meant something. Just before she pressed on the door to enter the kitchen, it dawned on her.

Stepping into the kitchen, she caught Liam's attention. "Sweetheart, remember how Mommy and Daddy have been teaching you about colors?" At his nod, she continued. "Think now, does someone in this room have on the same color as the butterfly you saw?"

"You do, Mimi," he said, pointing to her blue top. "And Auntie Janice and Auntie Lu."

Both ladies were wearing red. "Thank you, Liam." She gave him a big hug. "And I see red too," she said with a grin. "Right there on your face where you've been eating up all the strawberries."

The little guy giggled.

Tess gestured for LuAnn and Janice to follow her into the pantry. "Liam says he saw a butterfly in the house, and he said the colors of the butterfly match what the three of us are wearing. Where else have we seen a red, white, and blue butterfly today?"

"There was that crazy fairy at the parade," Janice offered. "I still don't think that was a good fit for a patriotic parade even if it did match the requirements for the theme."

"So if we find out who marched in the parade in that costume," LuAnn said, "then we will have the name of Liam's butterfly."

"Exactly." Tess said as they exited the pantry. She looked around the room. "It's rare that we're all together, so can I enjoy this just a little longer before we go chasing after this clue?"

"Of course," LuAnn said.

"Shouldn't we tell the agent?" Janice asked. "He's the professional."

"We will tell him," Tess said. "But right now I really don't want the inn turned into a crime scene. If we can deliver a suspect, maybe he'll be nice and not close us down for a few weeks while he and his buddies investigate."

LuAnn nodded. "I like how you think."

"All right," Janice said grudgingly. "But if there proves to be anything dangerous going on, we're heading straight to the Feds, got it?"

"Got it," Tess and LuAnn said in unison.

An hour or so later, Tess waved goodbye to Lizzie and her family and then turned to Jeff Jr. "What's wrong? You've been quiet, and that's not like you."

"I'm worried about you."

"About the Feds?" She shook her head. "I'm not going to jail. I promise."

"No, about this whole thing with the inn. When you told Lizzie and me you were going to do this, I thought at first you were probably just looking for something to fill your time, which wasn't a bad thing. I did have some doubts as to the financial end of things, but you're a pro at hospitality management and you did Dad's books for years. That part of it, I got used to after the initial shock of my mother becoming an innkeeper wore off."

"Shocking, was it?" she said with a grin. "Well I'm glad I can still raise eyebrows at my age."

"Stop teasing, Mom. Things are happening now that none of us saw coming. You have to be a little worried about all of this. Liam has a great imagination, but he saw something and we both know it. And the delay while this investigation is ongoing? What's that doing to your budget? I know you had to have projected an opening well before it will be ready now."

"Yes, there have been unexpected delays, but I teach in my classes to expect those things. No, I don't like having to wait so long before the inn can open. And no, I really don't like the fact that my grandson has been drawn into some weird mystery that the FBI is now trying to solve." Her laughter held no humor. "That certainly goes beyond anything I thought might happen when the ladies and I decided to do this inn thing."

"Well I'm guessing a human butterfly wasn't on the list of suspected delays," he said.

"There you go." Tess patted his arm. "The Wallace sense of humor has returned."

"I tend to lose my sense of humor when my mother is in danger, and that goes beyond any financial loss. I think I'll give that contractor of yours a call. Maybe he can fix the time line with the other workers so there won't be any delay."

"Leave Thorn alone. He's busy enough, and there's nothing he could do about this anyway. And don't worry, I won't be moving in with you if we don't make a go of the inn." She mustered a smile. "I promise."

"Well sure, promise me that but don't promise that you'll take this threat more seriously."

"There is no threat," Tess reminded him. "This is about a quilt that was found in the inn. Nothing more." She paused to let out a long breath. "Everything will be fine."

"That's supposed to be my line, Mom." He looked back at the inn where several more federal agents were now securing the entrance.

"You can't always be my protector," she told him. "And everything *will* be okay. This is just temporary."

"Is that what Agent Butler told you?"

"It's what I know," she countered. "Thank you for coming out and driving us in the parade today. Your dad would be proud of what a great job you've done on the old truck."

Jeff Jr. smiled. "It was a labor of love. Every time I felt like I was ready to give up on the never-ending project and sell the thing, I would think about how much Dad and I loved working on it together." He looked away. "It's going to sound weird, but when I'm driving the truck I feel like Dad is riding along with me."

Tess leaned into her son's arms. "That doesn't sound weird at all."

"I miss him, Mama."

He hadn't called her Mama in years. Not since he held a meeting at the age of five where he announced that from now on he was to be called Jeff or Jeff Jr. but never Jeffy. Apparently along with this came his first very adult decision to start referring to her as Mom.

Until now, she hadn't realized how much she missed hearing him call her Mama.

She snuggled into his shoulder and closed her eyes. "Oh honey," she managed. "I miss him too."

"Hey, stop that."

Tess stepped back at her son's sharp words. He pressed past her to confront the same fellow who'd ridden with them in the parade. What was his name?

"I don't remember who you are, but you are not filming me or my mother without permission," Jeff Jr. snapped. "Especially not today."

"Barrett," Tess recalled just as Jeff Jr. reached him. "His name is Barrett something."

"Barrett George," the cameraman called.

Tess hurried toward the two men as Lizzie and Michael's van turned around at the corner and drove toward them. "What in the world?"

Michael stopped just a few inches short of them and rolled down the window. "Oh, good. In all the excitement I completely forgot to ask you if this guy ever got around to telling you the big news."

"Is everything all right out there?" LuAnn said from the door. "I thought you'd all gone home."

"What's wrong?" Janice called as she followed LuAnn out the door. "Lu and I were just grabbing what the agents would let us take when we saw all the commotion out here."

"Hold that thought, Michael." Tess turned toward her friends. "He let you take things out? I thought we were supposed to leave with only our handbags."

LuAnn shrugged. "He just said for us to show him what we were taking so he could log it in."

"Then we need to be sure to get *our* quilt. It's in the kitchen, I think. Would one of you mind checking? Oh, and if I left any of the paperwork for the new sink and plumbing, would you get that too? I need to add those costs to the spreadsheet."

"Sure. Let's both go," Janice said to LuAnn. "This looks like a family moment."

Tess let them leave without comment and then turned back toward the group gathered in front of the inn. "Okay so where were we?"

"I was about to throttle this guy for intruding on a moment with Mom. Seriously, man," he told Barrett. "That wasn't cool filming us. I don't care who you are."

"Hey look, sorry, man," Barrett told Jeff Jr. "I do a lot of filming to get a little bit of usable film, so I'm not always paying close attention to what's going on in every frame."

"Not good enough," Jeff Jr. said. "None of that better show up in the news. I'll sue."

"News?" Michael turned his attention to Barrett. "Guess you never got around to telling them you're with that television show. I'm with Jeff. Not cool, man."

"What show?" Tess asked, a thought dawning. "Surely not *Quilt Mysteries?*"

Barrett looked sheepish. "That's the one. I heard the word got out that we were coming, so I decided to get some location shots discreetly before I brought the whole crew in. I did come over to the inn to tell the ladies after I left the parade grounds, but that guy in a suit was talking to you and it looked serious."

"Which you also filmed," Tess said. "I saw you."

"I was shooting exteriors of the inn."

Jeff Jr. did not look appeased. He did, however, take a step back and cross his arms over his chest. "I won't be signing any releases, so don't plan on using anything with me in it."

"If you're with the show, why not identify yourself earlier?" Tess ask, skepticism rising.

"You saw me show him my ID," he said, indicating Michael. "I was about to when that fire engine started making all the noise. After the parade you disappeared too quickly for me to speak up."

That much was true as Harper had needed to find a potty quickly and would only agree to go with her Mimi. By the time they found an empty porta potty and the deed was done, the crowds had dispersed and it was time to go back to the inn.

A wail went up inside the van. "Naptime," Lizzie said. "We'll catch up with you later at the fireworks. Jeff, you make sure Mom is okay."

"Already on it," Jeff responded, keeping his attention focused on Barrett. Or whatever the guy's real name was.

She held her hand up to her ear indicting that Tess should call her. Tess responded with a nod and then waved as they drove away.

Finally, she turned back to Barrett. "Let's start at the beginning. And I mean the very beginning. Who are you really, and what's your name? And remember, I have a team of federal agents combing my inn for evidence right now. I have no problem calling them to come out here and investigate you as well."

CHAPTER EIGHTEEN

Barrett handed over his press card. The size of a laminated driver's license, the card bore Barrett's picture and his name along with a bright yellow banner that ran along the top. Inside the banner was the word PRESS in large letters. Beneath that: Producer, Art & Antiques Network.

"Oh," Tess managed.

"We got the things you asked for," LuAnn called.

"That agent is a nice man," Janice added. "He told us he would...what's wrong?"

Tess walked toward them holding the press card out at arm's length. Janice and LuAnn met her midway down the walkway, and she turned the card toward them.

"Goodness gracious goat!"

"Hey can I get you to say that for the cameras, Mrs. Eastman?" Barrett called. "That'll make a great promo."

LuAnn snatched the card from her and stared at it. "You're sure this is real?" At Tess's nod, she squealed. "Then I'm with Janice. Goodness gracious goat!"

"I had hoped to interview the three of you inside the inn, but that doesn't look possible." As if to illustrate the point, another dark car pulled up and two more men in black pressed past them to enter the inn. "Maybe we could set up a live shot out back?"

"Not until I get that patch of weeds under control," LuAnn said. "There's really no good place right now since it is all overgrown."

"What about down by the river?" Janice said. "There's an entrance down there to the inn that goes under the street. It's terrifying, but these two say it does still go through."

"That's just a patch of weeds too, Janice," LuAnn said. "Probably not the best for filming."

"True," Barrett said. "Although I am fascinated by the idea of a tunnel. Maybe we could arrange a time for me and my crew to go film it. I figure I will need to have the right lighting to capture it on film."

"Definitely," LuAnn said. "And prepare to get dirty because it's a pretty grubby place."

"I would imagine," he said. "But interesting all the same."

Another vehicle pulled up, this one very familiar. Thorn jumped out and hurried over. "Your son just called. What in the world is going on, Tess?"

"That rat," she said as she shook her head. "I told him not to call you."

"I'm your contractor. When something happens at the inn, you're supposed to call me." He turned to Barrett. "Do I know you?"

"I doubt it, man. I'm not from around here." He stuck out his hand. "Barrett George."

"No," Thorn said slowly. "I know you. It'll come to me." He returned his attention to the ladies. "Who's in charge in there? I'll just go see if I can help."

"Agent Butler is his name," LuAnn said.

"And whatever you do," Tess added, "don't make jokes. He frowns on those."

"Duly noted," Thorn said as he gave Barrett one last long look and then walked away.

"So," Barrett said, his attention still on Thorn. "I assume you ladies know why *Quilt Mysteries* is in Marietta."

"The River of Life," Janice said. "But we don't have it."

"Exactly," he said. "And you don't have the inn for a backdrop either, but we do have the city of Marietta. The way I figure it, the ladies who sewed that quilt back then must have been proud of their town. Why don't we celebrate that with a little walkabout?"

"What is that?" Janice said.

"That's just the four of us walking," he said. "We could go walk in the footsteps of the women who made the quilt. I've got a selfie stick for my GoPro. That ought to provide some good footage. Are you ladies game?"

"Sure," Tess said as the other ladies agreed.

"Great," Barrett said. "Now the bad news is I will need to go back to the hotel and prepare for the shoot. I figured I'd be speaking to you inside so that's the sort of equipment I brought. Plus we've got the crowds gathering for the picnic and, later, the fireworks. Would you mind if we wait until Monday morning to do the filming?"

They agreed on a time and place, and Barrett entered the info on his phone and put it away. "Now there's just one more thing I need to ask of you. Please don't tell anyone about this. I know I'm pretty much compromised as far as the surprise element on my crew's arrival, but only you and Mrs. Rector know I'm here right now. It would make my life much easier and guarantee our filming will have as few unwanted guests as possible if we keep this to ourselves."

"Yes, that's fine," Tess said.

"Just one thing," Janice told him. "I want a guarantee from you before we agree to this interview. We have a business to run, and an appearance on your program would certainly help our business to get off the ground. Can we have a promise from you that you will mention the Wayfarers Inn and show it prominently in your piece on Marietta?"

Tess exchanged glances with LuAnn. What in the world had gotten into their meek friend?

"You have my word," he said. "Without the inn, there wouldn't have been a quilt. I can't imagine filming here and not showing the place of the River of Life's origin."

"Fine then," Janice said. "We'll do it."

After Barrett was gone, Tess giggled. "Impressive," she told Janice.

"I didn't think you had it in you," LuAnn added.

Janice's eyes narrowed. "Are you making fun of me?"

"No," they both hurried to say. "We love you," Tess added. "We're just surprised at how assertive you were with him."

"I can be assertive," she protested. "I got us the job of grand marshals."

"True," LuAnn said. "And Marietta an antique fire truck."

"It's just that you can kind of be, well…" Tess bit her lip searching for the right word.

"Timid?" Janice offered.

"Yes, timid." Tess embraced her dear friend. "We love you for it. Never change."

Janice smiled but Tess had the sneaking suspicion her friend's feelings were hurt. Thus, she went out of her way to make Janice laugh at the picnic later that day and spent extra time seeing that she was enjoying the fireworks. By the end of the evening, she was pretty sure Janice was back in good spirits.

Still, she had to marvel at how her friend had managed to find it in herself to do some of the things she'd done in the past few days. At this rate, she'd be leading them in a jaunt through the most claustrophobic of tunnels one day.

No, Tess decided with a grin. There were just some things about Janice Eastman that would never change. And that was a good thing.

God created all three of them with traits that made them unique. He only gave one of them the need to organize and make lists and one of them the ability to write a business plan and manage a hospitality-based endeavor. And only Janice would ever be Janice.

They were a team. They were the Inn Crowd.

Now they just needed a fully functioning inn to run.

CHAPTER NINETEEN

Despite the fact that Pastor Murphey's Sunday sermon was on being patient and waiting for the Lord, Tess spent the rest of the day eager for Monday to arrive. Janice was busy with family, and LuAnn had taken a day trip back to Clarksville to attend a baby shower for one of her former students.

The absence of her friends left Tess alone in the big house she rented with nothing to do but think about the knots in the mystery that refused to unravel. She'd never been one to enjoy being alone, and perhaps that was why she chose to work in the hospitality industry.

When Jeffrey was alive, he was company enough but they still entertained regularly. Before his retirement as general manager for the golf course in Stow, she was often called upon to host gatherings for anywhere between a dozen to more than a hundred people, so a solitary day with nothing to do but wait for Monday to come was foreign to her.

Finally she decided a walk would be just the remedy. She put on her walking shoes and drove down to the riverfront park where she intended to begin her walk. The remnants of the Fourth of July celebration had been cleaned up, the only evidence of the celebrations the trampled sections of grass where fireworks viewers had been seated.

Tess made her way across the park with the cool breeze blowing off the river. There was a slight chop to the water today, likely owing to the change of weather that had been forecasted for next week. Storms were coming, the perky weather girl had warned. So be prepared.

Storms were always coming. Unfortunately there were just some storms that a body couldn't prepare for.

She stepped carefully over the old tree limbs and continued her hike as a few joggers ran past. Trees here and there cast spindly shadows in the early afternoon sun, and the warm scent of summer surrounded her.

Woodbine, roses, and lilacs bloomed profusely, their colors a beautiful contrast to the green grass that grew wild around the trees. Up ahead she spied the entrance to the tunnel and wondered all over again what this place might have looked like to weary travelers and frightened escaped slaves.

She let out a long breath and slowed her pace until she reached the tunnel entrance. Just across the road she could see the inn. Today only one black car guarded the entrance, which gave her hope that Agent Butler would return her key sooner than promised.

Her phone rang, and she pulled it out of her pocket to see that the caller was Justin O'Hara. After dispensing with greetings, he got right to the point.

"My buddy was able to enlarge that image in our photograph," he told her. "You're not going to believe who it was."

"Try me," she said.

Tess pulled her car to a stop in the alley and looked up at the windows that marched across the back of the old downtown buildings. Unlike larger cities, Marietta's downtown area emptied out when the businesses closed.

While there were plenty of spaces above the storefronts, only a few were used as dwellings. And one of them was right in front of her.

She stepped out of her car and then paused. Justin had emailed the photograph to her, and there was no doubt who had been skulking around. The question was no longer who but why.

And though she knew she should wait until LuAnn and Janice could accompany her, waiting was not her strong suit. So she climbed the iron staircase and came to a stop in front of one of two apartments on this block.

The other apartment door was just to her right, divided from this one by a wall that ran between the buildings. While this entrance had a simple iron railing around it and just enough room to place a straight chair and a small plant, the other apartment had been lavishly decorated with the latest in patio furniture and filled with blooming plants in colorful pots.

Before she could knock, the door opened. "I wondered when you'd pay me a visit." Harry stepped back to usher her inside an apartment that appeared to be an extension of the Antiques and Salvage Mall downstairs. The walls were brick and floor-to-ceiling windows opened on the street that was nearly empty this time of day.

Where most might have had a television in their entertainment center, Harry's was filled with books. More books decorated a beautiful antique credenza and spilled onto stacks on the floor. A dining table in front of the windows had been set for two, and the smell of something deliciously Italian was coming from the kitchen.

"I'm interrupting," she said, though this would not deter her from completing her mission.

He glanced at the grandfather clock in the corner and smiled. "Not for a while," he told her. "So sit and let's talk, shall we?"

Tess seated herself on one of the burgundy velvet wing chairs that flanked the old brick fireplace, and Harry chose the other. "All right," he told her as he regarded her with an unreadable look. "I'll just remind you that I still cannot give you that address, but I'll tell you that I did give it to that FBI fellow. If you want it, you'll have to wrangle it out of him."

"Having met Agent Butler, I doubt I'll be able to wrangle anything out of him," she said. "But thank you for letting me know. Maybe I'll try."

He shifted positions, his expression softened. "So if that isn't why you're here, then what can I do for you?"

She sighed. Although she had prepared for this conversation, she still didn't like confronting such a nice man.

"You can tell me why you were in my inn on the day the fire alarms went off."

Harry sat back, his iron-gray brows gathering. "I don't understand."

Tess reached into her pocket and retrieved her phone then pulled up the photograph. Without a word, she passed her phone to Harry.

The clock ticked loudly as Harry stared at the phone. Finally he handed it back to Tess without comment.

─────◦◦◈◦◦─────

As Prudence neared the farmhouse, Patience met her, squawking furiously. The door was open and the house was empty but marked by some sort of violence that had left furniture broken and crockery smashed.

She went from room to room shouting but no one responded. Her family was gone.

Finally, Prudence went back to Jason's chair and collapsed. "No time for this," she told herself as she rose once more.

Though the hour was early, Prudence walked all the way into town and dared to present her bedraggled self to the maid at Captain Markham's grand home. Though several members of the captain's staff had attended the quiltings at the inn, this woman had not.

"The captain is gone, and his lady is yet abed."

"It is urgent, and not for me but for my husband and son," Prudence protested. "I ask only that thee deliver a message, nothing more."

The maid looked down her nose at Prudence, likely for good reason. Her skirt's hem was soaked, and her skirts splashed with mud. Tears stained her face, and her hair had long ago fallen into disrepair.

"And what would that message be?"

"Please tell Mrs. Markham that Violet's friend wishes to speak with her. Moses is in danger."

"Wait here then," she told Prudence before slamming the door and locking it.

Prudence remained at the door for a moment and then, despairing of a swift response, went to sit on the steps. She'd nearly given up when the door opened and the maid appeared with a message.

"You are to go home and wait."

"But I had hoped—"

"Just go home and wait," she snapped and then stepped inside and closed the door.

Prudence did as she was told. By the time she returned home, the fog had burned away and the sun shone through the trees. Patience greeted her with her usual exuberance and danced circles around her as she tried to walk up the path to the farmhouse.

"Get thee behind me, goose," she snapped when she nearly tripped over the frantic bird. When Patience had tried the last of her patience, Prudence stomped to a stop.

The goose chose that moment to go off honking toward the river. After a few steps, she returned repeatedly to where Prudence stood watching her.

Finally she gave up and followed the bird until the path met the river. There Patience turned to follow the shore, and the goose.

She stumbled over a tree root and landed face first in the dirt. Her elbows surely bleeding, Prudence sat back against the tree. Even the goose was gone now. She was truly alone.

With nothing left to do, Prudence called out to the Lord. Then she began to cry.

A familiar sound cut through her sobs. The thin cry of a baby echoed around her. Prudence rose. "Moses?" she called, knowing the babe could not respond.

Oh, but he could cry for his mama's voice.

Which he did, though his cries were still far away. She called again and turned toward the sound.

Which came from across the river.

"Mrs. Willard?"

Prudence turned at the sound of the distinctly male voice. "Captain?" she asked. "Is that you?"

"It is." Captain Markham strode toward her on the path, his sword gleaming in the dappled sunlight. "Where is the child?"

She wiped furiously at her tears, fully aware her hands were muddy. "Over there," she said. "Across the river."

The captain stood silent for only a heartbeat. "I hear him," he said. "A trick of the water. Sound carries a long distance across it."

At the reminder of how far her precious child was from her, Prudence's lip trembled. She struggled and failed to take a breath that did not come with a ragged wail.

"Settle yourself," he told her. "You risk your child's life. Now stay where you are. Perhaps wash your face while you wait for my return."

"What are you going to do?"

"Something that I will deny with my dying breath."

The captain returned an interminable amount of time later. "Follow me."

Prudence fell into step behind him, stopping only when he did. "There," he told her. "That vessel is ours."

Captain Markham waited while the boat's owner helped her aboard. Then he joined them and sat without speaking. A moment later, they were gliding across the Ohio River. At once she heard her son. Then he was silent. And then she heard him again. It was enough to cause her to cry out herself. But she did as the captain asked and remained silent.

Then the boat touched something solid, and immediately Captain Markham's boots were on Virginia soil. "Stay," he said, leaving her with a stranger in a place where she could easily be taken.

Though she tried not to, she watched the man who had rowed the boat as his eyes scanned their surroundings. Was he an abolitionist like her or did he ascribe to the opposite doctrine?

Or was he a man like the captain who took his pay from parties who insisted he end the activities of the Underground Railroad whether he agreed with those activities or not?

Prudence gathered her arms around her knees and rested her head. Though sleep eluded her, she closed her eyes and prayed for her family. For Amity. And for the captain.

After a while, her companion in the boat sat up straighter, his hands on the oars. "You'll not leave without my family," she told him.

"Quiet," was his only response.

CHAPTER TWENTY

Tess watched several expressions cross Harry's face. Then he rose. "If you'll excuse me, I need to stir the sauce."

Not what she expected. Tess watched the old man shuffle across the wide plank floors and disappear into the kitchen. A minute went by and then two. Finally she stood, tucked her phone back into her pocket, and followed him.

The kitchen was tiny, a galley design that was likely put in well before the advent of any sort of modern convenience. Though the stove had four burners, they were squished together so closely that the pot Harry stirred took up two of them.

Though it was early afternoon, the room was cast in shadows. Sparks of light from the gas burner and a small light on the metal vent hood were the only illumination, but apparently this was enough for Harry to complete his task.

The wall containing the stove also boasted a small refrigerator like the ones she saw on old black-and-white television shows. Between it and the stove was a beautiful antique porcelain sink that was likely original to the building and would probably fetch a pretty penny in the shop downstairs. One of those old metal kitchen stools that doubled as a stepladder sat against the unadorned wall beside an old metal Coca-Cola sign.

A long narrow window looked out onto the alley and provided the only natural light in the room. Tess reached over and switched on the fixture overhead, illuminating the room and the tears streaming down Harry's face.

"I never did anything like that before," he said without looking at her.

Tess moved closer to take a seat on the stool. "What did you do exactly?"

He continued to stir as if he hadn't heard her. Finally he ceased stirring. "I think that's fairly obvious. I went into the inn uninvited."

"Yes," she said gently. "You did. But the question is why?"

"Because I promised I would," he told her. "For love. And that's all I will say about that. Please don't push the issue."

"Promised who? And why?"

He moved his hand to continue stirring. "As I said, I will not answer those questions, Tess. Prosecute me for breaking and entering if you must, although to be fair I did walk in through an open door. But I had no right to come in. So call the cops." He shrugged. "I did the crime so I am prepared to do the time."

"That's not necessary," she said. "I only want to find out what it was you were looking for in the inn. You see, my friends and I are investigating a mystery, and we're just curious if perhaps you have something to do with what we're looking into."

"Something to do with that strongbox that you and Margaret both wanted?" he said.

"That is part of it," she said. "But since you know who you sold it to, then you must know it wasn't either me or Margaret."

"I know it wasn't Margaret because she has tried for two days now to use her feminine wiles to get me to talk." He paused to slide her a sideways look. "An old man like me enjoys that kind of attention, so I'm not complaining, mind you."

"I imagine she can be persistent."

"You have no idea." He shrugged again. "But as to you, well, I can't say if you did or you didn't. The buyer only gave me a post office box and a corporation that no one without a proper warrant will get out of me."

"But that Agent Butler now knows."

"Correct."

She bit her lip. "Harry," she said slowly. "You said you were in the inn without permission for love. Would that be love of Margaret? Because if that's the case, I just feel like I should warn you that if she doesn't care for you unless you find a way to give her the strongbox, then you probably need to reconsider being in a relationship like that."

Harry let go of the spoon and shook his head. "No, Tess. I don't disagree about Margaret, though."

"If not love of a woman, then what?"

He went back to stirring. "I can't say."

"Can't or won't?"

Harry continued stirring. Finally Tess decided she'd gotten all the information she was going to get out of the old man, so she rose to leave.

"You know where to find me if you decide to come clean about why you were in the inn."

"Yep," he said without looking up from his work. "And you know where to find me if you decide to call the cops on me."

She stood there a moment longer and then went out to fetch her purse. When she turned to go, she heard him call her name and looked up to see him standing at the kitchen door.

"Won't," was all he said before disappearing back into the kitchen.

Tess let herself out and then paused on the tiny patio to retrieve her keys from her purse. A glint of light between the boards of the small porch caught her attention, and she leaned over the rail to investigate.

There, at the bottom of a Dumpster stuffed with trash from the antique store, something red and blue sparkled in the sunlight. She hurried down the stairs and then opened one side of the Dumpster to find a jumble of boxes and trash bags. Pushing them out of the way, she finally reached the item that had caught her attention from upstairs.

She pulled on what she decided was some sort of fabric, but it refused to budge from its resting place beneath the heavy bags and boxes. Finally she managed to wrangle the bags out of the way, and after giving the fabric another yank, it tore free.

Tumbling backward with a length of sparkly fabric in her hands, Tess landed beside her car on her backside. Stunned, she sat for a moment until she could be sure any damage she'd done was superficial and did not involve broken bones.

Then she turned her attention to the material in her hand. She recognized the stretchy fabric as the same sort she used to wear in ballet class as a child, but this was covered in red and blue sequins.

Tess went back to the Dumpster where she spied more of the material wedged between several smelly trash bags. Holding her nose, she climbed into the Dumpster and freed the fabric.

Climbing out, she spread the two pieces on the hood of her Honda. The smaller one that she'd torn out first fit nicely at the bottom of the larger piece. When placed together, they appeared to form the top of a leotard.

Or possibly a costume that Liam might call a butterfly.

She was about to go back into the Dumpster for more of whatever the garment was when the garbage truck came rolling around the corner. "No, no, no," she said as she stepped between the Dumpster and the truck.

The driver of the truck stopped and got out. "Are you crazy, lady? Move out of the way so I can get this job done and go home to my family."

"Not crazy at all," she said. "I'm conducting an investigation, and the contents of that Dumpster are part of what I'm looking into. When Agent Butler of the FBI learns what I have, I'm sure he will confiscate the contents, so let me save you some time and ask that you just move on."

He shook his head. "You look like a nice lady, but I've been working overtime to get the city cleaned up after the parade. Do you have any idea how much trash a city of this size generates on parade day?"

"I'm sure I don't."

"It's a lot. Why do you think they have me working on a Sunday? And I really don't want to argue with you, but my day isn't getting any shorter. Please just move out of the way."

She stretched her arms out in an attempt to protect the Dumpster from being emptied. "We both have our jobs to do. I'm just asking you to do yours tomorrow. Or maybe the next day. That's not such a big thing to ask, is it?"

"Can't do it, ma'am." He shook his head. "Look, here's what's going to happen. I'm going to get back into my truck, and I'm going to back up to that Dumpster and empty it. Nothing you say or do will change my mind. If you want to follow me to the dump and look through it after I've done my job, then there's nothing stopping you, but I cannot wait any longer. Got it?"

Tess sighed. One thing she prided herself on was reading people. And this guy meant business.

"Got it." She moved out of the way. "And which dump do you deliver to?"

Tess arrived at home to find both LuAnn's and Janice's cars in the driveway. Stepping inside with the scraps of cloth in her hand, she found them in the kitchen.

"What in the world happened to you?" LuAnn said as she turned to face Tess. "You look like something the cat dragged in."

"More like someone who climbed into a Dumpster." Tess dropped the two pieces of fabric onto the table. "But it was worth it. Look what I found."

Janice shook her head. "I don't understand. Those just look like scraps."

"Scraps of something that has been cut up." She pointed out the straight cutting line along the top of the larger piece. "Someone tried to destroy this."

LuAnn moved closer then wrinkled her nose. "And for good reason. Tess, honey, maybe it's time for a shower?"

She waved away the comment. "Don't you see what this is? I found this in a Dumpster. It looks very much like something that would have been worn in the parade."

"Yes, I can see that," Janice said.

Tess grinned triumphantly. "Remember that fairy we all commented on?"

"The one we planned to try to identify," LuAnn supplied.

"We may not know her name," Tess said. "But now we know where she got rid of her costume."

"How does that help?" Janice said. "She could have dumped her costume anywhere. And where's the rest of it? What you've got there isn't much to go on."

"The rest of it was in the Dumpster, I'm sure of it. I just couldn't get it out before that infuriating trash man insisted on emptying the thing." She let out a frustrated breath. "I mean, I understand the city generates a lot of trash during the parade, but did he have to empty that Dumpster right then? I say he did not."

"Tess," LuAnn said gently. "Why don't you just sit down, honey? You seem to be, well..."

"Sounding crazy?" Janice offered.

"I was going to go with overwrought," LuAnn said. "But now that you mention it, yes, you're sounding crazy."

"I am, aren't I?" She looked down at her clothes that were stained with whatever had been in the Dumpster. "And I probably don't smell so great."

Janice's brows rose. "I wasn't going to mention that, but as long as you have, no, you don't."

"You look like you actually climbed into the Dumpster." LuAnn laughed. "Which surely you..." She shook her head. "Oh Tess. You didn't."

"I did. But I had to," she protested. "And if I hadn't we wouldn't have this clue."

"Right," Janice said. "So maybe while LuAnn and I make a pot of coffee, you should consider a shower?"

"Great idea," LuAnn said brightly. "And maybe you could put those clothes directly in the washing machine?"

"It's that bad?" Tess asked.

"It's worse," LuAnn said. "We're being nice."

After Tess had showered and started a load of laundry, she returned to the kitchen to find that LuAnn had made some of their favorite almond pecan coffee. She poured the heavenly brew into mugs and placed a plate of Janice's famous sugar cookies on the table between them.

"All right," LuAnn said as she doused her coffee with sugar. "Janice and I have some questions for you."

"Fire away," Tess said as she took a sip of coffee and smiled. "I am in my happy place right now."

"Good, because we're not too happy with you going off and investigating clues without us present. You could have been hurt."

"You were both busy, and the clues came to me. How could I have been harmed? This is Marietta. It's the safest place I've ever lived."

"It might be," Janice said. "But what if that garbage truck had shown up while you were inside that Dumpster? Have you considered that?"

She hadn't. "Well, it didn't," served as her only defense.

Both LuAnn and Janice gave her looks that told Tess exactly what they thought of that statement. Finally Janice shrugged. "We've been wondering what led you to a particular Dumpster and caused you to climb in."

LuAnn took a sip of coffee and nodded. "It would helpful to us if you start at the beginning. Maybe at the point where you decided to take off looking for a Dumpster?"

"Actually the story starts before that." She went to retrieve her phone and then pulled up the picture that Jason sent her.

"That's Harry from the Antique and Salvage Mall. What was he doing in the inn?"

Tess reached for a sugar cookie and shrugged. "He wouldn't tell me."

"You confronted him?" LuAnn demanded.

"Alone?" Janice added.

"It's Harry," Tess said. "Harmless Harry who sold us that box with Prudence Willard's memorabilia and found the lantern that used to be on the front of the inn. How much danger could I have possibly been in?"

LuAnn turned the phone around to show her the photo. "Harmless Harry was, at the least, trespassing. At worst, he had some other purpose for being there. Whatever the reason, Harry doesn't look very harmless here."

"And why does he have that name on his shirt?" Janice pointed to the circle just barely showing at the bottom of the photograph. "Did Justin's friend enlarge that too?"

"I asked him that," Tess said. "But at this level of resolution, the name was blurred out."

"See," LuAnn said. "Harry doesn't wear a uniform, so not only was he in the inn for some unknown but probably illegal purpose, he was also in disguise."

"Not much of a disguise if he didn't bother to hide his face." Tess took the phone from LuAnn and set it on the table. "Okay, I know. I should have waited until you two were with me. I promise I will be more careful in the future."

"Okay," Janice said. "So you went to Harry's place to confront him. What did he say?"

She shrugged. "He didn't deny it was him. All I could get him to say was that he did it for love."

"Love?" LuAnn shook her head. "What does that even mean?"

"He wouldn't tell me. All I could get out of him was that he was fine if I needed to call the cops, but he wasn't going to say anything else." She shook her head. "He looked sad about it. He was even crying when I followed him into his kitchen."

"Sad like someone made him do it?"

"Possibly," she said as she thought of the blackmail the Bickerton sisters had mentioned. "Do you think he's the one Irene and Thelma are worried about?"

"Maybe so," Janice said. "But then, they said the victim was someone who meant a lot to them. I never thought there was any kind of connection between them and Harry."

"Me neither," Tess said.

"I'm writing all of this down," LuAnn said.

"Then you can put down that he told me it wasn't Margaret who caused him to do it. Apparently she's been throwing herself at him in hopes of getting the address of the person who bought the strongbox."

"Why? We have the box," Janice said. "Knowing who bought it won't help her in the least. However, it would help us."

"She knows I found it," Tess said. "So my guess is if she figures out who the strongbox belongs to, then she can buy it from that person and become its rightful owner. If that's the case, then we would have to give it back to her."

"That's pretty sneaky," Janice said. "But Harry isn't budging?"

Tess shook her head. "According to Harry, the only person he's given the address to is Agent Butler."

"Okay," LuAnn said. "Were you able to find any clues at Harry's place?"

"Just one," she said. "His table was set for two, and he was making the most delicious-smelling spaghetti sauce."

"Interesting," LuAnn said. "Dinner for two with spaghetti."

"Reminds me of that Disney cartoon with those two adorable little dogs," Janice said. "What was the name of that movie?"

"Stick with the topic, Janice," LuAnn said. "If Harry owned up to being in the inn for love and he's making a romantic meal that has to simmer all day, maybe the three of us need to do some surveillance?"

Janice grinned. "As in hide out to see who Harry is dining with? I think that's a great idea."

"I'm in," Tess said with a grin. "But I think we're going to have to take one of your cars. Mine might need some airing out."

CHAPTER TWENTY-ONE

Are you sure there were two place settings at that table?" Janice peered over the steering wheel and tugged at the dark scarf she wore to hide her pale hair. "Because it's well past time for dinner, and no one has shown up."

The trio had decided to take Janice's car since hers sported dark paint and dark interior. Janice parked a half-block down from Harry's place in a spot where the streetlights did not reach.

"Yes, I'm certain there were two. Just as certain as I am he was cooking a pretty special meal. Be patient," Tess said. "Maybe Harry eats late."

LuAnn pressed the button on her fitness tracker, highlighting a screen that showed the time was close to nine o'clock. She passed the information on to the others and waited for their response.

"Maybe he keeps his table set all the time," Janice offered. "Some people do that, you know."

"If you could have seen his apartment, you wouldn't say that. Think bachelor pad meets book lover meets owner of an antiques and salvage business." She shrugged. "Then add in the fact he's well past the age to be only just beginning to receive social security, and you get the picture. He set that table because he was expecting company."

"Okay," LuAnn said. "Then the way I see it, we have two choices. We can give up and go home, or one of us can walk up those stairs and see what's what. Tess, maybe you can come up with some reason to talk to him?"

"Like what?"

"You left your purse? Your sunglasses?" LuAnn shook her head. "Be creative. It will be less weird for you to go back up there than it would be for either of us to just show up. Besides, it's late."

"Oh, all right." Tess reached for the door handle just as a car turned into the alley. "Duck!"

The car rumbled past and then slowed to a stop in front of the apartment next to Harry's. When the car door closed, all three of them peered up over the seat to see a man heading for the stairs.

"Who is that?" Janice said.

"Wait just a minute, and he'll be on the porch where the light is on," LuAnn said. "We should be able to see him then."

He bounded up the stairs, taking them two at a time. "That rules out Harry," Janice whispered. "Or anyone else over the age of forty, but why do we care since he's not visiting Harry?"

Tess gasped. "Because he's visiting Wendy Wilson."

"The Sassy Seamstress?" Janice said.

"She's looking pretty sassy right now," LuAnn said. "Look at how she's kissing him."

"I'm more interested in how she's keeping us from seeing his face right now," Tess said. "I wish she would just turn a little more to the right so the porch light is shining on them."

The couple disappeared into the apartment and the door closed behind them. "Oh, shoot. Did anyone see him?" LuAnn said.

"Not me," Janice said.

"Me neither," Tess responded, "and now Harry's lights are out. I'm guessing the old guy has gone to bed. That answers whether we need to disturb him tonight. Or Wendy." She giggled. "Wendy told me she didn't have any friends in Marietta, so I'm glad she's found someone."

"She found him pretty fast, don't you think?" Janice asked. "We haven't known her very long." She started her car. "Okay, then. Time for us to go home."

"Aren't you curious who he is?" LuAnn asked.

"Lu," Tess said. "Let's not be those busybodies, okay?"

"So you are curious," she said with a giggle. "I'll just write down the make and model of the car and the license plate number."

"Whatever for?" Janice said as she shifted the car into Drive.

"Just curious," LuAnn said as she scribbled in her notebook. "You never know when a fact you just learned will become important."

"Or completely useless," Tess said with a laugh. "But I'm curious too. However, unlike you two, I'll just ask her next time I see her." She paused and then smiled. "Which will be tomorrow since I need to tell her how much we appreciated the gift of the quilt and show her the photos, which I'm about to print for her, of it on the truck."

The next morning, Tess opened the Honda's trunk only to discover the strongbox was still inside. She should probably turn it over to Agent Butler, but that would have to come later. Right now she had another mission in mind.

Tucking the envelope of pictures in beside the strongbox, she closed the trunk and then looked at her car. Only then did she recall her warning to the ladies last night about her vehicle needing some airing out.

She walked back inside and called to LuAnn. "Do you want to make a trip to the Sassy Seamstress with me?"

LuAnn looked up from the book she was reading. "Give me a second to change clothes and get my purse."

Ten minutes later, Tess and LuAnn walked out into the garage. "I'll grab the pictures," Tess said as she walked over and pushed the button on her key fob. The trunk opened to reveal absolutely nothing but her walking shoes inside.

"LuAnn!"

Her friend came to stand beside her. "Where are the pictures?"

She shook her head. "Worse, where's the strongbox?"

"Tess," LuAnn said under her breath. "The strongbox was still in your trunk? How could you have left it there?"

"I know! This sounds awful, but I just completely forgot. I have no excuse." She paused, fingers trembling. "In fact, I only remembered about it when I opened the trunk to put the photos in. I thought maybe I would deal with it when we got back." Tess shook her head. "But it's gone."

"Okay," LuAnn said as she looked around the garage and then stepped out onto the driveway. "I don't see anyone lurking around."

"If you'd just stolen a priceless artifact and a bunch of pictures, would you hang around?"

"Well, no," LuAnn admitted. "But how could anyone get into your trunk? Was the car locked?"

"No, but the garage door was closed."

LuAnn shook her head. "And it's still closed. It appears someone has figured out how to open your garage door. And knew you had that strongbox in the trunk. Can you think of anyone who might have seen you put it in there?"

Tess gave the question some consideration and then nodded. "Just one person," she said. "Grant Grimes."

"And he's a Realtor, so that might explain how he would know how to get a garage door open."

Tess picked up the phone and dialed Grimes Realty. Saffron answered the phone, and Tess asked for Grant.

"He's not here right now," she said. "Would you like to leave a message, Mrs. Wallace?"

"No message, Saffron," she told her as she hung up.

"Let me guess," LuAnn said. "Out of the office."

Tess started dialing again.

"Who are you calling?"

"Janice," Tess said. "I know she won't want to miss this."

Before she could complete the call, her phone rang. "Hello, Irene," Tess said when she answered. "What can I do for you?"

"Remember that topic we were going to discuss?" she said.

"The blackmail?" Tess offered.

"Yes, that's right. Well, forget about it," Irene said. "Now you have a nice day, dear. Tell those nice friends of yours that Thelma and I would love to see you all sometime." She paused and seemed to be speaking to someone in the background. "Yes, and when we see you, it won't be to talk about that thing we said we would talk about."

"All right," Tess said. "Well, then thank you for calling." She looked over at LuAnn. "I'm supposed to forget that Irene and Thelma were going to invite me over to talk about the fact someone is blackmailing someone special to them."

"Well," LuAnn said, "all right. Did she say why?"

"No, but she would love to see the three of us sometime. She wanted me to let you know that when they do see us they won't be willing to discuss that whole blackmailing thing."

"Okay, then." LuAnn shrugged. "What's our next move?"

Tess lifted up her phone. "We call Janice and then we go find Grant Grimes."

When LuAnn pulled up in front of Janice's house, she was waiting outside. While Tess briefed her on the events of the morning, LuAnn drove over to Grimes Realty.

She pulled in just as Brad stepped out of the building. "Hey there," he said. "I was just leaving. How can I help you ladies?"

"We're looking for your brother. Have you seen him today?" Tess asked.

"No, but I can let him know you're looking for him," he said.

"No," they all said in unison.

"All right, then." Brad shook his head. "I'll go on to my appointment. I'm meeting the aunts. Apparently they've got something important to talk about. Know anything about it?"

"Blackmail." LuAnn nudged Tess. "Tell him what they told you."

She relayed the information and then shrugged. "So that's all I know. I'm guessing the person they're worried about isn't you."

"No, but I may know who it is." He held up his hands. "And don't ask. I don't want to say anything until I'm sure, but you never know when a fact you've just learned will be important."

Tess's breath caught. *A fact you just learned.* Hadn't LuAnn said the same thing last night outside Wendy's apartment? The apartment that shared a Dumpster with Harry's building.

"Ladies," Tess managed when Brad returned to his car. "I think that license plate LuAnn wrote down last night just got important."

They did remain in place. And then a great noise rolled toward them, a symphony of men shouting and dogs barking, and one tiny baby's cry.

Her companion remained on alert, but his attention shifted to Prudence. "Not a muscle will you move," he asserted. "I'll shoot you before I allow you to cause me to be caught. Nod if you understand."

At her nod, he went back to his watch. Finally a short distance upriver, a man broke through the trees. Jason.

In a moment, the boat was back afloat and moving upriver toward her husband. Before they reached him, Jason began wading toward them.

Then she heard the cry again. "Moses," she whispered. "My precious son."

As the vessel neared her husband, the cries grew louder. Only when the boat was close enough to see him did Prudence realize Moses was bound to Jason somehow with only his little face visible below his father's open shirt collar.

Though her husband once could swim well, likely the combination of his injuries and the son he carried kept him from making the attempt. So he hurried along the river's edge with the water at waist level.

The shouting continued, as did the barking. Then came the first shot.

Had she not been wearing skirts that would have drowned her, Prudence might have jumped in and closed the distance between them. For if they were to die, better to die in her husband's arms.

So she waited, arms outstretched until Jason could hand Moses to her and then climb in. A proper welcome would wait, for where was Amity?

"They were behind me," Jason said as if knowing her question. "Markham sent me this direction, and he and Amity went the other."

"Thee are unharmed?" She ran her free hand over his chest.

"Other than an ache to the back of my head, I should heal up just fine. And blessed be the Lord for somehow giving me the ability to run home to my wife."

"We are not home yet, Husband," she told him, her light tone belying the deep gratitude she held at the moment.

The man at the oars pulled a looking glass from the bag at his feet and used it to scan the shoreline. Another bullet screamed past as the vessel turned away.

Prudence stifled a scream, and Moses began to cry.

"Like as not he's starved," Jason told her.

Without a word, the man rowed for a distance of some half a mile, possibly more. Prudence could not be certain, for she could only rest her head on her husband's shoulder and content herself with his embrace while she settled her hungry son.

"There," Jason said softly, and the man at the oars nodded.

Prudence followed the direction of her husband's gaze and spied a man wading into the water up ahead. Something trailed over his shoulder.

"Amity," she said softly. "Please be alive."

As they neared and the captain began to swim, Prudence spied her friend's broad smile. Indeed she was quite alive and well, a fact she confirmed when Captain Markham hoisted her into the vessel.

"Prudence," she exclaimed. "And Moses! Oh, Jason, you're all here. I tried to hide the baby but he cried. I think they expected we were hiding folks at the farmhouse. They certainly were looking."

"Quiet, woman," the stranger hissed.

Bullets again flew as the men who'd been chasing them emerged onto the shore. Dogs were set on them, but none could reach the distance where the vessel now floated. Captain Markham dove for the boat but his hands slipped. Then came the bullet that tore through his shoulder and sent him plummeting beneath the murky surface of the river.

This time Prudence did not bother to hide her scream. Amity joined her, as did Moses. Another bullet splattered the water just beyond them. "We go," the oarsman said. "I'm not getting paid to die."

As the vessel turned away from where a pool of blood was forming, Jason kissed his wife and then dove into the water. Had she the strength or the ability, Prudence would have fetched Jason back. But she had neither, so she could only watch as the man she loved more than life itself disappeared beneath the rippling water.

"Turn back," Prudence demanded. Amity echoed the cry.

The oarsman ignored them.

Prudence swiveled to see Jason bob to the surface. "Turn back," she said again. "Else I will tell all who will listen that thee are guilty of leaving a captain of the United States Army to drown."

"He's done drowned," the man said. "And ain't nobody going to believe that fancy fellow was with me for any good reason."

Jason went under again then quickly came back up. This time he was not alone.

CHAPTER TWENTY-TWO

Tess reached into her purse and pulled out the clear plastic zipper bag containing the two fabric scraps she'd retrieved from the Dumpster then shook it. "Still think it was dumb for me to go Dumpster diving?"

"Yes," both of them said.

"But I do see your point," Janice said. "Now that we know Wendy lives in the building near where those fabric scraps were found, then they do become an important piece of evidence."

"I say we go show these to Wendy," Tess said. "If she's our parade butterfly, then it should be obvious when we show this to her."

"So which lead are we following?" LuAnn said as she backed out of the parking lot of Grimes Realty. "Grant the thief or Wendy the butterfly?"

They turned the corner and the Sassy Seamstress came into view. "I think we've got our answer," Janice said. "Look, there's Grant talking to Wendy out on the sidewalk."

Tess craned her neck to see the tall silver-haired man shaking his head while the dark-haired young woman spoke in what appeared to be a rapid fashion. By the time LuAnn parked the car and turned off the engine, Wendy had stormed

233

inside and Grant was climbing into a 1970s era orange Camaro convertible.

"Grant," Tess called before the younger Grimes brother could drive away. "Could I talk to you for a minute?"

"It's not a good time, Tess," he said over the roar of the engine. "Maybe later today?"

She thought of the interview already arranged with the producer. "I can't. So maybe now? I'll make it fast."

He turned off the engine. "Okay, what can I do for you, pretty lady?"

Tess looked around and saw her friends watching from the other side of the street. She returned her attention to Grant and then added a smile. "Two things, actually. First you can tell me where my strongbox is, and second, who is blackmailing you?"

His mouth opened as if to speak, and then he shut it tight and turned on the car. A moment later, he threw the Camaro into gear and roared away, narrowly missing Harry's truck.

"Ever the charmer, Mrs. Wallace," Harry called as he parked in the spot Grant just left.

She shrugged. "I cannot imagine what I said to set him off."

Harry turned off the truck's engine and then climbed out. "If you're here to try to change my mind, I said everything I intended to say last night."

"No," she said. "But I did wonder how your dinner went."

His face fell. "I do see why you're having trouble getting a man to have a conversation with you. Good day now. I have a store to open."

She watched him walk away, then turned around to see Janice and LuAnn walking toward her. "He didn't look happy," Janice said.

"Neither did Grant," LuAnn added.

"I'm two for two," Tess quipped. "What say we go in and talk to Wendy? What are the odds I'll make it three for three?"

Janice laughed. "I don't like those odds. I assume you didn't get any information from either of them."

"What they didn't say spoke volumes. Grant took off like a crazy man just because I asked about blackmailing and the strongbox. Harry snapped at me after I merely inquired how dinner was."

"Interesting," LuAnn said.

Tess nodded to the front door of the Sassy Seamstress and the Closed sign now showing. "So is that."

Janice went to try the door and found it locked. "It was just open." She leaned against the door to look inside and shook her head. "She's gone."

"She couldn't have gone far," Tess said as she took off power walking. "Janice, you watch the front door. I'm going to go check out the back."

"Stay out of the Dumpster," LuAnn called. "I don't want to have to get that smell out of my car."

Tess made her way around the building just as Wendy was coming out the back door of the shop. "Wendy, stop," she called. "We need to have a chat."

Of course she ignored Tess completely, climbed in her red Mustang, and roared off down the other end of the alley.

Retracing her steps, Tess found Janice and LuAnn waiting by the car. "I'm three for three. So how about I treat you two to an early lunch before we meet with Barrett?" She paused. "Or do you feel the need to run away too?"

The three of them climbed into the car and drove over to the Galley Restaurant at the Hackett Hotel. They had just taken a seat and ordered glasses of water when Brad walked in and headed toward them.

"Congratulations, ladies. Not much gets my brother riled up, especially when it involves pretty ladies, but you have managed it."

Tess spoke up. "That was me, Brad," she said. "These ladies are completely innocent. And all I did was ask him about the strongbox and quilt that are missing from my trunk."

"And about the blackmail," Janice added.

"Well, yes, that too."

Brad exhaled and shook his head. "May I join you? I think we've got some catching up to do."

"Please do," Tess said. "Your meeting with your aunts must not have taken long."

"I never got there," he said. "Irene called me on the way over and said for me not to bother coming."

LuAnn set her menu down. "Did you ask why?"

"Of course," he said. "But I got some nonsensical answer that basically added up to me forgetting they had ever mentioned anything about blackmail."

"So the same answer I got when she called me." Tess sat back in her chair. "Brad, what do you think is going on? You said you had an idea."

He glanced around the dining room, now deserted as the lunch crowd had yet to arrive. "You know that I've been managing the Bickerton accounts for a while now, but I'm not sure who in the family is aware of that. A few months ago, a major withdrawal was made from the aunts' trust account. Irene's signature was on the check, but when I confronted her about it, she professed ignorance. Given past history, I assumed our cousin was behind it."

"But he wasn't?"

"No," he said. "He's been working pretty regularly offshore and banking what he makes. He showed me proof, and I believe him. After what happened last month, he seems to be a changed man."

"So you think Grant took the money out and signed Irene's name to the withdrawal?"

Brad sighed. "I hate to think that's true, but the evidence does support that theory. Or, maybe there's someone else out there who would have the access and reason to take the money." He shook his head. "At this point, I don't know."

"So," Janice said. "Why do Irene and Thelma think there's a blackmailer? Is it because of the missing money?"

"That's what I asked them, and neither would give me a straight answer. If they know anything other than that the trust fund amount is greatly reduced, then no one is saying so."

A waitress returned with a glass of water for Brad and took their orders. When she left the table, Brad continued.

"I know you ladies are good with investigations, so maybe you'll have a different perspective than I do. Grant can be frustrating and he certainly does have his faults, but I just cannot figure out a scenario where he would be behind the missing money. So is he a jerk sometimes? Sure. But a jerk who would steal from his aunts? And technically he would be stealing from me and our cousin since we're all heirs. So, no, I really just don't see it."

"Unless there is blackmail involved," LuAnn supplied.

"The kind of blackmail that would put him in a position to cause him to do something he would never do," Brad added. "But as of yet, I cannot figure out what that would be."

"It seems to be the day for conundrums," LuAnn said. "Tess, tell him about Harry and Wendy."

Tess recounted her story of the visit with Harry and her encounter with the Dumpster and then retrieved the bag from her purse. "I don't suppose you recognize this?"

Brad laughed. "I am no connoisseur of fabric, but that looks like something that would have been part of the red, white, and blue parade."

He held the bag up to the light as the waitress arrived with their salads. The waitress smiled. "Are you looking for more of that too?"

"The fabric?" Tess said as Brad handed it back to her. "Yes, actually. Where can I find some?"

"Can I see it again?" the woman said after she delivered the salads to them.

Tess handed her the bag. "It's torn, as you can see."

"That happens when those little girls start getting silly." The waitress passed it back to Tess. "My daughter's dance team had to wear them in the parade. We were responsible for buying the fabric to dress it up. The only place in town that had it was the Sassy Seamstress. Weird thing was, they ran out. One day I went in and there was half a bolt. Next day when my daughter's best friend tried to buy some, it was gone."

Janice frowned. "So the Sassy Seamstress sold this fabric?"

"Oh sure. They've had it at least since the spring. When the new girl took over, she kept a few of the old bolts, but got rid of a lot of them. Seemed like a waste to me, but I guess if you're flush with cash, you start over." She scrunched up her nose. "Probably best she got rid of some of that stuff since it likely smelled like fish."

They shared a laugh with the waitress. Once she had walked away, Brad's expression turned serious.

"I'm sorry," Brad said. "I've been doing all the talking about me and I haven't asked what the status is regarding the inn. Is it still under federal control?" He made a face. "I was sorry to hear about that. I know that must have created a nightmare for the timeline for renovations."

"Thorn assured me just this morning that the contractors are ready to work as soon as they can get in," Janice said.

"But we have no idea when that will be." Tess traced her finger around the rim of her water glass. "Agent Butler has been very apologetic, but apparently the Feds like to be thorough."

"It must help that the FBI is on the case, though," Brad said. "Maybe they can provide some answers as to why that quilt showed up at your inn." He paused. "That reminds me. I've done some checking about your plumber, Tom Davis."

"Oh?" Janice said.

"Did he tell you that he was arrested for theft?" Brad leaned forward. "You'll like this. He stole a valuable quilt. And even more interesting? The quilt was being featured on the *Quilt Mysteries* show when it disappeared."

"You're kidding."

"Nope," Brad said. "It happened a few years ago in Cleveland, where he's from. Tom has kept his nose clean ever since, at least according to the records I was able to find."

LuAnn retrieved her notebook. "That certainly adds another black mark against our plumber. First his note ends up sitting on top of a stolen quilt and now this? It adds up to something fishy."

"Speaking of fishy," Tess said. "What do you know about Wendy Wilson? And yes, I know that was a stretch, but I cannot go into that building without thinking about how they used to sell bait in there alongside the bolts of material."

Brad seemed to consider the question for a moment, and then he shrugged. "Nothing beyond that she paid cash for the building about six months ago in a very hush-hush sale and has pretty much kept to herself."

"See, that's unusual to me." Tess shook her head. "When you opened Grimes Realty with your brother, you both were known in Marietta."

"For better or worse, we were," he agreed.

"Okay, but even though you were known, you advertised your business. You printed calendars, bought ads in the paper, made business cards, sponsored Little League teams, or whatever, right?"

"We did most if not all of that. Don't get me started on what we sponsored, or for that matter, the things we elected not to sponsor. Like the time Grant thought it would be a great idea to put our company logo on the porta potties at the county fair. I'll leave it to you to figure out what the slogan was going to be."

"Tess has a point," Janice said when she stopped laughing. "Have any of you seen a single ad for the Sassy Seamstress? Because I haven't, and I am the perfect demographic. I sew, quilt, craft, and spend a good portion of my fun money buying supplies for these activities."

"You'd think she would have at least put a float in the parade," Brad said. "Or accepted the invitation to ride on the fire truck with you ladies."

"She acted like being out in a crowd was terrifying," Tess said. "Again, why is she in a service-related business if she feels uncomfortable around people?"

"Something doesn't add up," LuAnn said. "Especially since we saw her arguing with Grant a little while ago. Grant took off and wouldn't speak to Tess, and then Wendy did the same."

"Why would my brother be arguing with Wendy? How does he even know her well enough to have a conversation, much less an argument?"

LuAnn's phone dinged. She retrieved it from her purse and then put it back again. "That was my fifteen-minute warning. We need to get the check and head over to our meeting place for the interview."

"You've asked good questions," Janice said to Brad. "So maybe you can let us know if you find the answers?"

"I'll do that." He nodded to the door. "Now go on and get out of here. Lunch is on me."

After the appropriate amount of arguing and three sets of thank-yous, the ladies gave up and handed over their checks.

"Don't forget the senior discount," Janice said as she grabbed her purse.

"Oh good heavens," LuAnn said as she followed her friends out the door into the afternoon sunshine. "Did you ever think you'd live to see the day when one of us would say that to the other? Or to a man?"

"I, for one, am very glad we've lived that long." Tess stalled on the sidewalk beside the car. "Before we go, can we pray that what we're about to do and say in this interview glorifies God and not us?"

"I think that's a great idea," LuAnn said. "Janice, as a pastor's wife, why don't you start?"

Right there on the sidewalk in front of the Galley restaurant, the ladies gave thanks for the opportunity that awaited them and prayed that the inn would be a sanctuary for all and a place where God's love was always felt.

"Amen," they said in unison and then piled in LuAnn's car for the short drive over to meet Barrett.

"I wonder what he'll ask us," LuAnn said. "I've never seen the program, have you?"

"I binge-watched the first half of last season on Netflix with the kids at Stuart's house yesterday," Janice said. "I really liked it."

"Wow," Tess said. "Your kids watched a quilt show with you? They must really love you. Mine would never have turned off Sunday afternoon football for anything craft related."

"It's not about the craft of quilting," Janice said. "It's a little bit like that show *Mysteries at the Museum*."

"Oh, I love that show," LuAnn exclaimed.

"So do I," Janice agreed. "The format is similar on *Quilt Mysteries*. Each episode starts with the background of a famous quilt, or maybe one that just has an interesting story. They'll show where the quilt is, as in what museum has it now, and then they talk about who made it or whatever the mystery is. It's fascinating."

"It must be to keep your kids watching," Tess said.

"To be fair," Janice admitted, "they were all taking Sunday afternoon naps, but they were in the room and a couple of times one of them actually commented about something on the show being interesting. Anyway, I just thought I would study up on what the show was like so I could be prepared. I never taught speech, although I did sub in the class a few times, but I have never been on television except for sitting in the front pew while Larry was preaching."

"I'm glad you thought of that," Tess said. "Any suggestions for your friends who haven't seen the show?"

Janice grinned. "Just answer the question he asks and don't elaborate."

"That's what I was told when I had to testify in court last year," LuAnn said.

"You had to testify in court?" Tess shook her head. "Whatever for?"

"One of my students needed a character witness, and since she was an A student, I was happy to oblige." She paused. "But it was very intimidating. I hope being interviewed is not like that."

CHAPTER TWENTY-THREE

B arrett smiled. "We are doing an interview but nothing formal," he said. "I want you three to just talk. We'll have a conversation about things that you'll add to and maybe I will add to. Or maybe I'll just ask questions and you will answer. At some point, I want us to take a walk around town. Any hopes we can get into the inn?"

Tess shook her head. "Unless I get a call while we're filming. Otherwise we'll still be waiting."

"We can always add those interior shots when the camera crew arrives. In the meantime, let's see how it goes, shall we?" He paused. "Okay, so I'm just going to do a little intro so I know what we're doing and when we did it, and then I'll turn the camera around on you and we will start the interview. Any questions before we begin?"

"I have one," Janice said. "Are we doing the same kind of interview that Maybelline Rector did?"

"Maybelline Rector?" Barrett shook his head. "What do you mean?"

"When I found out we were going to be interviewed, I watched a number of episodes so I could know what to expect. Most shows have two types of interviews. There are the people who are experts, and then there are people who pretty much just fill in with information they thought was true so the expert can correct them."

Barrett appeared flustered and a pale pink color rose in his cheeks. "I, um, well…" He shook his head. "Yes I guess you're right. We do generally format our show that way. Have you studied film?"

"Just your show, so the answer would be informally, I guess," Janice said, obviously pleased with herself. "And only most of one season. Which also makes me wonder where Gwen Billings is."

The red flush that had begun earlier deepened. "Miss Billings and I had a creative difference of opinion about the direction this season should go. I'm afraid she won't be at this taping."

"A pity," Janice said. "She seemed so knowledgeable when she told those stories of how the quilts were made and all the work that went into them. It was just fascinating to listen to her."

"Not if you had to listen to her all the time," he muttered. "But I digress. It's possible we may bring her back, or maybe we will find another host. Are you available, Mrs. Eastman? You certainly seem knowledgeable."

"Me? Oh goodness gracious goat. I could never do anything like that. But thank you for asking. You've made my day, Barrett."

"I'm glad I could do that. Now, I'm turning on the camera and we're going to talk about quilts and Marietta and the inn and whatever else you three would like to discuss. Remember, I'm doing an intro first so don't say a word until I give you this signal." Barrett held up his right hand and pointed toward the sky. "Everybody good?"

At their nods, he set the camera on the tripod and then pushed a button to begin filming. "Hello all, and welcome to another episode of *Quilt Mysteries*. This is Barrett George and today we're sitting beside the sparkling Ohio River in beautiful Marietta, Ohio, where—"

"I'm just so excited to listen to him say that in person," Janice whispered.

"And cut." Barrett turned around. "Please, Mrs. Eastman," he said with a broad smile. "No talking, okay?"

"I'm so sorry," Janice said. "I just got kind of overwhelmed. I've heard this on my television—technically my son's bigger-than-a-minivan size television with picture-in-picture and 3-D thingamadoodles—and it just seems surreal that you are here. Now. And I'm here. Now."

Tess reached over to touch her. "I've heard that when someone gets nervous, they tend to babble."

"Am I?" At Tess's nod, she affected a chastised look. "I am so sorry. Please continue, and I will keep my mouth shut until you point at Jesus."

He shook his head. "Point at…oh, yes." He looked up. "At Jesus. I get it. Okay, starting over from the top and no talking, got it?"

When they had all answered appropriately, Barrett pressed the button and filmed the intro, ending with, "and now I would like to introduce you to the innkeepers of Wayfarers Inn, the lovely Tessa Wallace, LuAnn Sherrill, and Jan Eastman."

"Excuse me," Janice said. "I know you haven't pointed at Jesus yet, but my name is Janice. I never go by Jan. My mama always said she gave me the full name of Janice Ann and it was fine not to use the Ann because most folks don't use that middle name, but I shouldn't ever shorten my name to Jan because that's not the name I was given."

Tess leaned over. "Janice, honey? Babbling again."

Janice pressed her fingers to her lips and said a soft, "Oh."

Barrett put on another smile. "You know, I think we will tidy up that intro back in the studio. Why don't one of you start by telling us what you know about the River of Life quilt? Is it true that it was made here in Marietta?"

He pointed his finger toward the sky in what Tess would forever think of as the Jesus gesture. "And go," he whispered.

"Yes, it's true," LuAnn said, taking her cue from Barrett. "Not only was the quilt made at our inn, but it was also made by women who were aiding the cause of the abolition of slavery and the Underground Railroad."

"How so?" he asked, giving LuAnn a chance to offer up what she knew regarding the history of the inn, specifically how it was used during the period when the Underground Railroad was active in Marietta.

Occasionally Janice added a tidbit here and there regarding the construction of the quilt or gave her opinion on something related to the differences in quilting in the nineteenth century and today.

Tess sat back and let her friends speak. They were doing such a great job that the last thing they needed was her to offer up an opinion on anything. Plus they were speaking with such love: Janice and her crafts, LuAnn and her history. Oh, how she was blessed to have such wonderful friends.

From her vantage point, on her right-hand side she could see the river as it flowed past. On the left, the foxglove and goldenrod set off the edge of the woods with the perfect counterpoint to the dappled shadows of the forest.

She looked into the camera and maintained her smile until Barrett's gaze found her. "Do you have anything to add, Mrs. Wallace?"

"Only that I cannot wait to share Wayfarers Inn with guests once we have the building approved for opening. Everything about the inn has been done with the history of the building in mind. We especially love that the quilt you're investigating today was made right there in the parlor. How wonderful to be appointed treasurers of such a beautiful old inn."

Barrett shut off the camera and shook his head. "That had very little to do with our mystery, but you're very well spoken on camera. Have you had media training?"

"Hardly," she said. "I taught hospitality courses at a community college. But the three of us did have a singing group, and I was a cheerleader."

"I see where the enthusiasm comes from," he said. "So now we're just going to walk around the city and cover some of the places that have historical value. Are there any suggestions as to where we should start?"

"I've got a suggestion." Tess turned to see Maybelline Rector marching toward them, hands on her hips and her high heels occasionally sticking into the soft ground. "You were supposed to be interviewing me. I am the expert, not these women."

Tess groaned. Then her phone rang.

"Agent Butler, please tell me you have good news." She moved away from the noise of Maybelline and Barrett's discussion toward the trees and the parking lot beyond in order to better hear the agent.

"I've got good news, and I've got bad news." He paused. "The good news is we've cleared the inn as a crime scene, so you're welcome to return and continue renovations whenever you're ready."

"That's not good news," she said with a giggle. "That's great news. I can't wait to tell LuAnn and Janice." It was her turn to pause. "But you said there's bad news?"

"Yeah, I heard you guys were going to be on a television show about quilts." The sounds of Barrett and Maybelline's discussion were getting louder, so she moved closer to the parking lot. "We're actually filming now down at the park by the river. Well, we were, but there was an interruption."

"Hey sorry about that. We can finish the conversation later."

"No, it's fine. Barrett is busy working out his differences with the director of the Underground Railroad Museum, so I've got a few minutes."

"Okay, well in that case you ought to know that—"

The rumble of a muscle car's engine drowned out his words as Grant Grimes roared into the parking lot and screeched to a halt. He was out of the car and heading her way in an instant.

"I'm so sorry, but I didn't hear a word you said." Tess stepped out of the shadows so Grant could see her. "Can I call you back?"

"What was that? Sounds like trouble."

"Oh, most definitely trouble." She clicked off her phone and stowed it in her pocket. "Grant," she said as she stepped into his path. "Got a minute?"

He continued walking. "Not right now, Tess."

She fell into step beside him. "I just want to know why you didn't stick around and answer my questions earlier."

He stopped and swiveled to face her. "Because I've been trying to talk to that guy, but every time I think I know where he's going to be, he gives me the slip. I thought I had him when Maybelline was bragging over at the chamber of commerce breakfast that he was interviewing her this morning, but he never showed. My guess is he saw my Camaro out front and bailed."

Tess glanced over at Barrett, who had his hands full placating Maybelline. "Looks like he's not going anywhere just now. What possible reason would he have for hiding from you?"

"How much time do you have?" He shook his head. "It's a long list, but none of it is good."

"Okay," she said. "Then let's talk about me for a minute, please. I really would like that strongbox back. And that quilt was not mine."

"Look, I'm sure you're a nice lady. And you know what? If I saw you walking down the street, I'd take a second look because you've got it going on. But right now you're not making any sense." He crossed his arms over his chest and looked down at her. "So just cut to the chase. Why is it you think I took a box and a quilt from you? This ought to be good."

"They were in my trunk, and then I went inside to wait for LuAnn. When I went back out to the garage, they were gone."

"And why do you think I did this?"

"Because whoever came in the garage had to come in the garage door. I left it closed. The only explanation is that someone who knows the garage codes opened it." She shrugged. "Besides, I know you're being blackmailed. Maybe your blackmailer told you to take those things in exchange for satisfying whatever debt you've got with him or her."

"Again, how did I do this, Tess?"

"You've got the house next door listed. So of course you're going to know the codes in the neighborhood."

He stared down at her with the strangest expression. "That makes absolutely no sense."

She let out a long breath. If Grant was lying, he was an extremely good liar. "I just thought maybe..."

"Is your code 1234?"

Tess's eyes widened. "See, I was right! You do know."

"No, Tess. That's the default on every garage door in that neighborhood unless the homeowner changes it. That's what the builder programs in all his homes. It is also the code that is built in to the device if you were to buy that brand and put it in yourself. It doesn't take a Realtor to know this."

She shrugged. "I rent, so I guess my landlord needs to change it."

"I can do that for you," he said. "If you trust me. And as long as you don't need it today, because right now I have got to go see a man about a big problem he's about to have."

"Thank you," she squeaked out. "And I'm sorry."

"Well, I'm sorry you lost your belongings," he said over his shoulder as he walked away. "I hope they turn up."

The sound of another engine much like Grant's rumbled across the grass. Tess turned around to see a Mustang pull into the parking lot and come to a stop beside the Camaro.

"Well now," she said under her breath as a dark-haired young woman jumped out and raced across the parking lot yelling for someone to stop.

"Wendy?"

Tess crossed the distance between them, meeting Wendy on the edge of the parking lot. "What's wrong?"

Today she wore a denim skirt and a white T-shirt with the sleeves rolled up and *I'm Sew Awesome* decorating the front of it in glittery gold letters. Her flip-flops were dusted with the same gold glitter.

"I cannot believe he's doing this," she said. "I told him not to, but there he is messing everything up. That's why I didn't want to tell him."

"Whoa now," Tess said. "You're not making any sense."

"Not now, Mrs. Wallace," she said. "Remember how I prayed you'd be my friend? Well, right now I need my friend to understand that I cannot talk to you."

She stormed away toward the loud discussion that had now become a three-way argument. Tess made her way back to the picnic table where LuAnn and Janice had settled to watch the show.

"What did I miss?" Tess asked.

"A lot of yelling but not much that makes sense," LuAnn said. "Oh, but Maybelline did get Barrett to agree to turn on the camera and give her an interview. It had just started when Grant rolled up."

"So as far as we can tell, the camera is still filming," Janice said. "I wonder if this will go viral like your hunky fireman picture."

"Janice, please," Tess said. "I prefer not to be reminded of that."

"You took advantage of her and you know it. It's what you do," Grant was saying to Barrett.

"Look, man, you're crazy." Barrett tried to reach for the camera to turn it off, but Maybelline stood in the way. "Move, woman," he told her. "Interview is over."

"You're right. It is over," Grant said. "And so is that show of yours, but you knew that, didn't you? You got cancelled at the end of last season. All of this was just to try to get back in the network's good graces."

"What's this?" Maybelline said, hands on her hips. "You interviewed me under false pretenses? You will be hearing from my lawyer." She stormed past without sparing the ladies so much as a glance.

"He couldn't have been cancelled. Barrett?" Wendy turned her attention toward the producer. "Tell him that's not true. After all we did to get the funding for this show and all the hard work you put into research and finding copies of the quilt and the box that was made for it, how could that even be right?"

"Know what's not right, Miss Wilson?"

Tess turned around to see Agent Butler walking down the hill with two other men in black. "Uh-oh," she said to Janice and LuAnn. "Which of those three made the Feds mad this time?"

"Are you sure it was them and not us?" Janice said.

"What could we have possibly done?" Tess said. "Just a few minutes ago he called to say the investigation is over and we were getting the keys to the inn back. I just hadn't had a chance to tell you."

"The investigation is over?" LuAnn said, clapping her hands. "That's wonderful news!"

"Mrs. Wallace," Agent Butler called. "A word, please?"

"He hasn't drowned," Prudence said. "And I do not care who believes thee or me. The story will be told. Are you willing to chance a charge of murder?"

The man said nothing as he turned the boat back in the direction of Jason and the captain. Jason had somehow managed to keep the captain's head above the water, but Prudence could see her husband was soon to be going under.

"Get as close to them as you can manage," she said. "Should a bullet come, I'll gladly take it on thy behalf if it saves my husband."

Amity moved to sit beside her. "As will I."

"No." Prudence handed Moses to her. "You will guard Moses."

"With my life," she said as she took the child.

Once the vessel was near enough, Prudence reached out to Jason. Rather than take her hand, he shoved Captain Markham in her direction.

"Hold him in place until I can climb in and pull him to safety."

Prudence nodded in agreement and did as he asked, but she knew what Jason would see soon enough. Samuel Markham had no need of saving. His soul had already flown to Jesus.

The commotion had alerted Marietta authorities who met them on the Ohio shore. Though the man who rowed the boat was greeted as a hero, he strangely disappeared when it came time to thank him for his efforts.

Despite her bedraggled state, Prudence pressed past the crowd to make her way to Violet's door. This time the maid admitted her without question. Silent footsteps led her upstairs to a darkened bedchamber where her friend rested, eyes open and tears flowing.

Prudence fell on her knees beside the bed. "The fault is mine alone," was all she could manage before her tears prevented more of the apology she had practiced all the way from the river.

Violet's hand covered hers and together they wept.

Three men who were known to procure slaves without care of status or color were prosecuted for the abduction of Jason and Amity, two free citizens of the state of Ohio. Being but a babe, the taking of Moses did not count against them though Prudence felt that to be the most heinous of their crimes.

A fourth was hung from a tree by the river for the murder of Captain Samuel Markham. Seven months after his father's death, a son, Samuel Markham, Jr. was born with the fair hair of his father and his mother's green eyes.

The quiltings continued, as did the work that went on beneath the ladies who studiously pretended an interest and skill in such things. Rumors abounded that there would soon be war. That the men and women who risked their lives to bring souls to safety and freedom would soon go back to their plows and their very ordinary lives.

And then one day the Markham widow arrived for a quilting, her arrival causing a gasp among those assembled. After a proper greeting and introductions, Violet seated herself beside Prudence at the end of the frame and retrieved an elaborate sewing kit from her reticule.

"It appears you have some skill at sewing, Mrs. Markham," Amity observed after a while.

"I was raised with a thimble in my hand," she said. "And though my mother despaired of me becoming a proper lady thanks to the company I kept, she did instill a love of needlework in me that I've missed exercising."

"Miss it no more," Prudence said with a gleam in her eye. "Thee are most welcome to join us at any time. If thee don't mind the company thee will be keeping here."

Amity's eyes widened at what she surely thought was an inference to the activities downstairs. Only Violet and Prudence knew otherwise.

And though the others might make feeble attempts at sewing pretty stitches, the corner of the quilt that was Violet Markham's to sew blossomed with intricate stitches. While the others pulled out their work and did it all over again, Violet continued to add more stitches, beautiful beads that shimmered and sparkled, and even threads of gold and silver.

The other ladies called it the Markham corner. Prudence called it a miracle.

Chapter Twenty-Four

See, Tess," Janice said under her breath, "it's us again."

At the sight of the federal agents, Barrett George took off running. What the producer didn't realize was that before he was a real estate agent, Grant Grimes was a star running back at Marietta High. And while his running back days were far behind him, he had the advantage of knowing where the edge of the sidewalk fell off just near the entrance to the tunnel.

Barrett went tumbling down into the river while Grant stood on the shore appearing to be debating whether to jump in or let him drown. Then the younger Grimes brother jumped in and hauled the producer back onto solid ground.

After a moment, Wendy hurled herself into Grant's arms and cried.

Leaving Barrett to the federal agents, Grant escorted Wendy back to where the ladies were seated. Janice pulled a tissue out of her purse and handed it to Wendy.

"I'm afraid this won't help you," she said to Grant, who was soaked with river water.

Wendy dabbed at her damp eyes—her damp distinctive blue eyes—as a jolt of recognition hit Tess. "Grant," she said slowly, "is she..."

"We're pretty sure," he said. "Unless Barrett was lying about that too."

"He wasn't." Agent Butler handed Barrett over to one of his associates as Grant and Wendy embraced. "I've seen the birth certificate. Congratulations, it's a girl."

"Okay so what just happened?" Janice said. "I thought Saffron was Grant's daughter. Wendy is too?"

Grant gave her a sheepish look. "Her mom and I were college sweethearts. I was an idiot, and she broke up with me. I had no idea." He shrugged. "Then I got a call, and here we are."

Wendy stepped out of Grant's embrace. "It was Barrett's idea for me to call him. He said it would add authenticity to the story of the quilt if it also contained a secondary story line about a father and daughter reunion."

"I don't know about authenticity," Grant said, "but if he's the reason you contacted me, then I'm glad I didn't let him drown."

Wendy's smile began and then faltered. "I didn't know he'd stolen the real quilt. I thought we were just planting copies to call attention to the show. I would never have done those things if I'd known."

"Like sneaking through the inn wearing your parade costume?" Tess said. "Why did you do that?"

"Barrett said he'd left the quilt on the top floor. He complained that the plumber kept messing with his hiding places. Said it was like the guy was out to get him."

"He was," Agent Butler said. "You would be too if your half-brother let you take the fall when a valuable quilt was stolen.

And yes, I see your surprised faces. Tom Davis's half brother is Barrett George Davis. He dropped 'Davis' and used George as his stage name when he left Cleveland for Hollywood. And if you're wondering why Tom's note was sitting on the strongbox, we were all supposed to think Tom stole the thing. That's when the show was going to reveal the theft and solve it. The problem was, between Grant and that lady from the museum, Barrett was having a little trouble keeping out of sight. So when he tried to film at the inn, he couldn't get in without someone seeing him."

"Because of the fire alarm." Tess shrugged. "But who set that off?"

"Tom. He admitted it to my associate. He said he wanted Barrett off his back. Said he knew Barrett would get around to blaming him for something. He's a good guy and that plumbing company is his fresh start." Agent Butler shrugged. "Don't blame him for the deception, but Tom's going to have to come clean with you."

"There's plenty of time for that. How did Barrett and Tom know about the quilt?" LuAnn said.

"Apparently the Davis brothers' father was a Civil War history buff who took his children to Marietta on multiple occasions. He was especially keen on visiting the Underground Railroad sites."

Tess nodded. "So Barrett knew all about the history of our town and presumably the River of Life quilt."

"That is what we've determined," the agent said.

"He needed help, and when a sweet girl with ties not only to Marietta but to the River of Life quilt wrote his show and told him what a big fan she was, he knew this was how he was going to get his show renewed. Because what better way to get a show that solves mysteries back on the air than to create a theft and then film yourself finding it? We've got enough on Davis to keep him in custody for a long while."

"Custody?" Wendy shook her head, her face pale and streaked with tears. "I guess I ought to be arrested too."

"You probably should," the agent said. "But for what? The part where you told your new father that you needed money for your business so he went and got money out of an account that was meant for all the Bickerton heirs?"

"What?" Grant's head snapped toward Agent Butler. "I did no such thing."

The agent shrugged. "Someone did. If not you, then my suspicion is that Barrett did it. If Miss Wilson let him anywhere near a writing sample of yours, then the rest was easy."

"You mean like the card that went with the frog?" Tess offered. "The one with the green ink?"

Wendy groaned. "The card went missing. And then suddenly it was back in the shop where Mrs. Wallace found it." She turned to Tess. "That's what upset me that day. I wondered why someone would just take the card, but now I see."

"I have a question," Tess said. "How does Harry fit into all this?"

"Harry?" she said with a smile. "Such a precious man. He cooks for me because he says I'm too skinny. He heard me arguing with Barrett about going into the inn and getting the quilt. I refused, but I was so upset that Harry said he'd go get it."

"Why did he wear the shirt with the logo?"

"Barrett was pretty specific about that. Turns out that he wanted to film the quilt leaving the inn and play with the film to make it look like his brother Tom."

"So the shirt looked like something a plumber would wear."

"Exactly." She shook her head. "I'm such an idiot. Harry should never have gotten mixed up in this."

"Wendy, you'll need to make that right, but Harry likes you a lot, so I doubt you've lost a friend," Tess said. "But I wonder if you might know where a few other things are that went missing. Like the strongbox that Harry sold and some Fourth of July pictures of the red, white, and blue quilt you gave us?"

Wendy looked stricken. "The box. Barrett got it out of your car this morning, Mrs. Wallace. He was hoping you would mention it was missing in the interview so he could find it for you and be the hero of the show. He took your pictures too."

"That brings me to the bad news I was trying to tell you on the phone," Agent Butler said to Tess. "The strongbox has to go back to the archives. It's government property, and we will need to confiscate it."

"I do understand," LuAnn said, "but can I get the pictures back? They were just snaps of us in the parade showing the quilt."

"That shouldn't be a problem," said the agent. "However, there is one more piece of bad news."

Janice groaned. "Oh no, what now?"

"It's about your Fourth of July quilt. We confiscated it during our initial search of the inn and sent it back to the archives for further examination. Our experts have dated that textile as possibly older than the River of Life. The material was dyed using early nineteenth-century techniques."

"But we rode in a parade with that quilt draped over the tailgate of a truck," Tess said with her own groan. "It's a miracle it wasn't harmed."

"Apparently the seamstress knew what she was doing," he said.

"That would be Prudence Willard." Wendy smiled. "She's very important in Marietta and Underground Railroad history, but most people haven't heard of her."

"I have," LuAnn said.

"So have Tess and I," Janice added. "Some of her things are preserved in the Marietta Underground Railroad Museum."

"I would love to see them," Wendy said. "She was also very important to my family."

"How so?" Tess asked.

"She and my great-great-great-grandmother had a shared history that was written down and passed through the generations to me." Wendy paused to wipe her eyes with the tissue. "That's how I came to know about the River of Life quilt and why I wanted to share the Fourth of July quilt with people who would honor the history behind it."

"It would have helped to know that history," Tess said.

"I did plan to tell you," Wendy said. "But then everything started happening, and I just never managed to."

"So the River of Life quilt," LuAnn said gently. "You learned about that from your family history?"

Wendy nodded. "And from that, I met and fell in love with Barrett George."

Grant wrapped her in his arms again. "He won't bother you anymore. I'll see to it."

"So will we," Agent Butler agreed.

"Wendy," Tess said. "Who was this relative of yours?"

"Captain Samuel Markham, Sr. and his wife Victoria lived in Marietta for a short time. The captain lost his life saving Prudence's husband and child, and Victoria gave her support to the quiltings. With a war hero's wife in attendance, no one dared challenge what went on at the inn." Wendy shrugged. "I have Victoria's journals that began after she left Marietta to move back to Virginia, but oddly she refers to herself as Violet. Maybe a nickname of some sort?"

"I would love to read those," LuAnn said. "It sounds fascinating."

"Oh, it is."

"I hate to break up this party," Agent Butler said, "but I have a prisoner to interrogate." He shook hands all around. "I'll be in touch," he said to Tess.

"Wendy," Tess said as she watched him leave, "can I ask you a favor?"

"What's that?"

"That you stop hiding and come around to see us at the inn occasionally, okay?"

Wendy smiled. "Okay."

"And bring that journal," LuAnn added.

"Hey everyone," a familiar voice called. Tess looked up to see Brad walking toward them. "What did I miss?"

"Other than a new niece and a solution to the mystery?" She shrugged. "Not a thing."

The women sewed on that quilt for almost a full year. Because the men who worked below in the tunnel and in the rooms beneath where the frame was placed needed a distraction, the women sewed on.

There were rumors that the ladies were so intent on making the quilt just right that they tore out more stitches than they kept in. Others said the length of time it took to complete the masterpiece was proportional to the intricacies of the pattern.

The truth, though it was buried deep in the legend that became the River of Life, is that the sewing of that quilt took just as long to complete as the freeing of those slaves who lived on the other side of the river. And with a hero's widow in attendance, the ladies were never disturbed.

As with any legend, it wouldn't do to have reality intrude. Thus, Jason used his skills as a carpenter to build a special box that would hold the fabled River of Life. Unlike the other work he'd done, he made sure the hinges on the strongbox went unoiled and soon became unusable. When a Union Army battalion marched through, the quilt was sent off as a gift from the citizens of Marietta to the abolitionist president, thus ending the quiltings but adding to the legend of the famous quilt.

Only Jason and Prudence knew that there were two identical strongboxes. One held the fabled quilt with one beautiful corner that was never to be seen, while the other was empty.

One day when war ended and freedom for the slaves had been declared, the Markham widow and her son simply disappeared. Where she'd gone was a mystery.

Their whereabouts were no mystery to Prudence. Thus began years of visits to the little town where Prudence and Violet began their lives, and where someday Violet would come to the end of hers. It remained to be seen which of the two little boys would be well behaved and which would be the one who gave his mother gray hairs, but Violet and Prudence certainly could guess.

And as to the quilt the abolitionists called the River of Life? Over the years the legend was lost with time. But Violet recorded everything in the hopes that someday the River of Life quilt would go home again to Marietta and the inn.

It took five generations to accomplish the task.

Dear Reader,

Thank you for joining LuAnn, Tess, Janice—and me!—as the mystery of the River of Life quilt was solved. Contrary to what some readers might think, many mystery writers get all the way to the end of the book before they determine which of their cast of characters to pick as the culprit. Yes, it's true! I had so many potential perpetrators in mind when I began writing River of Life that I had a hard time eliminating the ones who could not have committed the crime. Finally, when I settled on the culprit, I was almost surprised that he was the one. Were you surprised too, or did you guess correctly? If so, congratulations! You're a great sleuth!

In addition to the contemporary story of the Inn Crowd, there is a more serious aspect to the Wayfarers Inn series. I am honored to tell the story, however fictional, of just a few of the people who toiled invisibly along the stations of the Underground Railroad. While most of their names have been lost to time, the efforts of those who risked their lives to deliver precious souls from the horror of slavery should never be forgotten.

As much as I enjoyed creating the story for *River of Life*, I could never have written this book without the help and encouragement of some very special people. Special thanks to my husband, Robert Turner, for all he does as patron of the arts, and to Tracey Bateman for providing insightful critique. Also, many thanks to Trish Caldwell Landsittel who provided a wealth of information regarding the history of Marietta, Ohio. Finally, I cannot let the opportunity pass without bragging on Susan Downs, Caroline Cilento, and JoAnne Simmons, as well as the rest of the amazing Guideposts team. I am blessed to be in such great company.

I hope you'll join LuAnn, Tess, and Janice next time for another mystery and adventure at the Wayfarers Inn. I can't wait to see what kind of trouble the Inn Crowd gets mixed up in. Can you?

Enjoy!

Signed,
Kathleen Y'Barbo

ABOUT THE AUTHOR

Bestselling author Kathleen Y'Barbo is a multiple Carol Award and RITA nominee of more than eighty novels, with almost two million copies in print in the US and abroad. A tenth-generation Texan, military wife, and paralegal, she has been nominated for Career Achievement Awards as well as Readers' Choice Awards, and is the winner of the Inspirational Romance of the Year by Romantic Times magazine. To connect with her through social media, check out the links on her website at www.kathleenybarbo.com.

THE VISIT THAT ALMOST
DID NOT HAPPEN

In *River of Life*, I mention the visit paid to the city of Marietta by the famous General Lafayette. While General Lafayette's visit to Marietta in May of 1825 is well documented in the annals of local history and commemorated on a plaque where the illustrious Frenchman first set his foot down in the city, many do not know that the visit almost did not happen. In fact, the general and his party very nearly were lost to the waters of the Ohio River thanks to the sinking of the steamboat *Mechanic*, the vessel chartered to deliver the general to Marietta.

In a letter written on April 15, 1859 by Captain Wyllys Hall to Doctor S.P. Hildreth and found in the Ohio Historical Society publications, the entire story unfolds as told by the ship's captain himself. The tale begins with the *Mechanic* departing Nashville, Tennessee, to begin the journey toward Marietta with the general and a group of others aboard.

The day was May 6, 1825, and the dignitaries aboard also included Governor Coles of Illinois, a number of American generals, and other dignitaries. The *Mechanic* was local to Marietta, having been built by John Mitchell on the Little

272

Muskingum River less than ten miles from the city, and the captain knew the waters between Nashville and Marietta well.

Three days later on the Ohio River, with the clocks striking midnight and the change of the crew's watch still in progress, the steamboat ran upon a snag that pierced the bottom of the boat and ran through the main deck. A crewmember who minutes before had been sleeping in the forecastle was driven up unhurt to the main deck with the snag.

While the captain supervised the evacuation of the passengers, his trusted clerk, John Hunt, was given the task of removing the captain's portable desk containing books, papers, and approximately one thousand dollars in cash. Unfortunately, as the ship's deck tilted sharply, Mr. Hunt stumbled and the desk fell into the river.

All of its contents—the valuables entrusted there—were lost to the river. According to Captain Hall, the only items salvaged from the sinking steamship were a venison ham and a few breakfast biscuits. Much to General Lafayette's relief, a portion of his belongings were later retrieved from the river and loaded aboard another vessel for the trip to Marietta.

SOMETHING DELICIOUS FROM OUR WAYFARERS INN FRIENDS

Author's Note: While Harmless Harry gets the credit for this sauce in the novel, the real credit goes to my grandmother, Katie Aycock, who passed this recipe down to me.

Harmless Harry's Italian Meat Sauce

Ingredients:

½ cup onions, sliced

2 Tablespoons olive oil

1 pound ground beef

2 cloves garlic, minced

2 1-lb cans (4 cups) canned tomatoes

2 8-oz cans (2 cups) Italian-seasoned tomato sauce

1 3-oz can (⅔ cup) broiled sliced mushrooms

¼ cup chopped parsley

1½ teaspoons oregano or sage

1 teaspoon salt

¼ teaspoon thyme

1 bay leaf

1 cup water

In a large skillet, cook onions in hot oil until almost tender. Add ground meat and garlic and brown lightly. Add remaining ingredients and simmer uncovered 2 to 2½ hours or until the sauce is nice and thick, stirring occasionally. Remove bay leaf and serve over cooked pasta. Serves 6.

Read on for a sneak peek of another exciting book
in the series Secrets of Wayfarers Inn!

All That Remains
by Tracey Bateman

November, 1858

Rain fell in torrents, bringing waves crashing—over and over—to the bank of the Ohio River. Hidden behind a large oak on the Virginia side of the river, Prudence waited alone, praying for the package that was to arrive tonight.

Two packages, one bulging with precious cargo, the note had said. Two adults, one of them heavily pregnant. Prudence always felt the weight of her responsibility to keep the runaways safe even more when they had little ones, even if they were still tucked in their mothers' wombs.

Thunder shook the sky, matching the roiling of her stomach, and she thought of her own secret, hidden deep inside her body. Another life she alone was responsible to protect. She hadn't told Jason yet. She would wait a little while longer. Not until she was sure the Lord would allow them to keep this one.

If only Jason could remember why they had accepted God's call in the first place. Prudence knew his concern was born of love, and that was the reason she couldn't admonish him for a lack of faith on nights such as this, when the pain in his leg held him at home while she carried out the task. He would have faced the pain to come with her, but if she found herself in a situation where she must run, he would only slow her down. The admission felt like a betrayal, but they both knew the unspoken truth.

Each time she received new instructions in the hollowed-out oak tree, Jason hovered as she waited for the cover of darkness. Prudence could always feel his prayers as the danger rose, peaked, and finally subsided. Yet they were never fully out of danger. He would pray every minute she was gone and would not relax until they were safely tucked beneath the quilt she'd stitched with her own hands. He would hold her—too tightly—until morning.

But first she had to focus her thoughts on the package that should have already arrived. Prudence tried not to surrender to the sin of worry, but she couldn't resist the frown pulling at her lips as she looked through the brush toward the dock where her small boat lifted and crashed down with the waves. The storm had begun only a few moments ago, after she had rowed from the Ohio bank and tied the small vessel securely to the dock. How on earth would she ever row safely back to the other side in this weather? *Oh, Lord*, she silently prayed. *Calm the winds and waves, if it be Thy will. If* not, she had to believe God would keep them safe in the midst of the storm.

A branch snapped behind her and she froze, then whipped around.

"Friend of a friend?" a voice whispered from the shadows.

"Friend of a friend."

"My father would be absolutely furious if he knew you were a woman." The amused voice accompanied the figure of a man as he stepped out from behind a tree, his coat collar high and his hat low to protect him from the persistent rain.

"Wh-what do you mean, sir?"

"I mean, ma'am," he said, his shadowy form large and fearsome, "that we've lost five of my father's slaves in the past three years. And unless I miss my guess, that circumstance appears to be largely your doing."

The sickening feeling that rolled inside of her had nothing to do with her pregnancy, but it threatened to release the contents of her stomach all the same. His voice, his words, the way he spoke. This man was not a slave. Prudence's hands shook, causing the lantern to sway as she took a step closer and raised the light to get a view of his face.

She gasped and shrank from him, taking a step backward as she looked up into the pale eyes of a white man. Fear tightened her gut, and she thought of her poor Jason waiting for her at home. She thought about the dear child deep inside of her. She swayed, blackness swirling about her. As she felt herself fading from consciousness, she thought about the precious human cargo she had expected to meet tonight and help on the journey to freedom. Where were they?

Almighty God, into Thine hands I commend us all.

Marietta, Ohio
August

Janice Eastman reached with leaden arms through the foggy veil of her dream world, searching for something solid to hold on to as she awoke. Anything that explained the buzzing noise invading her slumber.

She sat up slowly, and her surroundings began to make sense. Goodness, she'd fallen asleep in the wing chair again. That explained why her neck felt so stiff. With a sigh she glanced toward the sound that had drawn her from another dream about her late husband, Lawrence. In her dreams, he disapproved of her buying an inn with her two best friends. In real life, she would have seriously considered his thoughts on the matter, and he very likely would've won the argument. But he'd flown away to heaven without her, so he could just keep his opinion to himself as far as she was concerned.

The buzzing started again, and this time she recognized it for what it was. Lifting her cell phone from the table next to the chair, she saw her daughter's name staring back at her. A slight smile touched her lips as she answered. "Hi, honey. I'm sorry it took so long to answer. I was dreaming about your father again. You'd think after a year..."

"Dreaming?" Stacy interrupted. "Mother!"

Janice sighed. "Oh, I know I shouldn't sleep during the day. I dozed off for just a few minutes." *What time is it anyway?*

"Mother!" she said again. "Where. Is. Larry?"

"Larry?" Janice popped to her feet. "Oh my word. Larry!" How on earth could she have gone and fallen asleep when she was supposed to be taking care of her five-year-old grandson?

"I can't believe I let you talk me into letting you babysit in that run-down warehouse."

Let her? Stacy had begged her to babysit, even though she knew full well an interior designer was coming today to help them decide on decor. Plus, they were expecting a linen and bedding delivery this afternoon. It hadn't even been convenient to keep an eye on the wandering little boy. But she'd agreed to it, because that's what parents and grandparents did when their kids were in a jam. "Don't worry, Stace," she said with more calm than she felt. "I'll find him pronto and call you right back."

"Wait—Mom! Don't hang up!"

But Janice pressed the button to end the call without acknowledging she'd even heard. The last thing she needed right now was a scolding from her own daughter.

She hurried toward the kitchen. "Larry!" If there was one thing her grandson liked above all else, it was getting into Miss LuAnn's cookies when Nana wasn't watching closely enough.

And this seemed to be an opportune moment for the sneaky little guy. Janice smiled, picturing the guilty look in his big brown eyes. A bit of clanging reached her ears as she pushed open the door and stepped inside ready to bust him with cookies in his hands.

"Good gravy, Janice." Tess Wallace, Janice's lifelong friend and one of three partners in their inn venture, whipped around from the stove, then caught herself on the counter as she stumbled. The cup of tea in her other hand clattered against the saucer, but righted itself with barely a slosh. "You nearly scared me to death. Warn a girl next time."

Janice scanned the kitchen from one end to the other, ignoring the admonishment. She had no time for that. "Where's Larry?"

With a shrug, Tess limped her way to the wooden table, spilling a bit more tea into her saucer before she reached her chair. "How would I know? I thought you were watching him."

Not very well!

"I fell asleep, and he ran off." She cast a quick glance at Tess's ankle and debated whether to ask for help. Tess could do pretty much anything most of the time, and Janice relied on her in awful situations such as this. What an absolutely terrible time for Tess to hurt herself!

Guilt stabbed Janice's conscience. And what a terrible thing for her to even think. The night before, Tess had stepped down hard in a hole left by the landscapers. By the time LuAnn and Janice had heard the cries and reached her, the sprained ankle had already begun to turn color and swell. She shouldn't even be getting her own tea, let alone traipsing around after a five-year-old boy. But what else could Janice do? LuAnn was out. "Stacy's going to have a cow if I don't call her back soon."

The phone in Janice's hand buzzed and Stacy's name popped onto the screen as if summoned by the words. Janice pressed Decline, and had to force herself not to beg for Tess's help. She hated to admit it, even to herself, but she was no good in a crisis.

"He's probably off chasing a moth around the house. Or exploring. You know how he is." Tess waved aside Janice's fear as though it were nothing. The way her friends dismissed her sometimes really burned her up, but the three of them had been besties—as the kids these days liked to say—since their first year of college, when they were practically kids themselves, so no sense making waves now.

"I'm sure you're right." She gathered in her bottom lip, trying to decide where to start first in the mammoth house. They were in the midst of renovations. Opening the Wayfarers Inn as a bed-and-breakfast had seemed like a wonderful adventure when Tess suggested it a couple of months ago. Janice had championed the idea and once LuAnn, their history buff friend, had discovered the treasure trove of history between the walls, there was no stopping them. Living with Stacy had gotten more than a little tiresome, and moving in with Stuart, her thirty-six-year-old son, hadn't been an option. As the town coroner, he got calls at all hours, and a woman Janice's age needed her sleep—but not when she was supposed to be keeping an eye on her grandson!

The sound of chair legs scraping against the floor pulled Janice back to Tess. Her friend rose without even sipping her tea. "I'll help you look for Larry. He has to be around here somewhere. Where have you looked?"

Janice hesitated, then took a deep breath and shook her head. "Tess, sit down. You can't walk around. You'll make that ankle worse. Just stay here and let me know if he shows up looking for a cookie."

"Don't be ridiculous. Of course I'll help. Where have you looked so far?"

Janice opened her mouth to continue the argument, then gave in. There was no time to argue.

"This was my first and only real thought. You know how he likes to sneak sweets."

Tess's eyes took on that merry glint she got when she was amused or delighted. "He does at that."

Janice sent her friend a grateful smile.

"Where did you last see him?"

"Oh, playing on that tablet thing of his. He was just right there with me in the living room. Next thing, I was waking up and he was gone."

"Okay, stay calm. The last thing we need right now is for you to panic."

Janice frowned and pulled herself to full height—which wasn't much—and squared her shoulders. "I do not panic."

Tess slung her arm around Janice's shoulders. "Of course you don't."

Shaking her off, Janice gave a huff. "Stop patronizing me. I have to find Larry before Stacy blows a gasket."

Tess frowned. "Are you okay?"

"I'm fine. Let's just find my grandson."

They searched the bottom floor first, from the kitchen to the café just outside the door. Janice cast a nervous glance to the door heading into the basement. Surely, he wouldn't have gone down there. She glanced to the old elevator that had been boarded up until they discovered it a few weeks ago. It was the only part of the first floor that was not yet completely finished. Largely because they were trying to decide whether to fix and use the ancient thing, or if it should be taken out and turned into a closet on each floor.

"Don't you even worry about the elevator," Tess said, her intuition intact as always. "You know it's closed off tighter than a drum." They walked, slowly, past the bar and through the other café door into the sitting area. "Have you checked the living and reception areas really well?" asked Tess.

"Not really. I sort of pan—...well, I thought he'd most likely be in the kitchen." She ignored the sudden smirk on Tess's face, and sucked in a full breath. "Larry Eastman! Are you in here?" she called, as she left Tess standing at the door of the room. She looked behind every piece of furniture Larry could possibly hide behind.

"Well, he's not on this floor." Tess turned and limped out of the room into the foyer and cast a worried glance toward the stairs.

"Wait here," Janice said. "You can't do steps."

"Of course I can. You go on ahead, and I'll be up there before you're finished searching the second-floor rooms."

There was no way Larry could have gotten into the rooms, but she grabbed the keys from the drawer in the bar just in case. By the time Tess reached the open space on the second floor, Janice was ready to head up to the third floor. This time, she insisted Tess sit herself down and wait. "As much as I appreciate the offer, Tess, you're slowing me down," she said firmly. "Stay here and rest that ankle."

She searched the danger zones first—which covered pretty much anywhere on the third and fourth floors. As a general rule, Tory Thornton, their contractor, had declared the top two floors off limits, even or maybe especially to the three owners, as the workers restored and renovated—trying to keep as much of the original wood, blown-glass windows, and bits of history as possible. It was a slow process and the workers had been a bit on edge lately, especially since there had been yet another problem with the wiring.

But Janice ignored the irritated looks. Only Robin, the one woman on the crew, showed her any sympathy. No one had seen hide nor hair of Larry, and he seemed nowhere to be found.

When she returned from the fourth floor to the third, Janice stared with exasperation right at Tess, who had not stayed put, but had climbed the steps.

"Tess! You have to sit. That ankle's as big as a bowling ball."

Tess shook her head, splashing red curls around her face. "Absolutely not until we find him." She glanced at Janice's hand as the phone buzzed for the fifth time in fifteen minutes. "You better get that before she calls the cops."

With a sigh, Janice prepared herself for an earful and touched the screen. "Yes, Stacy. We are still looking."

"Mom! It's been over twenty minutes." The panic in Stacy's voice went straight to Janice's heart. And truthfully, she was about to dial 911 herself.

"We haven't looked downstairs yet." Tess groaned as she hopped the bottom step and landed with a grunt on the first floor.

"Tess is going to look in the basement, and I'm heading to the backyard. If we don't find him in a few minutes, we'll call the police. But you know he's probably chasing butterflies or exploring." Her words echoed Tess's statement from moments ago.

"Don't patronize me, please. Just find my son!" The line between them went dead.

"I can't go into the basement." Tess swept a gaze to her swelling ankle. "The steps are a lot steeper and deeper than these, and the railing isn't as sturdy."

"Well, then who's going to…"

"Janice, you know I would if I could. But you said yourself I can barely walk."

Janice gasped as she looked in horror at the truth in her friend's sad eyes. "You know I'd die down there by myself! I don't even like that spooky place when you and LuAnn are with me."

Tess took Janice firmly by the shoulders, giving no indication that she was even a tiny bit concerned with Janice's fears of the dark, tight spaces, or spiders, and steered her toward the basement door. "You can do it. This is for Larry."

Gathering in a shuddering breath, Janice glanced back at her friend. Of course Tess couldn't take those stairs. Still… "Do you think one of the workers might…? Robin seems nice."

"Goodness, Janice. They're on overtime as it is. They don't have time to form a search party…unless we can't find him, then I suppose we'll have to call the police."

Vines of fear slithered up from Janice's insides and wound themselves around her heart. The all-too-familiar beginning of anxiety began to tighten her chest and spread toward her shoulders. She stopped short a few feet from the basement door, forcing Tess to do the same behind her. Pressing her hand to her chest, Janice shook her head.

"Don't," Tess said firmly in her teacher voice as though Janice were one of her former students. "You don't have time for an anxiety attack. Panic later. What if Larry fell down the stairs? Are you just going to leave him there?" Tess snatched up the flashlight from the accent table next to the basement door and handed it over. "Take this in case the lights go out. Besides, you might need to look in the tunnel and it's dark as midnight in there."

The thought of her little grandson finding his way into that dark place where a century and a half earlier escaped slaves had stealthily made their way to the river beneath the inn, only elevated her anxiety. And Tess could've been a little less bossy about it, but that didn't mean she wasn't right.

"Take a deep breath," Tess said, her hands getting decidedly heavier on Janice's shoulders. She reached around and switched on the light over the stairs. That helped some.

Reaching up, Janice patted her friend's hand. "Go rest that ankle before it gets any bigger. I'll be fine."

"I'll wait right here at the top of the steps so you don't feel like you're alone down there."

Janice nodded, drew a shaky breath, and stepped down onto the first step. Her head spun a little, and she wrapped a white-knuckled grip around the railing. One foot after the other.

Tess fell back to her typical attempt at encouragement. "Remember, there's nothing to fear but fear itself."

"That never helps," Janice called back.

"God hasn't given you a spirit of fear," Tess called down as Janice reached the midway point.

"That helps." She'd meant it facetiously, but then realized it actually did help. How many times had she quoted that same verse in Second Timothy to her children when they were afraid? Did she trust God or didn't she?

"Make me brave," she whispered to the heavens. "Larry!" she called out. "You down here, baby boy?"

As she reached the next to the last step, Janice heard the distinct sound of scraping, then a clatter and the slamming of a door. An instant of fear shot through her, followed by a wave of relief. "I heard something," she called up to Tess.

"Oh, thank the Lord."

"Larry! Where are you?" She moved toward the sounds she'd heard, picking up her steps. She frowned as she noted chunks of what looked like mud trailing along the basement floor. Had Larry somehow gotten out through the front and come around to the back door and tracked in dirt? Making a note to check the lock on the door leading to the loading area, she continued toward the scraping noise she had heard.

"It's okay, sweetie. Come on out. Nana's not mad." Not too much anyway, and more at herself for falling asleep than at the wandering boy.

There were eight small rooms, four on each side of a narrow hallway. She stopped short in front of one of the small bedrooms, which they now knew were used to hide weary slaves while they waited for transport up the river toward Canada. The entrance to the tunnel was hidden under this room. Surely Larry hadn't found his way to the passageway. How would he have even known about it? Janice didn't remember him ever being around when they'd shown it off to friends and family. Knowing she was going to have to go into the room and possibly the tight dark space, Janice steeled herself and took in a deep breath, then pushed the door open. "Larry?"

No answer.

She switched on the light and looked around while her eyes adjusted. She frowned. The beautiful mahogany antique rocking chair Tess had discovered at a flea market of all places, and which LuAnn had lovingly restored, was tipped on its side. Was that the clatter she'd heard? Strange. If the door slamming had been this door, then Larry must've been in here and gotten spooked when he heard her call. Thank goodness the chair appeared to be in one piece. "Lawrence John! You best show your little behind pronto or Nana's going to spank it."

She should have done it last time he ran off after a bluebird. He'd just wanted to see how far it could fly without landing, but for goodness' sake, he'd gone two miles before they'd found him. She knew he didn't mean to be bad, he just had the most vivid curiosity about anything in nature. If he made it to adulthood without absently walking off a cliff, he'd likely be one of the most brilliant minds of his generation. But first, she had to find him.

In trepidation, she noted that, not only had the rocking chair been upended, but the stool that had been built by the original owners of the inn to hide the tunnel was also on its side, revealing the gaping hole. Her legs shook as she walked to the stool next to the cot-sized bed they'd installed in all of the rooms down here—although this room would ultimately be off limits, except for guided tours, because of what lay beneath the floor.

Kneeling, she shined the flashlight down the hole. At first glance, it appeared as though an adult couldn't possibly fit, but she knew from earlier examinations that it widened after the initial descent. Her heart sped up and the familiar numbness spread across her jaw from left to right the way it did when she was about to go into a full-blown panic attack. Oh, mercy.

"Jesus, help me." There was absolutely no time for this. True, she had just about every fear possible, particularly of dark, closed-in spaces, but she had to find the strength to take the plunge and go find her grandbaby before he got more lost or, worse, hurt. What would Lawrence do if he were here? Janice rolled her eyes at her own question. She knew what her husband would have done. Barged right in with the arm of the Lord as his strength, and found his namesake safe and sound.

"Well, Lawrence Eastman, I'll just show you, mister."

She negotiated the narrow stone steps into the tunnel, never more aware of the extra twenty pounds she'd packed on since Lawrence died. She gripped the flashlight as though it were her last line of defense against an evil so terrifying she was starting to fear that the tightness in her chest might actually be "the big one," instead of just panic. Taking the steep steps one at a time, she pressed her empty hand against the brick wall to steady herself.

"Janice!" She heard the faint sound of Tess's voice from the top of the stairs. "Are you okay down there? You can come back. I found Larry."

She found Larry? Then who had knocked over the chair and stool? And what was Tess doing in the basement? Distracted, Janice's foot missed the second to last step. The jolt sent her to the ground and she landed hard on her backside, the flashlight flying from her hand. Everything went black.

Janice stayed put at the bottom of the steps, knowing Tess was just above her. An entryway, no more than three feet wide, separated the bottom step from the tunnel where the flashlight had likely rolled, but she couldn't move, even with the light from Tess's flashlight shining above her.

Her imagination had always been her greatest weakness in times such as this. Not that there had ever been a time as wretched as this, except maybe during a couple of tornado warnings when Lawrence insisted they hunker down in a closet till it passed. But at least then she'd had her children to be strong for and her husband's strength to lean on. Right now, she was too utterly petrified to reach into the darkness and feel around for the flashlight. She knew it hadn't gone far. But there was no telling what she would grab. A snake? A rat?

Merciful heavenly Father, help me. She had to get out of here before she had an absolute panic attack.

"Janice? What are you doing down there?"

"Hang on," Janice called up. "I dropped the flashlight. Be there in a jiff."

She breathed in a steadying breath and forced herself to crawl into the tunnel. The bulky flashlight couldn't have rolled far. She inched her palms along the cold stone floor, her knees and hips protesting being placed in such a precarious position.

Against her nature and, frankly, her better judgment, she slid her palm along the floor until she made contact with an object she assumed was the flashlight.

"Found it," she called, inching her fingers forward, trying to find the handle. But as she felt along the object, she realized in one, awful, terrifying moment that this was no flashlight.

With an ear-splitting scream, she chucked the object into the blackness, shooting to her feet without one thought for her poor knees or hips. As she rubbed her hands furiously on her pant legs, she heard sounds coming from her mouth she'd never experienced before.

There wasn't any doubt. She'd grabbed the arm of a human skeleton.

A NOTE FROM THE EDITORS

We hope you enjoy Secrets of Wayfarers Inn, created by the Books and Inspirational Media Division of Guideposts, a nonprofit organization that touches millions of lives every day through products and services that inspire, encourage, help you grow in your faith, and celebrate God's love in every aspect of your daily life.

Thank you for making a difference with your purchase of this book, which helps fund our many outreach programs to military personnel, prisons, hospitals, nursing homes, and educational institutions. To learn more, visit Guideposts Foundation.org.

We also maintain many useful and uplifting online resources. Visit Guideposts.org to read true stories of hope and inspiration, access OurPrayer network, sign up for free newsletters, download free e-books, join our Facebook community, and follow our stimulating blogs.

To learn about other Guideposts publications, including the best-selling devotional *Daily Guideposts*, go to ShopGuideposts .org, call (800) 932-2145, or write to Guideposts, PO Box 5815, Harlan, Iowa 51593.

Sign up for the
Guideposts Fiction Newsletter
and stay up-to-date on the books you love!

You'll get sneak peeks of new releases, recommendations from other Guideposts readers, and special offers just for you . . .
and it's FREE!

Just go to Guideposts.org/Newsletters today to sign up.

Guideposts®

**Visit Guideposts.org/Shop
or call (800) 932-2145**

Find more inspiring fiction in these best-loved Guideposts series!

Tearoom Mysteries Series

Mix one stately Victorian home, a charming lakeside town in Maine, and two adventurous cousins with a passion for tea and hospitality. Add a large scoop of intriguing mystery and sprinkle generously with faith, family, and friends, and you have the recipe for *Tearoom Mysteries*.

Sugarcreek Amish Mysteries

Be intrigued by the suspense and joyful "aha" moments in these delightful stories. Each book in the series brings together two women of vastly different backgrounds and traditions, who realize there's much more to the "simple life" than meets the eye.

Mysteries of Martha's Vineyard

What does Priscilla Latham Grant, a Kansas farm girl know about hidden treasure and rising tides, maritime history and local isle lore? Not much—but to save her lighthouse and family reputation, she better learn quickly!

Mysteries of Silver Peak

Escape to the historic mining town of Silver Peak, Colorado, and discover how one woman's love of antiques helps her solve mysteries buried deep in the town's checkered past.

To learn more about these books, visit Guideposts.org/Shop